Searching for Love

MARION DANTE

ISBN: 978-1-9996471-0-0
Also available as an e-book

Cover design by Andy Bowden

DEDICATION

To my parents Frank & Patricia (nee Colivet) Dante
& my brothers Tim & Des RIP

Marion Dante is the author of:

Dropping the Habit
Her autobiography

Novels

Searching for Love
A Love as Strong
Camino Tales

SEARCHING FOR LOVE

Love and the gracious heart are a single thing...
one can no more be without the other that the
reasoning mind without reason.

Amore e 'l cor gentil sono una cosa,
sì come il saggio in suo dittare pone,
e così esser l'un sanza l'altro osa
com'alma razional sanza ragione.

Source: *La Vita Nuova (1293)* Chapter XVI
by Dante Alighieri (tr. Mark Musa)

1

MOTHER'S GUILT

*W*ithout opening her eyes, Frankie stretched out, grabbed her alarm clock and banged down the button before pushing the clock under her blanket.

Oh! What day? What day is it? she asked herself as she rolled over in her cosy bed. *It's Saturday. It's holidays! No more school for ever. You silly clock. You've woken me up.*

She felt the sun's warmth on her face and she opened her eyes. Her dreamy thoughts flashed back to last evening. *My first disco. John and Margaret. The music, dancing with the boys, that kiss, the way he hugged me. Was it temptation? Yes, it was pleasurable. Was it sinful?* A little inner voice reminded her: *the sixth commandment forbids... whatever is contrary to holy purity in looks, words or desires.*

Frankie eased herself out of bed, the word *desire*. Desires, desire. *What harm is it to imagine I am in your arms, John? Oh, I felt so transformed, so desired, so attractive.*

She dangled her feet and gradually let them touch the cold bedroom floor. She rubbed her eyes. A smile stole across her face when she glimpsed the dress that she wore last evening hanging on a hook on the back of the door.

Not wanting to wake her mam, she carefully opened her bedroom door and peeped into the kitchen.

She drew in her breath. A stench of stale smoke pervaded the flat. *Thank goodness, Mam must have put out her cigarette before she fell asleep.* She was stretched out in her armchair snoring. The kitchen sink was piled high with dirty crockery.

Frankie crept past her mother to pull back the green and black checked curtains. She had forgotten that the porridge pot was balanced on the draining board. She knocked it over. It fell onto an ashtray full of butts. Water and cigarette ends splashed on Frankie.' *Oh no!*'

Her mother pulled the coat that she had draped over herself tighter. She yawned, looked up and sleepily uttered, 'What the hell… ?'

'Sorry, Mam. I'll make you a cup of tea.'

'Good. Where? There it is,' she said, searching for the cigarette box. 'Now that you've woken me up you might as well switch on the radio. I wonder what disaster has happened today?'

Frankie's mother lit up while Frankie scalded the pot and made the tea.

'Tell me what you did with yourself last night, Frankie? The note you left me said something about a church.'

'It was a dance in the parish hall at the back of St Peter and Paul's Church in Tooting Bec. Father Dan runs it.'

'I suppose there were boys there, Fran?'

'I was with the girls from La Retraite Convent School. They are all very kind. A bit posh.'

'I'll ask you again. There were boys there too, weren't there?'

'Yes, but Father Dan has laid down strict rules. You know what priests are like, Mam.'

2

'Well I suppose with those beady eyes of yours and all your freckles, boys wouldn't be chasing you. What did you do to your hair, girl?'

'What d'you think, Mam?' Frankie swirled round. 'Do you like it like this?'

'You used my tongs to get it like that. Let me have a look at that face of yours. They're not your eye lashes. Did you use my make up, Frankie?'

'Sorry Mam. I am sixteen... besides, I didn't think you'd mind.'

'In my day you'd have had to be a lot older to doll yourself up and go out to a dance.'

'That was Ireland, Mam and that was then.'

'Ah well, with your looks and lanky limbs, I suppose there is no need for me to worry. Sure, you look so nervous. You're like a bird of prey, ready to pounce.'

'Thanks, Mam. That's not going to help now when I'll have to make myself presentable in order to find a job.'

'That's true, Frankie. Now we're getting down to brass tacks. Who do you think will employ you?'

'I thought I'd continue working in Ben Lyon's Hair Salon for a while until I find something better. I hate sweeping up the hair. Only getting half an hour to grab something to eat. I don't like to look at those horrible eels when I go into that pie and mash store to buy sausages and peas.'

'... and spend the little money you've earned. What use is that, Frankie, I ask you? We need money. The only money coming into our home now is the hard earned money I get from dishing out dinners in that fecking school.'

Frankie pulled her chair nearer to her mother. She felt a tear roll down her cheek.' I'm sorry, Mam. I'll try to find something. Maybe the priest could help me.'

'Don't cry, darling. I hate to see you cry. It's partly... No, it's all my fault. I've failed you.'

'No Mammy. No, you do your best.'

'After your father died, I went to pieces. One day you'll understand. You have no idea what it's like to have the misfortune to be left all alone in this world when your husband is taken from you. I'm not surprised that your brother went off to the other side of the world. Your sister hardly visits.'

'You've done your best, Mammy. You've reared three of us. Isn't that a postcard from Dom that you've stuck on the wall over the mantelpiece? And Mary is a credit to you. She's busy looking after her husband and their son. Now, you're crying.'

'Yes. I am crying, Frankie. I know, I smoke too many fags and I go out and drown my sorrows in the pub. All the money I earn is wasted. I'll never join my husband in heaven at this rate.'

Frankie stood.' That's it, Mam. I'll join the nuns. Then you won't have to worry about me anymore.'

'Now, Frankie, never let it be said that I abandoned you to the nuns, but on the other hand, if you feel God is calling you, I won't have it on my conscience that I prevented you from answering the call of the Almighty.'

'I've got all those brochures that the nuns handed out when they came to visit our school a few weeks ago, Mammy. I seem to remember them inviting us to an exhibition in Westminster Cathedral.'

'Well, it wouldn't do any harm to go and look around, would it, Frankie. When's it on?'

'I think it is today. I'll go and check.'

'The best thing about going to the nuns is that you'd be able to polish off your education, Frankie. Then, later, if you discover that you don't have a vocation... that God is not calling you to that life, you'd be at peace with Jesus for having tested your calling. Think of it as a finishing school. My younger sisters back in Ireland went to finishing schools. Times changed for the better for them.'

4

'I'll go and hunt out those brochures now, Mammy.'

'Good idea, Frankie.'

Frankie was feeling guilty because she had omitted to tell her mother about the boys at the disco. How could she explain how she felt when John kissed her? She closed her bedroom door and knelt down in front of a little altar with the statue of the Sacred Heart and read aloud the answer to question 213 of the Catechism of Christian Doctrine: *The sixth commandment forbids immodest plays and dances*. It is sinful to look at them.'

Then she put her head in her hands and prayed,

Dear God Our Father,

I ask your forgiveness for the pleasure that I enjoyed when I was with John at the disco last night. I also beg forgiveness for reliving those pleasureful feelings before I fell asleep. And oh, I promise to confess to my mam that I lost one of her earrings.

Frankie found the leaflets that the nuns had handed out to the girls in her class, on the shelf where she had put her old school books the night before. Opening one, she saw that the Vocation Exhibition did begin that Saturday in a side room at Westminster Cathedral.

Frankie's mother was still sitting in her armchair, smoking and tut-tutting to the news on the radio, when Frankie poked her head out of her bedroom. Frankie turned the radio down, 'That exhibition is on today, Mam. If it's okay with you, I'll find my way there. I'll have to go by tube and change onto the Victoria Line.'

'Lucky for you, I won at the bingo last night. Hand me my bag, will you? I'll give you a shilling for the fare and for a drink or a packet of biscuits.'

'Thanks, Mammy. I'll get washed and dressed and find my way.'

While Frankie was getting ready, she heard the kitchen tap running and the clattering of crockery. She wondered if at last her mother was doing the washing up.

To her surprise when Frankie came out of her bedroom ready to walk to Brixton Tube Station, she saw that her mother was standing by the sink with one hand leaning on the table.

'Frankie, I've been thinking. You're old enough now for me to get things straight with you.'

'Oh Mam, you've said enough. Don't worry yourself, really, I'm fine. Really I am.'

'I've decided to make a new start, Frankie. Take a good look at the draining board. I've made a clean sweep. The suds are still on my hands to prove that it was really me that washed that pile of crocks.'

'Maybe I should have done the washing-up last night, Mammy, instead...'

'Come on, girl, switch on that kettle. We'll have a cup of tea. Sit yourself down. I'll tell you a few things that I've been keeping from you until you were old enough to understand.'

While Frankie was making the tea she was hoping that her mother was not going to reveal some awful secret. She often wondered why she hardly ever wrote to her relatives in Ireland. It also puzzled her that while she said her prayers and kept the lamp to the Infant of Prague statue alight on the altar in the kitchen, she rarely went to Mass.

After taking a sip, Frankie's mother said, 'That's a fine cup of tea, Frankie. Nothing like Barry's Tea, especially when it's brewed properly.'

Frankie pushed the packet of fig roll biscuits in front to her mother. 'Your favourites, Mam.'

Frankie's mother put her hand over Frankie's. 'I might as well tell you straight out, Frankie. I have sinned.'

'Ah, Mammy... haven't we all? That's what Confession's for.'

'No, I mean proper mortal sins, Frankie... against the

sixth and the ninth commandments. The kind that involves going with another man. Now, I've said it outright.'

'Oh Mammy, don't cry.'

'No, Frankie. I don't deserve pity. I'm a sinner. I must do penance. What's more I've neglected you, poor crater.'

'Please Mammy; you don't have to say all this. You haven't neglected me.'

'Drink, dancing and boys... men can lead to...'

'I know, I know, Mammy.'

'I bet the nuns never spelt it out to you about consequences. Did they mention babies?'

'They did in a roundabout way. But sure I know all that, Mammy.'

'Good, Frankie. I've never admitted this before but I am proud of you. You've turned out to be a grand girl, you know, in spite of how I've treated you. There. I've said it.'

'No need, Mammy. I always knew. Really I did.'

'Frankie, when I look out of that window over there and see you walking down the road to school, you look like a blimming film star. Like Twiggy.'

'Oh Mam. Even with beady eyes and lanky limbs?'

'Yes indeed. And I bet you were kissed at that disco last night. You were, weren't you?'

'Oh Mammy, there's not much I can keep from you, is there?'

'Mothers have a way of knowing. Why's that? Because they've been there before, Frankie. I met your father at a dance.'

'Okay. Now as we're confessing, Mam, I hope you won't be angry with me, but I borrowed and lost one of your black earrings.'

'Those old plastic ones. Some old woman gave them to me. No matter. You're forgiven. Quit now while we're even, if I were you. Get out that door as quick as your lanky legs will carry you and make for Westminster Cathedral, will you.'

Frankie blew her nose. She patted her mother's hand. She felt grown up and ready to face her new world. She hopped down the stairs, ready to walk to the tube station.

2

CAREER OR VOCATION?

*O*ne hour after leaving her mother, Frankie walked up the steps of Victoria Underground station.

That can't be Margaret? Frankie wondered as she rounded the corner and caught sight of a tall, slim girl. An older man's arm was resting on her shoulder. He was talking to her. She was nodding. They reached the other end of the piazza. Frankie followed close behind them. She noticed that he almost pushed her towards the big heavy front door of the hall before turning and leaving her. The girl turned and waved. The man was looking at his watch as he strode off. When Frankie saw the girl's face she realised that it was Margaret.

Good. I won't be alone, thought Frankie. *She's calling me...*

'This is incredible, Frankie! What are you doing here?'

'I was about to ask you the same question, Margaret.'

'Well, our schools are very near each other and...'

'I know,' she continued, 'the nuns did the rounds of both our schools looking for girls to train as nuns.'

'Are you thinking of becoming a nun, Frankie?'

'Not sure, Margaret! My mother thinks it's a good idea.'

'Neither am I.'

'The nun who came to our school said that she was looking for *vocations*. At first, I thought she meant that she wanted to find girls who would help the nuns.'

'No, Frankie. My father told me that when the nuns say they are looking for *vocations* they are looking for girls who will eventually become nuns.'

'After last night, I'd have thought you'd be the last person to want to become a nun, Margaret.'

'It was great fun, wasn't it, Frankie? You let yourself go eventually, didn't you?'

'That's just it, Margaret. I felt so alive and excited. Now I'm loaded with guilt.'

'Don't! Let's not think about guilt. My father keeps quoting the Catechism, '*Immodest*…

Frankie joined in and they both recited, '*Immodest plays and dances are forbidden by the sixth commandment*'

'He would like me to have made up my mind when he returns.'

'So he wants you to become a nun?'

'He does. He's very persuasive. He's says he is not forcing me, but he was horrified when he saw the way I was dancing with Peter last night. I feel so guilty.'

'So do I. I woke up worrying about my feeling for John, Margaret. He kissed this cheek.' Frankie pointed. 'I told him that I loved him… oh, I feel so ashamed. That's what brought me here.'

'I must have looked guilty. My father was ranting on and on as we drove home. He said, "After all the money we spent in sending you to a highly rated, independent grammar school, Margaret. This is what you do. You put yourself in the way of temptation. The nuns must have warned you. Boys… young men only want one thing." He stopped when he turned off the ignition. As I ran up stairs to bed he shouted after me, "Examine your conscience, my girl. Be down here at nine ready to go to the Vocations Exhibition."'

'And he kept his word, Margaret. I'm glad you're here.'

'He frogmarched me here. Why can't we just have fun?'

'Maybe there is fun in the convent?'

'You must be joking, Frankie. No nice clothes. No boogying or hugging or...'

'Not much hugging in my house, Margaret.'

'So that's why you're here? You do want to become a nun?'

'I didn't say that, Margaret. I'm just looking.'

'Come on. Let's get it over with. My father will be back to collect me in an hour's time.'

'This vestibule is a good place to chat, Margaret. No one will bother us.'

'At least we can enjoy the sunshine here. Once we go through those doors...'

'We've got to go in, Frankie. Come on!'

Frankie watched Margaret as she approached a nun dressed in long blue robes standing at the entrance. In Frankie's eyes, Margaret seemed out of place in her tailored tweed jacket and beige knee-length skirt. She seemed to ooze confidence. Margaret waved her over. 'Come on, Frankie.'

'Welcome to both of you!' smiled the nun, as she ushered them through the double doors. Plunged into the interior darkness of the huge hall, Frankie looked from the vaulted ceiling to the parquet polished floor.

'It's like our school hall, painted green and brown. Our hall has small windows built into arches and brown wooden panelled walls, just like these,' observed Margaret.

Frankie pulled a cardigan from the bag she was carrying.

'Here, let me help you, Frankie. Are you cold? I was just about to take my jacket off. I feel warm in here.'

'I'm hot too. But I thought I'd better cover up. Didn't your nuns tell you not to go about with bare arms?'

'Oh yes. Spoil sports. It's a shame to cover over your lovely lemon-coloured dress. It's got cup sleeves. Your arms are partly modest, Frankie,' teased Margaret.

Another nun smiled as she approached them and handed them a leaflet.

'Hello girls. It is an imposing building, isn't it? See that lovely wooden gallery at the back with a coat of arms as a centre piece. Do you see all the words, 'Ne cedes Malis' and the stole and crosses and the three lions? All symbolic. Isn't that grand?'

'Does that mean, 'Don't give into evil,' Sister?'

'Good girl. You know your Latin. Yes, you're right. The stole is part of the priest's vestments. The crosses are there to remind us of the crucifixion. The lions… well they're often mentioned in the Bible. An interpretation claims that lions sleep with their eyes open. Similarly God is always watching over his children.'

'That's lovely. Thank you, Sister,' said Frankie.

'Take your time. Have a look round.'

'The stalls are numbered. Let's not start with the first one,' suggested Margaret.

'You can begin at number 16,' encouraged the nun. 'You're at liberty to start anywhere in this hall. You might want to wander round and get an overview. Up to you.'

'Frankie, see that smiley priest dressed in black with the white. What do you call that long white piece he's wearing down the front of his robe?'

She pointed to a young man at the stall opposite to where they were standing.

'I think that's called a scapular, Margaret.'

'He looks interesting. His Order seems to have men and

12

women members.'

'They're Dominicans. They're called that because St Dominic started that Order. Read the poster.'

Margaret bent her head near Frankie's and whispered, 'We're being followed.'

Frankie turned round. Quickly she thought of a question to ask the nun who had welcomed them and was now standing behind them. 'Are there religious Orders that just have women?'

'Oh yes. Let me introduce you to the Sisters of Mercy. By the way, what are your names? That's if you don't mind me asking,' continued the nun.

'Frankie. I'm Frankie...'

Margaret winked at Frankie and said, 'And I'm Joan.'

Frankie hoped that the nun had not noticed that she was about to explode with laughter. She walked on quickly.

'Don't give your real name, Frankie. You never know, you could be rounded up and coaxed into joining.'

'Too late, Margaret, for me. I mean Joan! That nun was just being kind.'

'Do you know why there are so many different types of nuns and priests? Look there are more displays. Are those men called monks? They're dressed in black and brown. Shall we just walk all the way round the stalls and count how many different habits that we can see?'

'Come here, young ladies. Let me answer your question,' called out an old bearded priest who came out from behind a stall.

Frankie nodded to the priest and whispered: 'Margaret, we'd better try to look interested.'

'All I wanted to tell you is that there are over thirty different Orders represented in this hall today. They all have their own distinctive habits. Some were founded many years ago while others were started fairly recently.'

'Where are the modern ones, Father?' asked Margaret.

'Two tables along on the right. You will find a teaching Order that has nuns and priests founded by an Italian priest.'

'Oh, I'd like to meet them. Come on, let's see what they are like, Margaret.'

'Frankie, if I ever agreed to enter a convent, the word 'modern' appeals as does, 'teaching'. Don't you think 'Italian' sounds romantic?'

'So you have considered convent life, Margaret?'

'Maybe. Sometimes I just want to leave home... get away from my father's strict rules. How about you?'

'There's a little alcove over there with two empty chairs. Shall we?'

'Perfect, Frankie.'

'It's cosy here, Margaret. I wanted to talk... '

'About nuns and home and...'

'Good! It might all sound silly but ... '

'Go on. I'm interested.'

'My mother's an alcoholic.'

'Lots of people drink too much.'

'They do. There's usually a reason. Well, my mother confessed why. Oh, Margaret, promise you won't tell anyone else?'

'Of course, I won't, Frankie.'

'Mum said that I am old enough to know that she has... well there is ...or was another man involved.'

'Really, Frankie? Is he still around?'

'I didn't ask. I couldn't. You see, she was crying and apologising. Then she noticed that I was wearing her mascara. She commented on my hair. She guessed that there were boys at the disco. I felt guilty for kissing and I didn't tell you...'

'Something worse?'

'I lost one of my mother's earrings.'

'She told you off?'

'She didn't. In fact, she said that she was proud of me.

14

She told me that she sometimes looks out of the window to watch me walking down the street. She says that I remind her of Twiggy!'

'Oh Frankie! Your mother sounds okay. Who hasn't got faults?'

'I know. And to think of it, a few months ago, I asked to speak to one of the nuns at our school about my mother and her problems.'

'Well you didn't know then what you know now, did you?'

'That's true. I don't regret speaking to Sister Philomena, who teaches at our school. Everything was so perfect that sunny afternoon last May. I was delighted when Sister led me into a walled garden where everything seemed so peaceful, perfect and heavenly.'

'Sounds lovely.'

'It was. I sat next to Sister Philomena on a garden seat shaded by an old oak. An intoxicating fragrance wafted from the roses and mingled with the sweet peas and delphiniums.'

'You paint a beautiful picture, Frankie. Might be too unreal?'

'No, not when she asked me about my mother. I told her that she is an alcoholic.'

'Oh Frankie, take my hankie. You need a big hug. Pull your chair closer.'

'I'm alright.'

'You don't need to tell me anymore, Frankie.'

'But I do need...'

'You sure?'

'Margaret, I think that my father died when I was two.'

'Do you remember him?'

'Vaguely. And my mother... well I suppose that's why my mother finds it so hard to cope. That's another reason why she struggles financially. She does her best but she seems to have lots of problems.'

'Was Sister able to help?'

'At first I could not understand why she asked me if my mother went to Mass on Sunday.'

'Nuns and priests always ask that. What did you answer?'

'I want to laugh now when I think back. Do you know what I said?'

Margaret nodded.

'These... I think these were my actual words: Some Sundays she gets to Mass, Sister. But she finds a glass of gin helps her more. And she loves her cigarettes. *Players*.'

'Is that true, Frankie? Your Mum doesn't go to church and she smokes?'

'After her confession to me this morning, I've made her sound awful, haven't I, Margaret? She still has some religion. I mean she goes to church when she is up to it. She makes sure I go too. We have a picture of the Sacred Heart with a candle underneath it on a shelf on our sitting room wall. I've always had a miraculous medal pinned on my vest. Look. Let me pull up my vest so you can see it.'

'No need, Frankie. I have one too and a brown scapular. My family are very religious. Too religious. That's my problem.'

'Your turn, Margaret. Tell me about your family.'

'Later. Tell me if this talk with the nun in the garden triggered off the idea of becoming a nun? Then I'll tell you about my family and its problems.'

Frankie was relieved to hear Margaret had family problems too. She was even happier that Margaret did not seem to despise her because of her poor background.

'Fine. I liked the way Sister asked me if I had any brothers and sisters.'

'Have you?'

'Yes. I have a sister, Mary. Dom's my brother. They've

16

grown up and moved away.'

'You lucky thing. You're an only child now, Frankie.'

'I am I suppose. My sister is married. She has her own problems. Rarely comes to our house. That's the thing. Mammy has brothers and sisters, too. I used to wonder what my mother did to alienate everyone. Now I am beginning to realise that she keeps them at a distance because she feels that she has disgraced the family.'

'Did Sister Philomena solve your problems, Frankie?'

'Do you know she actually said very little. Nothing really. I noticed that she was fingering her rosary beads. But...'

'So she said nothing. Did nothing and still you were... ?'

'Relaxed, intoxicated by the floral scent and the mesmerising scene around me. Then a nun emerged through a gate from a kitchen garden with a basket laden with carrots, spring onions and cabbage. Sister Philomena started to talk. Sounded like a speech. She pointed to the nun. 'It's thanks to Sister Joan's hard work and ingenuity that we have such a wonderful display of flowers and a supply of fruit, herbs and vegetables.'

'You said it yourself, Frankie. You were mesmerised. Maybe, hypnotised?'

'I suppose I was. It was all so relaxing and enticing compared to home. Now tell me about yourself, Margaret.'

'Thinking about enticing, Frankie. When we were looking at that Italian Order I noticed that they had a map of the world.'

'Yes, with dots in many countries. The nun said that they wore white habits when they worked in hot countries. '

'Are you thinking what I'm thinking, Frankie?'

'Wouldn't it be wonderful to get away from England? I've always wanted to travel.'

'Oh Frankie! We could travel. Do good and teach

people about God at the same time.'

'Sunshine. Beaches. Perhaps lions. Oh I hope there are no snakes, though, Margaret.'

'You are so funny, Frankie. I don't suppose they'd let snakes bite their missionaries.'

'St Patrick drove the snakes out of Ireland so we can clear them out of Africa or Mexico or...'

'Oh no! There's my father coming through the door. I'll have to go, Frankie. He'll be annoyed. He instructed me to stand outside and wait for him. Bye for now. Bye. Sorry.'

As Frankie remained sitting alone in the alcove she became convinced that if Margaret ever bumped into her again, she would most likely avoid her. Why would a girl who belonged to a rich family, who could afford to send their daughter to Le Retraite Convent Independent and Private Grammar School want to be her friend? She smiled when she remembered that while their pupils wore summer uniform dresses in pastel shades that looked lovely as they got on the bus, they were creased by the time they reached their Balham stop. Even though she attended Holy Family Secondary Modern School, the material used for their uniforms was much more crease-resistant.

'Would you like a cup of tea? I noticed that your friend left.'

Frankie was glad that it was one of the nuns from the Order that was started by an Italian who was offering her tea. She remembered that Margaret said that Italian sounded romantic.

'Yes please, Sister.' She followed the nun down to their stall.

'God has guided you here for a purpose. What is your name?'

Oh no, thought Frankie. Then she wondered if she should follow Margaret's example and give the nun another name. But she changed her mind, and replied, 'Frankie, Sister.'

'Sit down there in this lovely comfy chair and sip your tea, Frankie. Would you like a biscuit?'

Frankie felt that she was being won over. When she wanted a cup of tea at home in her house, she would most likely be sent to the shop for milk. There would never be a custard cream biscuit offered to her.

'You're a member of an Italian Order, Sister?'

'We were co-founded by an Italian woman. We have vocations from all over the world.'

'All over the world? In lovely hot countries? Africa, Australia?'

'South America, Spain. Many countries.'

'What kind of work do you do, Sister?'

'All sorts of work. We run clubs, teach, help and support young people.'

'Do you have to be clever to join your Order?'

'We train vocations, Frankie. Everybody has some God-given talent. We're a young Order. Look at our habit.'

The nun must have seen Frankie look at an older nun seated at the back of the stall who was wearing a long black habit.

'Let me introduce you to Sister Petronella, Frankie. Sister is Italian. She knew our Sister foundress. The priests teach the boys and the Sisters cater for the girls in our branch of our Order.'

'Buongiorno. Good day. Il Papa, the Pope changed our habit.'

'So you see, as Sister explained, The Pope has modernised us. The habit that I am wearing is grey instead of black. It's made from a lighter, washable material and it's shorter. It is a more practical habit especially for those of us who help people in poorer areas.'

'Poor people, Sister?'

'Poor, needy. Most people have needs. Some rich people don't even realise that they are needy too. Isn't that right?'

'I suppose we all have needs, Sister.'

'Your family is needy, Frankie?'

Frankie felt uncomfortable. She did not want to tell the nun too much in case she would not be accepted in the convent if she did decide to become a nun.

'I must leave now,' said Frankie, handing back her cup. 'Delicious tea. Thank you.'

As she walked out of the exhibition Frankie pondered on how people with very little money could be rich in other ways. She had not noticed any needy rich people. She wondered if Margaret might be needy at the same time as being rich.

3

SURPRISE ENTERING

'*Y*ou have to get a proper job! There is very little money coming into this house. The bit of money you earn at that hairdressing job is nearly all gone by the time you've paid for your lunch. Don't come home until you have a job that pays a good wage.' Blood rushed to her mother's face as she thumped the kitchen table. She added, 'I mean that, Frankie!'

'I'm going to the nuns, Mammy. There's free food there.'

That day Frankie wrote to the Italian Order of nuns that she met at the Westminster Vocations Exhibition for application forms. The forms arrived three days later. She filled them in and posted them immediately. The nuns promptly replied.

When Frankie showed her mother the letter of acceptance from the convent, she said, 'Thanks be to God and His Holy Mother! One less mouth to feed. We'll have the nuns praying for us too. Maybe they will help us as well? We're poor people.'

'The nuns have enclosed a list of what we have to take with us when we enter the convent, Mammy.'

'Merciful God, you'll need to inform them that we've no money to go buying anything, Frankie.'

'I don't think we'll have to worry too much, Mammy. I've to wear a black skirt and blazer and a white blouse on the day I arrive at the convent.'

'So your school uniform will do. That's good. What else is on the list?'

'I've got everything else… oh, except a case... and I'd need another white blouse. I've got stockings. These shoes are fine.'

'Now, Frankie I have a small case. It's been on many a journey back and forth to Ireland. You can have that.'

'Is that the old one on top of your wardrobe, Mammy?'

'Less of the old, Frankie. Just be grateful. As for the blouse, I'm sure we can find one in Oxfam.'

'Most of the girls in my class were glad to get rid of their uniforms. I didn't ever want to wear mine again.'

'Count your blessings that you have it now, Frankie.'

'I've noticed that the list states that everything has to be labelled. I think there is a bundle of 'Cash's' labels in your sewing box, Mammy.'

'Search and see. I suppose I could let you have my emergency nightdress and dressing gown.'

'What emergency are you preparing for, Mammy?'

'You'll learn child. Every woman has night clothes ready in case she has to go to hospital. Fortunately, you are my last baby. You'll find my nightdress and dressing gown in the bottom of the chest of drawers in my bedroom.'

'Oh Mammy, that's great. Thank you.'

Frankie was not surprised to find that her mother's night-wear was crumpled and smoke-ridden. She also wondered if the nuns would mind her wearing a bright red dressing gown.

True to her word, her mother bought her a second white blouse from Oxfam.

Two days later as Frankie was walking past the pub that her mother frequented, a woman came out to greet her.

'Hello, Frankie. Your mother is very proud of you. She's been telling us that you're joining the nuns. Congratulations. Now if there's anything... '

'Well, actually Mrs Kelly...' Frankie could feel her cheeks flushing, 'as you run the laundrette, could I...?'

'I'd count it as an honour to give your clothes a spin. It would be a privilege to help. Bring them down. I'll see that they'll be returned to you as good as new.'

Thinking that her mother would feel embarrassed if she knew, Frankie managed to sneak her school blazer and skirt, the smoke-ridden dressing gown and nightdress as well as her underwear down to Mrs Kelly in the laundrette.

That evening Frankie was in her room when she heard someone knocking on their front door. Her mother shouted, 'Frankie, come out here.'

When she opened her bedroom door, three faces were beaming at her. Two women were clapping their hands. Mrs Kelly was pointing to a big bag on the kitchen table.

'Frankie, we've come to wish you well in your new life. God will reward you for answering His call,' said an older buxom woman. Then she forced two five pound notes into Frankie's hand.

'We've had a whip round to help out with anything else you'll need. If there's any left over, you can give it to the nuns.'

'Thank you. I'm really grateful. Really I am.'

'Open up the bundle, Frankie,' said her mother pointing to the table.

Frankie hoped her mother wouldn't be ashamed when

she discovered that Mrs Kelly had laundered her clothes. Encouraged by her mother's smile, she undid the linen laundry bag.

'May God bless you, Moira! Everything is washed and pressed and as good as new. I always knew there's good in you. Now Frankie, see what it is to have good friends.'

Frankie was relieved.

On 29th August, 1966, the day that Frankie was to leave home, she came down stairs carrying her mother's old brown suit case. As prescribed, she was wearing her refreshed school uniform skirt and blazer. She had removed the school badge. Dressed like that she hoped that she would not meet any of her school friends. She heated the porridge that she had soaked the previous night. She heard her mother moving about in her bedroom. Then the door opened.

'Come here, until I give you a proper goodbye, Frankie.'

Frankie couldn't recall her mother ever hugging her. She cried into her mother's smoke stenched dressing gown.

'Mammy I'll miss you. Promise me that you will look after yourself, won't you.'

'You know I'd come with you to the convent today if I could only... '

'I'm not expecting you to come with me. We agreed, didn't we? You're not really up to it.'

'Here. Take this photo of you and me on your First Holy Communion day. I'll be down there to visit you as soon as I'm able to find a proper outfit to wear.'

'Thanks, Mammy. Didn't I look angelic? I'll keep that always.'

As Frankie left there were tears in her mother's eyes and when she looked up at the flat window to wave goodbye.

When Frankie looked at the clock in Putney Station, she realised that she was two hours too early. She left home as soon as she was ready because she wanted to reflect on her decision to enter the convent. She deposited her case in the nearby parish church porch and walked along by the Thames.

Why am I doing this? She pondered this question as she pounded along the river path. *What compelled me to apply?*

Frankie had no watch. Estimating the time, she returned to check on the church tower clock. She saw a black Volvo drawing up outside the convent gate. A man stepped out and carried a case to the convent door. A woman and a girl sidled out of the car and hugged each other. The man jumped back into the car and waved as he drove the woman away.

That looks like Margaret!

'Oh, Frankie!' shouted Margaret, as she ran across the road. 'D'you know, I had a feeling that you would be here. I hoped you would. I'm so glad, Frankie.'

Margaret hugged Frankie and sobbed into her blazer. Tears streamed down her cheeks as they embraced.

'Margaret, what decided you to enter the convent?'

'Oh it's complicated. My father brought home a pile of literature from the vocations day. Once he read that these nuns were primarily concerned with education, he approved of them. He wants me to use my qualifications to become a teacher.'

'I saw you hugging your mother. What did she say about you entering?'

'Frankie. Whatever my father says, goes. He rules. Poor Mum. She is religious but waited to discuss my future when my dad had gone out. Then we talked about there being lots of different *vocations* or *callings* in life.'

'So she didn't push you into entering, Margaret?'

'No, Frankie. But my father has to be obeyed. She thinks, though, that after a while I will return home.'

'Was your father in the army, Margaret?'

'No Frankie. Initially I couldn't believe what I

discovered about my father.'

'He was a headteacher?'

'The opposite. When he had to fill in the forms, it asked for my father's occupation. You'll never guess what he wrote down, Frankie?'

'Naval officer?'

'Turf account! *Bookmaker* to you and me!'

'Bookies... where you put bets on horses, Margaret?'

'Yes. I used to wonder why he often went out to work in flashy clothes.'

'But he was in tweeds when he took you up to Westminster Cathedral, Margaret?'

'Well, that's just it. Whenever he came up to our school, he would dress smartly. On other occasions he wore bright colours. It also accounts for the fact that I often heard my mother ask him about money. They used to argue. Sometimes we seemed to be well off. Other times money was a big concern.'

'We were poor all the time.'

Frankie was pleased to know that Margaret was not from a really rich family. Life was not as secure for her as she had thought.

'Tell me, Frankie, what made you choose this Order of nuns?'

'Tea and biscuits. Sister tempted me with them when you left with your father the other day. Because they're 'Italian'. They're romantic!'

'Wouldn't it be great if there was romance? You never know.'

'Stand back and let me take a look at you in your convent clothes, Margaret. Are they all new?'

'Yes. Mum insisted on buying everything new. Besides, our school uniform is navy-blue.'

As Frankie looked at her friend she thought that she looked very attractive in her new uniform. Her hazel eyes that drove the jiving lads crazy at the disco were still twinkling. Frankie felt jealous when she looked down at her own shabby outfit. Margaret must have realised how she felt because she immediately changed the topic.

'We must be the same age. When's your birthday Frankie?'

'I was sixteen on 13th May.'

'And I was sixteen only a few days later on 24th.'

'I don't even know your surname, Frankie.'

'Frankie Danivet. What's yours?'

'Blackburn. Margaret Blackburn.'

'Brothers or sisters? Have you any?'

'Same as you, Frankie. One of each. I love music. I play the clarinet. How about you?'

Frankie noticed that when she enquired about Margaret's family, Margaret cast her eyes down.

'I strum a small guitar.'

'Music is another reason why my father wanted me to join this Order of nuns. He says that he loves Gregorian chant. He told me that when he was young he lived near a monastery. He used to hear the monks chanting. He was pleased that the nuns in the school I used to attend continued to sing the Gregorian chant at Mass, in spite of the fact that many schools started a folk choir.'

'Do you like the Mass to be celebrated in Latin instead of English?'

'In our local church the Mass is still celebrated in Latin on some occasions. I understand it better when it is in English.'

'I don't mind either. Our parish has a Latin Mass too.'

'I love disco music. Remember how much fun we had jigging about that first night we met at the disco?'

'How could I forget!'

'I love all kinds of music, the Beatles, The Who, The Kinks, the Mamas and Papas... the whole lot... even the chanting of the psalms.'

'My mother loves music. Old fashioned stuff.'

'What kind?'

'She plays records like Mario Lanza singing *'Be my love'*. She loves John McCormack. She claims that he is the best Irish tenor. *'When Irish eyes are smiling... There's a tear in my eye'*. Of course she knows lots of Irish rebel songs as well.'

'Look over there, Frankie. Let's stay here for a while and watch them going in.'

'Goodness! See that podgy foreign looking girl with short jet black hair? Are those gold earrings that she's wearing?'

'The girl getting out of the car over there on your right, Frankie. She's carrying a tennis racket.'

'The letter definitely stated that no jewellery is allowed. You would have thought anyone entering a convent would have known that, Margaret.'

'It stipulated that everything has to be handed in. It warned you not to bring anything you did not intend sharing.'

'I hope I can keep the bible that a woman from my mother's pub gave me. She took the bus up to the Catholic Truth Society Shop in Victoria to buy it. It's gilt-edged.'

'They're making a move, Margaret. We'd better go. See that nun is signalling to us.'

'There is at least eleven or twelve girls now. Shall we run away, Frankie?'

'My case? I'll have to grab it from inside the church porch. Wait for me, Margaret.'

When Frankie walked up the stone path leading into the convent carrying her mother's old case, she was pleased that Margaret was waiting for her. She was standing next to the nun that had given her tea and biscuits at the vocation exhibition.

'Welcome Frankie. I saw you both at Westminster Cathedral. Come in and join the others.'

The nun stepped in ahead of them. Margaret whispered in a haunting voice, 'It's a big, black heavy door, Frankie. We'll never see the outside world again!'

'You may be right, Margaret. Did you see the size of the key she was holding? But don't worry, we have each other. We'll be safe.'

'Gather round and I'll explain,' said the nun who had welcomed them. She was standing on the first step of wooden stairs that led up to a large window on a landing half way up the stairs. A big white and blue statue of Our Lady was displayed on the window ledge. Beside the door leading out to the porch, there were three other beautifully carved wooden doors. The walls were wood-panelled. The entrance hall was painted light green. The parquet floor was highly polished. As she had not eaten since breakfast and it was now tea time, Frankie felt her tummy rumble as she sniffed the air. She felt excited and hungry. The air was sterile.

'Welcome to our convent. Jesus and his Mother Mary are welcoming fourteen new aspirants into our community today.'

Frankie felt Margaret grab her hand and squeeze it tightly.

'Please carry your cases over to the corner of the hall and then follow me into the refectory.'

'Look at the size of the cases those two in front of us have, Margaret.'

'We all had the same list, Frankie.'

'I heard you remarking on the size of the cases,' remarked the nun. 'This happens every time new aspirants enter the convent. People ignore the rules. I noticed someone wearing jewellery and someone else has a tennis racket. Yes. You.' Sister pointed to a stocky built, sallow-skinned, girl. 'I'm sure I'll find umbrellas and even galoshes, books and gilt-edged bibles. They'll all have to be handed in.'

Oh no, thought Frankie. Surely they won't take the bible my mam's friend went to such trouble to buy me. Frankie noticed some girls looking at each other but they said nothing as their shoes tip-tapped over the glasslike floor. She wondered why the girl next to her was wiping away copious tears. She was aware of sniffles coming from someone behind her. As far as Frankie was concerned, life could only improve. There were going to be regular meals, a tidy room, ready-made friends and no more money worries.

Anxious to be seated next to Margaret at a long wooden table in the Aspirants' Refectory, Frankie stood next to her. She caught a whiff of Margaret's perfume. It wasn't like the aura of '*Evening in Paris*' that she smelt from the blue bottle that her mother hid in her wardrobe.

Margaret whispered, 'This is a far cry from the disco, isn't it, Frankie?'

'Yes. We'll have to try and forget all that now, won't we?'

'Did you hear on the wireless that the Beatles are giving their last live concert today? I just love the Beatles and that song, '*I Wanna Be Your Man.*''

Frankie's mind momentarily floated away to be with Beatles and Ringo on the drums. She felt her body jigging to the rhythm in her head.

A chirpy twelve-year-old nudged Frankie back from her reverie. Leaning nearer to her, she said, 'Hello! You day-dreaming?'

'Oh! Sorry… miles away,' exclaimed Frankie.

Frankie started to take a closer look at the other girls round her.

'Did you hear what that tall stocky girl… woman was telling the others, Frankie?'

'I was distracted Margaret. What about her?'

'She sounds very posh. The other older girl near her was asking her questions. I heard her say that she is a convert to Catholicism. She has a degree in science. Her father is an officer in the Navy.'

'Gosh. She's a good catch for the nuns, isn't she, Margaret. She'll make up for the likes of me.'

A ruddy faced nun appeared at the end of the refectory. Clapping her hands, she began,

'Allora! We begin with saying your names? First, I say welcome to each of you. You are very welcome. I am called Suor... Sister Laura. One by one, you say your name. Don't look so worried. It's Francesca, forse?' She pointed to Frankie.' Hardly ever remember names first time, eh?'

'My name is Frances Danivet but everybody calls me Frankie.'

'Che bel name, Francesca! Only a few days now, on four September we celebrate the festa Santo Francesco di Assisi.'

'I was christened Anne Elizabeth,' enunciated the posh woman.

Frankie nudged Margaret. 'Everybody's looking at her. She sounds very grand, doesn't she?'

'Sister Laura seems to be unimpressed though,' replied Margaret.

Sister continued, 'I ask you form a coda... a line. I give each one a mantilla. A black one to cover your hairs in chapel. After we go into chapel to show you places there.'

Frankie was delighted to see that that she and Margaret managed to sit next to each other in chapel.

'Congrats! You're a quick mover, Margaret.' whispered Frankie.

'Open the first page of the book that you see in front of you,' continued Sister Laura.' You will see it is in Latin and English.'

'Look,' she said, 'on right hand side of your book, see

the words, 'We adore Thee, O Christ and we bless Thee who by Thy Holy Cross hath redeemed the world.' If you know the melody, you can sing with me.'

Margaret prodded Frankie and whispered, 'She's got a lovely voice, hasn't she?'

'Yes, but help me. This veil keeps slipping off my head.'

Margaret started to titter. 'It's slipping down over your eyes. You look so funny. Tie the strings tighter and pull it back further.'

Frankie realised that Sister Laura noticed that they were talking because she put her finger up to her lips to remind them to be silent.

Frankie was struggling not to giggle. She glanced at Margaret. Frankie put her hand to her face and whispered, 'We'd better be careful.'

Sister Laura genuflected, turned and signalled them to follow each other out into a dark stone-floored corridor. Aprons hung on pegs on a wooden rack attached to one wall.

The corridor led off the wooden panelled hall through which they had entered the convent.

'Servants' quarters. We'll end up here, I bet,' whispered someone behind Frankie.

When they arrived in another room with smaller windows, tiled floor, green walls and brown skirting boards, the girl whispered, 'What did I tell you?'

Another nun was already in the room waiting to address them, 'Ah, Aspirants, you have been introduced to the most important person in our convent. Jesus Christ, our Lord and Saviour; our raison d'être. I'm Sister Rita. Together with Sister Laura, we will be your assistants or guides in the Aspirantade. You know that this house is called an *Aspirantade* because when you returned your applications forms you declared that you *aspire* or wish to become members of this Order of nuns. You are beginning to try to discover what this entails while we will decide if you have the necessary qualities.'

Margaret leaned close to Frankie and whispered, 'Aspire? I'm perspiring! What qualities?'

'What have we let ourselves in for, Margaret?' asked Frankie.

'Collect your case now. I will lead you up to the dormitory where you can find your name on the bed and locker assigned to you. You can begin to unpack only those belongings that you need tonight: Your nightdress, dressing gown, slippers and a set of underwear. After that, you are to carry your case to the linen room. Make sure that your name is visible on your case.'

Looking at the state of my old case I don't think it needs a label, thought Frankie.

'Tomorrow we will set aside a time when each of you will be called to discuss the other items you have brought. It's 5:30 now. When the bell rings at 5:55, we will file down to the refectory. You are never permitted to talk in the dormitory. Of course, should there be an emergency, you may whisper to us assistants.'

Frankie was relieved that everything was going to be in order. She was also glad to be rid of her mother's tattered old suitcase.

'Military precision,' whispered a smart, older looking woman.

'That's exactly right, Hilary!' remarked Sr Rita.

As Frankie reached the top of the stone steps, she followed the others into a long corridor where Sister was standing, calling out names and giving directions.

'Francesc... Frankie, right and up steps. Jeanette, follow. Right. Margaret, right... Catherine left... '

'Phew! Thought we'd be separated,' whispered Margaret.

'Now to find our names.'

33

'Oh! Here's mine. Look at the size of the bed. So narrow and white curtains all round.'

'Silence! No talking up here. You keep rules, Margaret,' Sister Laura reminded the aspirants.

Frankie searched for a bed with her name. She walked to the top of the first part of the dormitory when she reached a T-junction and turned right. Half-way down she saw her name. Her bed was facing a window. It was one of twelve in that part of the dormitory. *Thank goodness for a window,* thought Frankie. *I won't feel so closed in. It's narrow and small and the same size as my bed at home but it is clean and tidy and I have a locker to store some of my clothes. It'll be peaceful and safe here. No need to fear Mam bringing another man back from the pub late at night,* thought Frankie.

After taking out a long cotton nightdress and dressing gown she slid the First Communion photo into her pillow-case and carried her case to the landing and left it with the others.

As they sprang down stone steps leading to the refectory someone said, 'I smell food! Stew? Can't wait.'

Frankie came into the refectory behind Margaret. Fortunately once again they had been assigned places next to each other. She reflected that there was so much to be grateful for. It was exactly six o clock. Food was going to be served. This made her feel secure especially when she remembered that she never knew when there would be food available at home. She looked at the other aspirants standing round two parallel tables as they prayed the *Angelus* followed by 'Grace before meals'.

'Be seated,' said the nun.

A young aspirant waved her hands over her head and said, 'Hello everybody!'

'No. No talking yet. We all sit down and keep silence while a few verses from the Bible are read. That will be followed by a short reading from the life of the Foundress of the Order, Saint Maria Educatrice.'

'Whose turn is it to read tonight?' asked one of the nuns.

Frankie saw that the aspirant who had shouted out, blushed and then looked as though she was about to cry.

Someone else called out, 'Sorry, Sister.'

Another aspirant said 'More silence!' and looked around at the others for sympathy. Frankie noticed that everyone avoided eye contact.

A much older Scottish aspirant, standing at a brown wooden lectern, read a short excerpt from the Bible and then began, 'The Foundress of the Order of Maria Educatrice is Maria Alberi. She was born in Gabbice del Mare in 1837. When she was only ten years old the direction of her life was determined... '

Frankie was incapable of hearing anymore. She started to yawn. She was very tired.

She noticed Sr Laura making a sign to two of the twelve aspirants who must have entered the convent the year before or maybe even earlier. They pushed their chairs away to stand. When they opened the refectory doors, a delicious smell of gravy and potatoes wafted in to the refectory.

'Food!' whispered someone. They returned wearing oven gloves and long white serving aprons. They placed oblong, aluminium serving dishes on serving boards at the end of the two tables, each set for twelve aspirants. One of the Sisters sat at the top of the table.

Margaret whispered, 'I think it's my favourite. Shepherd's pie!'

'I'm starving,' whispered Frankie.

Frankie noticed that no one seemed to be listening to the reading. The young aspirant next to her clanged her cutlery. Sister must have noticed that everyone seemed distracted because she rang a bell to signal the end of the reading.

'Girls... aspirants. I rang the bell to end the reading because I realised that you have all been travelling today. Some of you have had very long journeys. You must be very tired. You need to get to know each other during dinner.'

The plates were piled in front of the serving mats, together with the serving cutlery. As soon as the lids from the dishes were removed, a familiar aroma emanated. Frankie turned to Margaret to declare, 'We both were right. It's Shepherd's pie, gravy and carrots.'

Frankie began to look more closely at each girl sitting around the table wondering what they were like.

'Pass the plates up the table, Margaret. Mind, they're very hot.'

Frankie realised that the small mousey brown-haired girl with a fringe seated on the other side of the table was next to the chirpy young aspirant who had nudged her earlier.

Frankie muttered sotto voce to Margaret, 'The four opposite us look older. Do you think they might be teachers?'

A little brass bell was tinkled.

'Viva Gesu! Welcome! Long live Jesus and welcome to each of you. I am Sr Maria, referred to as Sr Superior because I am the Sister in charge of the Aspirantade.'

Frankie wondered how many more Sisters would be introduced. It was she who had entered the refectory tingling a little brass bell. Her olive skin and slight accent suggested that she too might be Italian. Frankie was surprised that she was dressed in a long, black habit. She remembered that an older nun was wearing that kind of habit at the vocation exhibition. while the other nun was dressed in grey.

Margaret pushed a note onto Frankie's lap, 'Thought these nuns were modern?'

Frankie scribbled on the back of a paper serviette, 'Explain later. Old habit.'

The long, all concealing, religious habit that this nun

was wearing draped elegantly round her slight, tall body. The starched white bando under her veil and over her bonnet gleamed immaculately as white as her pearly teeth.

She continued, 'You must be longing to get to know each other. Now you have permission to speak and to make friends. We are all here for the same purpose; to get to know and love the God who hopefully helps us to become a little holier each day. We are saints because we share His Life and aim to spread His wonderful love to each person with whom we come in contact. *Educare* in the Italian language, is the verb to educate. That means *to draw out knowledge that informs us and others.'*

Frankie saw that Margaret was taking notes and listening carefully. She felt exhausted but curious.

As soon as Sr Superior left the room, Sr Laura encouraged the aspirants to mingle.

'After cena... I mean 'supper' we have recreation. You can speak and get to know everybody.'

'Phew, that was a lot to take in, Margaret! I suppose the Latin you know, helps you to understand Italian? What did she say? Educare?'

'Yes, Latin helps but I'm definitely not a saint.'

Sr Laura clapped her hands for silence.' Now we go round the table. Each one say you're your name and where you come from. We start at this table because you were here last year. Alright? We start with you, Hilary.'

When the introductions had been made, a youngster seated next to Frankie asked, 'Can you remember any of the names? I know you are Frankie but... '

'You're Jeanette. You went to the school that is part of this convent. Is that right?'

Margaret nudged Frankie. 'I can't recall everyone's name but I know that there are five teachers and four of them are Scots.'

'Okay, Margaret! There's a Maltese nurse, who is sitting

two chairs on your right. A French girl is sitting across from her and the girl with the flaxen hair at the end of the table comes from Holland. Someone else is from Italy. I heard her speaking with Sister Laura.'

'There are one or two from England.'

'And from Ireland. I love to hear the Irish accent. Reminds me of home. I mean my home in Ireland.'

The ice had been broken. The talking and laughter grew louder. When the apple crumble and deliciously hot custard was eagerly consumed, Sr Rita rang the brass bell that she had placed on the mantlepiece under a large picture of the Foundress of the Order, Maria Alberi.

'I see you have already passed your plates to the end of the table. When I have finished explaining what happens next, you should carefully and noiselessly slide out of your chair and lift it carefully and quietly. Stand behind it while we thank God for the food we have been so fortunate to have eaten. Remember so many people, in this world of ours, go hungry.'

Frankie felt Margaret's face as she bent closer to whisper, 'Why do nuns always say that? Makes me feel guilty?'

Sister continued, 'The aspirants at the same table as those have been aspirants for over a year will clear and set the tables for breakfast and wash the dishes and pots and pans. Those of you, who are on Sr Laura's table, please follow her out to recreation. It's a lovely night. You can loosen your limbs and start preparing yourselves to become real educators like Saint Maria. When the washing-up is done, we will join you in the fun and games. When the bell is rung at five to nine, we will end the day with evening prayer in chapel with the Sisters.'

Margaret whispered to Frankie. 'That aspirant was right about military precision.'

Sister continued, 'After that the grand silence begins,

no talking is permitted. We go to our various dormitories while we recite the *Miserere*. Lights are out until we are woken by the Benedicamus Domino at 6 a.m. Now, please all stand for the Grace after meals.'

'Great! Not our turn to do the washing-up, Frankie.'

'Let's follow the rest outside. Someone said that we play games in a big yard. That there's a tennis court too.'

When all the new aspirants were outside in the yard, Sister Laura started to explain how to play Tre Punti, an Italian ball game. She held up three fingers.

Tre Punti. You say 'Three Points', explained Sister Laura as she waved her arms about as she walked between the two lines of aspirants facing each other in order to form two teams.

Frankie noticed that when the aspirants who had been washing-up came to join them, they had their mantillas or veils pushed into the belts of their black skirts. They wore white school blouses and black cardigans. Their shoes were lace-ups and they wore black tights. Their short hair seemed to be controlled by having being combed back and flattened. No one had a fringe nor was there any suggestion of style. Uniformity reigned.

'Enjoyed that, Frankie?' It was Margaret.' We needed as much energy as we did at the disco. It was fun even without those crazy lads. What do you think?'

As Frankie was about to reply, a bell tinkled to announce the end of games.

A childlike voice called out, 'But we haven't finished.'

Sister Laura replied, 'When God calls, we go. Important to obey. First lesson, Jeanette.'

'I'm sweating. Perspiring, Sister. May I run in ahead and throw water on my face?'

'No time. Take your mantillas and join the line.'

The girls donned their veils and followed a line of twelve nuns into chapel. A young nun with a high-pitched squeaky voice started the prayers, 'Let us bow our heads and examine our conscience and reflect back over our actions throughout this day.' After long pause she began reciting the same 'Act of Contrition' or sorrow that is recited at the beginning of the celebration of the Mass. When that ended, another nun intoned the hymn for the Divine Office: *Plaisir d'Amour*.

Frankie noticed that one nun's tuneful voice and clear diction stood out from the others. Although most of the new Aspirants probably had never heard that hymn, they were able to sing along because it was the same tune as 'My God loves me... '

Frankie prayed, 'Please God, help me to sing as well as that Sister.'

Three psalms were followed by a reading and then bidding prayers. Each of their names was mentioned in a welcoming prayer. Frankie felt that she belonged when she heard her name. Then an Italian nun prayed, 'Dear God, the father of our family, and Mary, our Mother, bless and console the parents of these aspirants especially tonight and reward them for allowing their daughters to follow your divine call.' *That's me*, thought Frankie.

When Frankie heard sniffling, she became aware that perhaps everyone else was beginning to realise that they possibly wouldn't see their families for a long time. She was glad when the blubbering was drowned out by the singing of a beautifully ancient hymn to Our Lady called *Salve Regina*. Although she didn't know the words, she followed them on a sheet that was handed to them. She had heard this hymn being sung on feasts of Our Lady by the nuns at her school.

Margaret had her head in her hands and seemed to be praying her own prayers.

Frankie nudged her to get up and follow the Sister who had genuflected at the end of the front bench and signalled to the aspirants to follow her.

The aspirants exited the chapel one behind another, genuflecting first in reverence to the presence of Jesus in the tabernacle on the altar. Then they followed her across the hall, along the stone-floored corridor and up the wooden stairs to the dormitories. Sister handed each of them an English translation of Psalm 51 entitled *Miserere*. She began reciting it as they located their cubicles. Each girl pulled the white curtains around her bed, folded back the white candlewick bed spread on her bed and began to undress.

The words of the psalm began with, 'Have mercy on me, O God, in your goodness; in the greatness of your compassion, wipe out my offence...'

This psalm sounded mournful. Frankie felt guilty for thinking that it was no wonder it was called the *Miserere*.

Just then Margaret lifted up Frankie's curtain, 'Frankie. Please... I think it's my periods. I've no towels... what now?'

'Oh no! You're in pain? Is Sister there? You can whisper. Go! Explain to her.'

Fortunately, Sr Laura was standing on guard at the door that led from the dormitories to the wash basins and toilets. Margaret stood in front of her and whispered, 'Sorry Sister, but I need sanitary towels. Please would you give me some?'

Sister looked puzzled. She whispered back, 'Ripetere per favore... Say again, please?'

By the time Margaret had mentioned blood, monthly and towels, nearly all the aspirants were aware of her predicament. Eventually Sr Laura produced pieces of cut-up towelling that obviously seemed to be what the nuns substituted for commercial sanitary towels.

After fixing herself in the toilet, Margaret slipped into bed. Frankie crept along to her cubicle, 'You alright now, Margaret?'

'Thanks, Frankie. My mother usually gives me a hot

cup of chocolate. She always comforts me at the time of the month.'

Lucky you, thought Frankie. *No such luck in my house. It's my mother who looks for comfort.* But she said, 'I don't think you'll be that lucky.'

'I hope I won't soil the mattress with the make-shift towelling, Frankie.'

'I'd better get back to bed before I'm caught. Try and sleep, Margaret. Goodnight.'

'Night, Frankie. Can you hear the sobbing coming from the twelve-year-old girl in the cubicle on my right? I'm probably not the only one in pain. See you in the morning.'

Frankie lifted the curtain between the beds and bent down and kissed Jeanette's forehead. She could not believe her eyes when she saw that Jeanette was cuddling a teddy bear. She rubbed her tears away with her sheet and tried to smile back at Frankie. Frankie blew her a kiss. Then she peeped out behind the curtain to make sure that Sister Laura was not in sight before going back to her bed in her own cubicle.

Frankie lay awake for what seemed ages worrying about Margaret. She was disturbed by daylight still showing through the white curtains round her bed. She began to think: *I know that my time of the month comes in the first week of each month. Margaret is cleverer than me. Why wasn't she prepared? I wonder if big changes in a person's life, like moving away from home, interferes with our body clock.* As she thought about Margaret missing her mother giving her a chocolate drink, she felt deprived. She could not remember her mother ever kissing her goodnight yet she longed to see her again, watching the television as she crept past her mother's armchair into her bedroom. She left her most nights drinking wine and munching crisps. The lights were turned off. She slid her hand inside her pillow case to feel for the photo of her mother with her on her First

Communion Day. It was safe there.

Where am I? Is that Sr Laura ringing a bell and calling out. What is it?

'Benedicamus Domino!' *I must have slept. What do I do now?* Frankie rubbed her eyes and stretched.

Margaret. I'd better check on her, thought Frankie.

Frankie crept into Margaret's cubicle. She could see that she looked weak and worried.

'How are you?' whispered Frankie.

'Oh Frankie. I want to stay in bed. I'm wet. I'd better get to the toilet. I don't suppose Sister remembers …'

'Take it easy, Margaret. Out you go.' Frankie supported Margaret as she stepped out of bed and began to hobble her way out of her cubicle. When they pulled back the curtain Margaret nearly collided with Hilary. Frankie tugged Hilary's dressing gown and made signs to her. She looked at Margaret clutching her stomach and must have guessed Margaret's predicament because she moved quickly ahead of them and signalled to others in the toilet queue that it was imperative to let Margaret into the toilet as soon as possible.

Frankie watched Margaret, her face contorted in pain, mouthing 'Thank you. Thank you.' She was glad that Hilary was so understanding.

Even after all the trauma, Frankie found that she was first in line outside the chapel. She congratulated herself. *In less than half an hour I have managed to turn my mattress, make my bed, negotiate my way to the wash room and the toilet, get dressed, make my way down the wooden stairs and across the hall to wait for Sr Laura.*

Although there were no mirrors, Frankie patted down her hair and hoped that her black mantilla sat well on her unruly short mousey-brown hair. As it was still early and the lights were not switched on, she couldn't properly check how she looked in the black skirt and cardigan, black lace-up shoes and brown Lyle stockings. She was certain that the collar of her blouse was down because she had firmed it into place as she waited for the others to join her in the queue.

When Sr Laura led the new aspirants into chapel, last year's twelve established aspirants were already in their places. Frankie noticed that Margaret held her head down as she knelt in the row in front of her. As soon as the morning prayers began, she leant back in her seat so that her back almost touched Frankie's praying hands.

Oh no. Poor Margaret must be suffering from period cramp. The nuns are looking around. They must have noticed that Margaret is struggling. Why aren't they doing something?

Sisters Laura, Rita and Maria looked from Margaret to the other eight nuns in the community. Sr Maria opened a side window, probably hoping that fresh air would revive Margaret. Frankie leant forward and whispered into Margaret's ear, 'Are you okay?'

Margaret swivelled round, her chestnut curls masking her face and replied, 'It's the pain... I...'

Frankie thought something needed to be done. She turned round to catch Sr Rita's attention and pointing at Margaret, mouthed, 'Could you get her an aspirin, please, Sr Rita?'

The aspirants sitting on the right side of the chapel, where Frankie, Margaret and Sr Rita were kneeling, were supposed to be responding to the first part of the *Hail Mary* with the second part: *Holy Mary*...But they were barely audible. In fact, the praying of the rosary was almost disrupted.

Frankie was relieved to see Sr Rita leaving the chapel but was horrified to notice that she glared back at Margaret as she left.

Frankie leaned forward again to whisper in Margaret's ear, 'Help is coming.'

Sister returned with a glass of water.

Frankie said, 'Aspirin?'

Margaret fainted, falling forward she banged her head on the chapel pew.

Some nuns sighed and tutted. Sister Rita moved in beside Margaret and had to almost carry her outside.

Frankie hoped that the nuns realised Margaret's condition and that she had been taken back to bed.

Even so, the rosary continued to be recited. When it was finished the priest entered the chapel to celebrate Mass at the same time as Sr Rita returned to her place. Frankie hoped that Margaret was coping. She also wondered why everyone was behaving as if nothing had happened. *Do they think Margaret is feigning illness? Surely nuns don't ignore pain? Even my mother wouldn't be that cruel.*

After Mass everyone filed out from the chapel. The Sisters genuflected and exited very quickly. Sr Laura beckoned the aspirants to form a circle round her in the hall.

She handed each a copy of the following prayer to recite:

Father, may everything we do begin with your inspiration and continue with your saving help. Let our work always find its origin in you and through you reach completion. Through Christ our Lord. Amen

She read out a list of jobs to be done: 'The sacristy, study, front and back stairs, entrance hall, three dormitories, bathrooms, toilets outside the dormitories and back parlour have to be swept, dusted and tidied. Two of you will go down to the kitchen garden to feed and water the chickens, clean out their coops, put fresh bedding down and collect their eggs. The rest of you are to prepare the vegetables and place whatever we will be having for breakfasts on the refectory tables. You have half an hour to do these jobs. Take your named apron from the peg along the corridor. Leave your veils in the lockers underneath.'

Frankie heard a few comments whispered, 'I wish I had

some food inside me before I had to clean toilets. I never cleaned our toilet at home.'

Frankie agreed. Then she heard another aspirant saying, 'By the time I put my apron on and get to those dirty chickens, it'll be time to come back.'

Sister suddenly stopped, looked round and asked.' Who's whispering? Listen to me.' She continued, 'For some of you this is the first morning doing these chores. Aspirants, who came last year, take new aspirant to their job and explain.' She turned to address those of who had recently entered. 'They will take you to the area of the house to be cleaned. Breakfast is served at eight.'

'Please Sister Laura, how is Margaret?' inquired Frankie.

'You no need to concern. Sr Rita decide… let her sleep.'

Frankie was glad that she had been given the job of sweeping the dormitory because she hoped that she would be able to check on Margaret. When she reached the dormitory she saw the curtain was drawn round Margaret's bed. As soon as the aspirant who came to instruct her had gone, Frankie tiptoed to her bed and pulled back the curtain to check on her.

'You okay, Margaret?'

Margaret opened her tear-filled eyes. 'I'd love a hot water bottle, Frankie. I'm so cold and my stomach... These blankets are threadbare.'

Frankie turned to see Sr Rita climbing the last step into the dormitory. She had her finger over her lips to indicate that silence was to be observed. Frankie took no notice.

'Margaret needs a hot water bottle, Sr Rita.'

Sr Rita brushed past Frankie as she gestured that she expected her to start the sweeping. Then she whispered to Margaret, 'You are not ill. Every woman goes through this process each month. Get up now. After you have eaten your breakfast, any unpleasant feelings will be forgotten.

Imagine if each of us behaved like this? You have a quarter of an hour to get to the refectory.'

Frankie, near enough to overhear, was horrified. Her mother would have said something similar but she hoped that the nuns would be more Christ-like and caring. She also thought that the way Sr Rita strode through the room made her seem arrogant and self-assured. Six feet tall, well proportioned, stern-faced and rather manly, she appeared to be more suited to the army than to the convent.

By the time the first bell rang at five minutes to eight, the other aspirants had removed their overalls and were standing behind their chairs in the refectory. Margaret managed to join them. Frankie noticed that she was pale-faced and gripping the back of the chair. *Was Sr Rita smirking and looking satisfied? Surely not.*

Once Grace was said and they were seated in the places given to them the previous night, the young Aspirant, Jeanette, on Frankie's right, remarked, 'I've never eaten porridge. That's what we're having. Do you like porridge, Frankie?'

'We always have porridge in my home, Jeannette. My mother told me that her father was a commercial traveller. He brought Flahavan's Porridge Oats to many a shop throughout Ireland. That's why we ate it every morning, summer or winter. I'd miss it if I didn't have it.'

'Did anyone hear me snoring?' enquired Hilary, seated opposite Frankie.

'Very loudly! All night. No I'm joking, Hilary. Besides I might have snored too.'

'The thing is, you can't hear yourself, can you?' remarked another aspirant.

'My sister always tells me that I snore. I know she does. I suspect I do too,' confessed another aspirant.

One of the Scottish teachers asked, 'Does anyone know

what we are doing today?'

Those who heard, shook their heads.

Porridge was no sooner ladled out and passed up the table than Sister Rita rang a bell and announced, 'After we have finished eating our breakfast, the aspirants from last year will do the washing-up and laying the tables in the refectory. Meanwhile everyone else may walk outside in the fresh air before we all assemble in the entrance. Then we will go to the study to be assigned places there. After that Sr Maria will tell you the various timetables and all the important rules that you will be expected to follow in this Aspirantade.'

Frankie noticed that tears began to trickle down the cheeks of a young aspirant standing next to her. She moved nearer and whispered, 'What's the matter?'

The aspirant blubbered, 'I want to go home. I made a mistake in becoming an aspirant. I just want to go home.'

'It's the first day. Why not give it a try? It's like the day when you started school. I was frightened too. You'll like it by tonight. Wait and see,' coaxed Frankie.

4

RULES AND REGULATIONS

*F*rankie noticed that Margaret looked better after eating the porridge and a slice of bread and butter. Although the tea was lukewarm and not properly infused, she thought it must have helped to revive her.

Stella, the aspirant from Malta suggested, 'Maybe, Sr Rita has forgotten what it feels like to be new to womanhood, Margaret? But wait until it's my turn. I sometimes faint. Periods take us all differently. I'm a nurse so if you need anything, I'm here.'

'Thank you, Stella. My mother usually has an aspirin ready for me. I have been taken by surprise this time.'

'Lovely to know that there is a kind nurse around if you need one, Stella.'

'When I was working in a hospital in Valletta I nursed the Provincial of this Order of nuns.'

'Did you say the *Provincial* ? Is the *Provincial* more important than the Sister Superior?' asked one of the other aspirants.

'I'm not entirely sure of the ranking in the Order. As I

understand it, Sister Superiors are in charge of a community of Sisters whereas Provincials are responsible for many communities in a set area.'

'That's called a province? Is that correct, Stella?' asked Margaret.

'Malta is a good distance away from England. Yet it is grouped with Britain.'

'You've got me scratching my head there, Frankie. All I know is that Ireland used to belong to the English province but it has so many vocations now that it is a province on its own. Malta used to belong to an Italian Province but is now allied to Britain.'

'Maybe, it is to do with numbers,' suggested Margaret.

'Anyway, I was so impressed by the great work that these Sisters provide for youngsters that I decided that I wanted to join these nuns. And here I am,' said Stella as she clapped her hands.

Frankie noticed that those sitting near them at the breakfast table were smiling as they listened to this older woman. She hoped that her remark to Margaret had consoled her. At least Margaret was glad that she had managed to get herself down to the refectory. She sensed that some of the other aspirants were about to ask her how she was when Sr Maria arrived through the door and rang a bell to gain attention.

'Please stand. When you have said your grace after meals go straight to the study. Sr Laura will lead the way.'

Frankie moved behind Margaret and managed to sit next to her again in the study. Sr Maria was sitting at the desk in the front of the room. When they were all seated, she rolled her hands inside the folds of the big, black, outer sleeves of her habit, tugged her bonnet down over her ears before she started to speak.

'Firstly, I will show you the timetable that we continue to observe during these few days before school term commences. After that I will explain some of the philosophy that underpins the way we behave in responding to God's call.'

Sr Maria then unfurled the following timetable. Resting it over a blackboard, she used a stick to indicate the various points.

Oh no! This is like school, thought Frankie.

6 a.m. Benedicamus, make your bed, wash, dress and descend silently to assemble outside chapel.

6:30 Morning prayers and the celebration of Mass

Sr Maria rattled on. Frankie reflected: *I need rules and security but I don't want to join the army. Time to wash. Time to sew. Lots of time praying in and out of chapel. Angelus. Examination of conscience.*

Frankie looked over at Margaret and thought she was taking notes. Then she passed her a folded note under the desk. Frankie very quietly unfolded the paper: *Time to confess. But no time to sin!*

Frankie had to control a fit of laughter. She scribbled: *Fold your apron. Blow your nose.*

Frightened that she would be seen, Frankie waited several minutes before she sneaked her note to Margaret. When she looked around the room she saw that most of the aspirants seemed to be doodling.

Frankie thought that Sr Maria must not have been a teacher because she appeared to be oblivious of the fact that no one was listening. How could she drone on in such a monotone voice?

Sr Maria had her back to the aspirants when Frankie heard her saying, 'Half an hour slots for baths throughout Fridays and Saturdays.' Frankie looked at Margaret who was squeezing her nose. Frankie mouthed, 'Smelly.'

Frankie felt restless and began rubbing her eye lids and then the palms of her hands against each other. When she looked round the room again, she saw that a younger aspirant was biting her nails. All the others, including Margaret, were now sitting bolt upright and appeared to be paying attention to every word that Sr Maria was saying.

What's wrong with me? Frankie asked herself. *Am I stupid? I'm not going to fit in. But if I left, what is there to go home to? A mother who is delighted that she no longer has to worry about me? I'm not intelligent enough to be a nurse or work in a bank. I'll just have to stick it out.*

Sr Maria coughed, put her hands into her big sleeves to straighten them again and adjusted the position of the crucifix hanging on a cord round her neck and beneath her white bib. Then she recommenced: 'While the teachers and students among you will begin the new school year, others will be working here in the convent.'

She's not finished yet! I can't take any more, thought Frankie. She glanced at Margaret and raised her eyes heavenwards.

'Jeanette Smith, Pauline Shaw, Margaret Blackburn and Frances Danivet will join Mavis Hurley, who entered last year, to continue their education at school.'

Frankie felt her jaw fall open. 'I'm going back to school? I'm no good at school. I dreamt of going abroad to somewhere hot,' she whispered to Margaret. Margaret smiled back at her.

Frankie was about to put up her hand up and protest. Then she thought, *I'm the odd one out here. Judging by the glint in Margaret's eyes, she is delighted to be able to continue her studies. No wonder, she had passed six O-level GCE subjects and three A levels.* Frankie remembered that her father chose this Order of nuns in the hope that she would train to be a teacher.

Sister continued, 'I can see that Margaret and Frances, having recently left school look a little surprised but we have been advised that appropriate subjects have been decided for you to study. We will inform you both later.'

What can I do to get out of this? thought Frankie. *I barely scraped through GCE ordinary level English Language, English Literature, Home Economics and History. What would I be doing if I don't continue my education? I would probably end up working in Woolworth's.*

'Stella Stanza, you are a nurse. Anna Bianca is a secretary while both Monique Valleau and Brigitte De Roos are excellent seamstresses. All four of you will use your skills here in the convent translating, sewing, typing and learning Italian, which is the language of this religious Order. '

Having listened to what those remaining in the convent would be doing, Frankie realised that going to school was probably going to be better than being assigned to doing domestic chores.

Sr Maria droned on. Frankie switched off again. She began to think about convent life. Regimented, with lots of rules. *When I left school I wanted to be free to do what I like. No order in my home. I'd be free but I couldn't live the chaotic life that my mother seems to be content with.*

Frankie closed her eyes and imagined herself back on her aunt's farm in Ireland. The sky was blue, the hills green. Lambs were frolicking about the field.

'Frankie! Frankie! Wake up. Take one and pass them on.' It was Margaret who had disturbed her nap.

'I want to tell you about uniforms,' continued Sr Maria, 'At home in the convent, all aspirants will continue to wear black skirts, cardigans and lace-up shoes, white, cotton blouses and the brown Lisle stockings that you have brought with you. Those who teach will wear the same.'

Phew! Just as well that I've got two blouses. I hope the nuns are better at keeping them white. My mam sometimes used to mix them up with coloured clothes, thought Frankie. Then she wondered if her mam missed her carrying the bag of washing down to the launderette. Did she have to carry it herself now? *I bet she persuaded someone else to carry it down now.*

Sister continued, 'However, only those of you who are students will wear the school summer and winter uniforms when attending school. In summer it will be a blue and white pin-stripped cotton dress. In winter it will be a navy blue pinafore dress, white blouse and navy blue cardigan.'

Frankie heard one of the young aspirants comment aloud, 'Good. I have already got the summer uniform.'

One of the Scottish aspirants behind Frankie said, 'That girl's too young to enter the convent!'

Sister Maria must have heard this comment because she seemed to stare directly at Frankie. Then Frankie heard the Scottish aspirants whisper to whoever was sitting next to her, 'If looks could kill.'

Too many rules. I hope Sister did not see me yawning. Maybe Woolworth's might suit me better after all. I would be free. I could make new friends. After I had worked for a while, my pay would increase. Frankie sighed. *I can't take more of this regimentation. I want to scream. If only we could stand up and turn around.* Frankie trailed her hands through her hair as these thoughts ran through her head.

Sister Maria sipped some water from a glass on the desk in front of her and continued, 'On Sundays and feast days you will wear a black serge knee-length dress with a white Peter Pan collar and three pearl buttons on the front of the bodice.'

Frankie thought that she heard a suppressed laugh from someone at the other side of the room. She was scared to look around. She thought about the dresses that the girls wore to the dance hall. If they only knew...

Margaret whispered, 'I adore lovely clothes. How am I going manage without them, Frankie?'

Frankie shook her shoulders in acknowledgement of their plight. Some of the girls were fiddling with their hair, other slumped in their seats.

Seemingly oblivious of the restlessness, Sr Maria continued, 'When needed, you will each wear the black gabardine coats that you brought with you and a black beret. Those who attend school will be supplied with a school beret and blazer.'

Frankie screwed up her face. She detested the fact that she would have to wear a school uniform.

Sister continued, 'You each have been given a black mantilla to be worn in chapel. Those of you who become Postulants on 8th March, the feast of our Mother Foundress of the Order, St Maria Alberi, will wear a chemise and a cape as well as black stockings and a special postulant's medal.'

'What's a chemise, Sister?' asked an older aspirant.

'All will be explained when the time is right, Stella,' replied Sister Maria.

'Good!' exclaimed someone else in the study. Frankie was pleased too. It was only then that she realised that once you became a postulant even though you were still attending school, you no longer had to wear a school uniform. *Thank goodness I will only have to wear a school uniform for three months!*

The young aspirant next to Frankie stretched her hands into air and let out a sigh. Frankie yawned. Frankie looked over at Margaret and noticed that colour was draining from her face. She nudged her and said, 'You need to drink water, Margaret.' Margaret nodded.

Frankie put her hand up and called out: 'Please Sister, may I get some water for Margaret? I think she is about to faint.'

Sr Maria pursed her lips and stared. She took out her fob watch, checked the time and announced, 'We'll break for ten... no, fifteen minutes, to allow you to make yourselves comfortable. Margaret, you may come forward first.'

Frankie looked to see if Margaret was able to take care of herself.

'Thank you, Frankie. I can't hold out any longer for the toilet. I'll manage. Thank you.'

When Sr Maria left the room, most of the aspirants called across to Frankie to thank her.

'I thought my back was going to break if Sister went on much longer. I resorted to tapping my feet to stop them from going numb.'

'If I yawned any more, my jaws would have broken.'

Frankie guessed that Margaret was being told to go for a walk in the fresh air. She asked Sister Laura who had come to supervise them, 'Please, Sister, may we all go out for a few minutes? If we do we'll be better able to listen to Sr Maria when she returns.'

'Please, Sr Laura?' echoed everyone.

Outside, Frankie was delighted once more that she was patted on the back and thanked for her initiative.

Frankie joined Margaret seated on a garden bench.

'Was it the thought of never wearing all your lovely clothes that made you feel faint, Margaret?'

'Oh Frankie, I have a wardrobe full of really trendy clothes at home. On the last day of school a few girls from my class went round to one of our friend's house. We ripped off our uniforms and changed into the fashionable clothes that we brought from home.'

'The girl's mother wasn't there?'

'Of course not! We had planned it all. One girl brought a mini skirt. I tried it on. My parents would have screamed at me had they known.'

'Well let me tell you, posh girl, we did the same.'

'Oh! What kind of clothes did you swop, Frankie?'

'Well you know by now that there was very little money in our house, Margaret. When my friends announced what they were planning, I had to think ahead. I was determined not to stick out like a sore thumb...'

'You've got a rich uncle?'

'No Margaret, but our landlady has a daughter who works in Selfridges. '

'Selfridges?'

'Yes. She brings home top fashion clothes on approval. Every now and then, I'm called down to my landlady's to try them on. But that's all I get to do because even though they usually fit me and I love them, we can't afford them.'

'That must be even worse than just seeing them in the shops.'

'Yes, but I had worked out that if they were soiled they could not be returned!'

'So you... how could you soil... ?'

'I pricked my finger and just one drop of blood... '

'Oh Frankie, how could you? What was the dress like... was it a dress? '

'It was fabulous! Selfridges had copied it from the San Francisco fashion show. It was a vivid yellow colour with bright swirling stripes and flowers. Really short with long puffy sleeves. Hard to describe. It had a matching head band. I loved it.'

'That's all the rage! Lucky you. Did your mother have to fork out the money?'

'Of course not. No. She told her pub friends about her stupid daughter and they each contributed to the cost.

'Oh, the bell's gone, Margaret. Talking of colour, it's come back into your cheeks.'

As they walked back to the find the toilets before returning to the study, Frankie reflected and smiled to herself. *Maybe after all, my mother taught me how to cope and find solutions when I face problems.*

Frankie was relieved to see that there wasn't a queue outside the bathroom toilets located on the same landing as the study. She even had time to sip some water from a glass on a table leading into the study.

Sr Maria was waiting for them at her desk in the study as they filed back to listen to the rest of her lecture. She too looked relaxed. She cleared her throat and began again, 'Now that you are refreshed, I am going to tell you a little about our Foundress, though I am well aware that you will have discovered many facts regarding her life already. It is good to remind ourselves that her lowly beginnings, far from being an obstacle, helped to drive her to do great things for God and for others.

Not as lowly as my background, reflected Frankie. She glanced at Margaret. She smiled back. Frankie felt that maybe Margaret was more understanding of what it was like to be poor.

Sr Maria droned on enunciating each word slowly, 'Our Mother Foundress Maria Alberi was born in Gabbice Del Mare near Ancona on March 8th, 1837 to a labourer, Giovanni, and his wife, Angela. As the first born girl, she was called Maria after the Madonna. You will know it was the custom at that time in Catholic families to offer their first born to enter the convent. Naturally when Maria was ten years old, it was no surprise that she felt that she had been chosen and was given a specific mission to fulfil in life. Just like each of you, she had what we call a 'vocation.

Frankie caught Margaret's eye and mouthed, 'Vocation? Have you got a vocation?' Then she pointed to herself and upturned her hands as if to ask herself if she had a vocation too.

Sister continued: 'Confirmation that Maria had a vocation came when she had a special dream or vision on the feast of the Immaculate Conception on 8th December.

'She dreamt that she was by the sea shore when she saw a whale swimming close to the beach. She was scared but also curious at sighting this wonderful mammal so near land. She ran back and hid near the entrance to a cave. Then she

58

saw Jesus appear in a boat calming the waves and blessing the whale. It seemed to her that the whale smiled and Jesus said, 'These creatures are here for a specific purpose. Just as massive mammals, friendly dolphins and fish as small as sardines follow their way of life, you too have your calling. My apostles, Peter, John and James, became fishers of men and women. You too can help others on the stormy seas of life."

'Sister, I hope you won't mind me interrupting you, but wasn't this just a young girl dreaming? What I mean is, we all have dreams. How is this any different?'

Everyone looked round to see who was asking this question.

Frankie was delighted to see that it was Anne Elizabeth, one of the teachers. *She is brave,* she thought, *challenging Sr Maria. That was exactly what I was wondering but I didn't have the courage to ask. Besides, everyone would find out how stupid I am.*

'A good question. Let me continue relating this story. Hopefully you will see that this was more than a dream,' responded Sr Maria.

'While Maria was still dreaming, her eight year old brother, Giuseppe, opened her bedroom door and shouted, 'Hurry up, the polenta is ready. Mamma said, come before it gets cold.' Maria came to her senses. She didn't know what to make of the dream. She arrived for breakfast still trying to puzzle out what it all meant.

'Maria! Maria! Mamma's pet!' teased her brother.

Maria didn't seem to hear.

Her brother pulled her hair saying, 'Wake up, wake up, sleepy head!'

Maria's mother noticed that Maria didn't seem to pay any attention to her brother's usual taunts and teasing, 'What's up with you this morning, Maria?'

'Mamma, I think I've had a vision. Oh, I don't know.

Perhaps a dream but… well it had Jesus in it.'

'We say our prayers. We pray the rosary. Your head must have been full of holy thoughts. That is why you dream about Jesus. What did you dream?'

'When Maria related the dream, her mother raised her finger to her lips, scratched her head and said, 'Cara figlia, per favore, it's better you don't go around telling people about this dream. You know the story of St Bernadette of Lourdes and what happened to her when she said she had seen the Madonna?'

Giuseppe laughed aloud, then stopped abruptly. He looked from his mother to Maria. 'Mamma is Maria going to change into a saint?' Then smiling, he continued, 'Maybe then she will stop bossing me about.''

'Giuseppe had a good sense of humour,' an aspirant in the front row called out.

Frankie clapped and Margaret bent over and tapped Frankie on her shoulder in approval.

'Glad you enjoyed it so far, aspirants, I've nearly finished.'

Frankie stretched out her arms as she whispered, 'There's more!' She saw Margaret press the palms of her hands together, sigh and stifle a yawn. The aspirant seated in front of her was tapping her finger on her desk.

Sister Maria did not seem to notice.

'While Giuseppe got ready for school, Maria's mother put her arms around her and warned that her friends and their parents would make fun of her if she went around telling people about the vision.'

Hilary, the teacher from Oxford, must have thought Sr Maria had come to the end of the story. She called out, 'Sr Maria, has the life of Maria Alberi been made into a film?'

Sr Maria responded, 'A good question, Hilary. The script for the film has been written. Hopefully the film will be released next year.

'Just the last part of the story, aspirants.'

Everybody was moving some part of their body. Frankie could hear yawns, legs swinging, coughing, feet tapping. Desk lids were being lifted and shut. She thought if this had happened at her school, the class would have clapped when Sister said she was nearly finished. She breathed in and out slowly as she leant over and whispered to Margaret, 'When will she ever end?'

Margaret raised her eyes heavenwards and squeezed her hands together.

'It must be nearly time for the bell to ring for midday prayers. I'm sure that we have been here for two hours, Margaret!'

Obviously unaware of the restlessness, Sister continued: 'You can imagine the type of conversation that went on between Maria and her parents trying to convince her that it was because she fed her mind with images of Jesus and his apostles that she dreamt of them. Maria's mother was frightened that Maria might be seeking notoriety by claiming that she was some kind of saint who received messages from God. For the days, weeks and even months that followed, Maria realised that it was better not to speak of this dream again. Her family hoped that it had been forgotten. Maria often recalled this dream and walked down by the sea looking for whales and puzzling what she was to do about the message she had received from the Lord.

'Now aspirants, isn't that a wonderful lesson for us?' said Sr Maria.

Frankie raised her hands over her head and swivelled her face in Margaret's direction. Margaret gave her the thumbs-up signed and smiled back.

Sr Maria must have noticed because she smiled at them and finished, 'Now aspirants, some of you know the rest of this extraordinary story. I am going to stop here so that you all get on with the work that will be assigned to you for the rest of the morning. For those of you who have either forgotten what happened next in Maria's life or the few who don't know, don't worry because you will be able to learn more about her life at the readings during lunch and at dinner. It's such a wonderful story. Our Order would not have been founded had Maria not followed her dream and received the message that Our Lord gave to her.'

When Sr Maria left the room Frankie laughed and turned to Margaret and sang, *'Whenever I want you, all I have to do is dream... dream, dream, dream!'*

'Yes Frankie... dream of boys... '

'Shish!...'

'... dancing and being held tight...'

'We'll be thrown out, Margaret.'

'Good idea? No such luck. Here comes Sr Laura with the list of our jobs.'

5

PARTICULAR FRIENDSHIPS

*S*ummer lingered. Frankie wished that the aspirants had been able to roll up their shirt sleeves while they were gardening. Sr Laura clapped her hands. 'Time to stop. Basta! Stop! 15 minutes tea.'

'I'm so hot, Frankie. Sister must be boiling in that habit. Why are we covered up so much? It's not to keep the sun off us. We've aprons over our dresses and we've been issued with heavy gardening boots. Some aspirants are wearing wellingtons. In this weather! '

'I'm going for a foot bath, Margaret. My feet are sweaty and smelly.'

'So are mine, Frankie. There are only six foot baths. We're going for our weekly walk this afternoon. They'll get hot again.'

'Okay. Thank goodness it's still holidays, Margaret.'

'We've been here a week already, Frankie.'

'We've knocked seven days off our sentences!'

They both chorused, 'We've been inside for a week!' as they shook out their garden aprons.

'Hurry up now, aspirants. Make sure you give the aprons a good shake before you hang them back on the hooks,' called out Sr Maria. 'We can't keep washing them.'

'I'm tired of all this gardening. Wait until I tell my father that I have sawn through a tree trunk, Frankie. He thought I was here to train to become a teacher. Maybe he'll want me home.'

'I'm looking forward to the walk.'

'This will be our first walk outside the convent grounds.'

'Good. We'll be able to have a good chat about what we think of life inside. '

'Inside… inside? We're prisoners, Frankie!'

'We are!'

'Margaret and Frankie, stop that laughing and hurry up,' called out Sr Maria.

Frankie was first in the hall after dinner, washing-up, recreation and prayers. Sr Rita stood on the first step of the stairs and faced the aspirants.

'When we go out for a walk, I partner you off in pairs. We form a long crocodile with one of us Sisters at either end of the line.'

'May we choose who we walk with, Sister?'

'Good,' commented Margaret as she nudged Frankie.

'Definitely not, Hilary. I have noticed that some of you are already choosing to be together. This is your opportunity to get to know other aspirants.'

Frankie overheard someone nearby whisper, 'I hope no one recognises me dressed in this uniform.'

Then she heard a snigger. 'They'll think we've been let out of an orphanage!'

Frankie nodded to Margaret in agreement. They smiled at each other.

Frankie watched how they were being partnered. She whispered to Margaret, 'Try to move to the other side of the room.'

'It's no use!' sighed Margaret. 'There's no rhyme or reason to this pairing.'

'Frankie, you are to walk with Mavis,' announced Sister.

Although Frankie was disappointed not to be partnered with Margaret, she was consoled that she was going to walk with another Irish aspirant.

'Isn't it grand to get outside and be able to chat freely, Frankie?'

'What part do you hail from, Mavis? Is that a Dub accent I hear? My parents come from Kerry.'

'Well, you're right there. I lived in Leixslip, outside Dublin on the road to Kildare.'

'Is that near where the diocesan priests train?' checked Frankie.

'Yes. St Patrick's Seminary and University,' Mavis assured her

'Wasn't there a picture of it lately in the *Universe*?'

'Yes, indeed. On the front page showing the Bishops at their summer conference. How long are you over here, Frankie? I can detect the lilt of Kerry or Cork in your accent. Were ye living on the border?'

'Oh, we've lived here a few years now. It must be all of five, Mavis. I hope you won't mind me asking you, Mavis...'

'Go right ahead, Frankie. No secrets among us aspirants.'

'Alright so. What drew you to these nuns? Have they got a convent in Dublin?'

'Yes. As you know, there lots of convent schools in Ireland, Frankie. The one I went to is in Cork. The nuns came to our school looking for vocations.'

'Was your school a convent school?' inquired Frankie.

'It was run by the Sisters of Education.'

'So why didn't you join them?'

'Because they didn't wear a proper habit. Although I

liked them, they wore a green costume. They didn't look like nuns. That's what my mam used to say, Frankie.'

'But surely... ?'

'Yes, of course there were more important reasons. I can't really explain. Can you? God calls, doesn't He?'

'That's so true. You just know. Quick, Mavis! Look over there! Did you see the swans?'

'There's lots swimming near that woman. I wish we had brought some bread.'

'It's so lovely to walk by the river, isn't it, Mavis?'

'Just going back to the reason why I choose these nuns, Frankie. I think what attracted me most of all was the life of Maria Alberi. The fact too, that this Order was founded in Italy, the heart of the Catholic Church yet it reaches out to people in many nations.'

'Didn't Maria Alberi have an awful time convincing her parish priest that God had given her a specific mission in life, Frankie?'

'She did. I can understand why he was sceptical. Anyone could imagine that they had a vision. Some folk just want attention.'

'Even St Bernadette encountered problems.'

'Yes, Bernadette kept saying that Our Lady appeared to her but those who knelt beside her saw nothing.'

'It was only when sick people were cured of their illnesses at Lourdes that eventually convinced the Vatican that Bernadette was a saint.'

'It was the miracles that persuaded them.'

'Well, it was the outbreak of typhoid that led Maria to help others. She succumbed herself. Again it was the miracles that ensued, that proved that she was a genuine saint.'

'Brava! I catch up with you before we arrive back home!'

'Oh welcome, Sister Laura,' responded Frankie as she

signalled her to walk between them.

By this time the crocodile was winding up the drive to the convent front door. Sister Rita clapped her hands and addressed them.

'I hope you enjoyed your walk. When you enter the house remember that the Sisters are observing the silence. Make your way quietly through the back entrance and continue into the refectory for tea.'

'The corridors are so dark and gloomy. Thank goodness the ref is bright and airy, Frankie.'

'Yes, in spite of all the brown woodwork round the walls and all that green everywhere. Do you know, Mavis, when we were ushered in here on that first night I thought it looked like a scene from Oliver Twist.'

'Indeed. Two long parallel tables and a top table facing down.'

'It's the bay window that throws light in here. What a lovely scene. Let's join the others.'

'Grand! That's a copper beech tree over there, isn't it, Frankie?'

'Think so. Great walk!'

'Sit next to me, Frankie.'

'Seat here, Mavis.'

As the noise level peaked, Sr Rita rang a bell to get their attention:

'Aspirants, I realise that having spent time chatting on our lovely walk, you are now more familiar with one another. I must put you on your guard against what we term 'particular friendships'. What we mean by this is that each of us must not form close friendships with any one person in particular. You recall that our life here on earth has only one goal. We are made for God and will not be happy until we are united with our Maker. Remember that our lives here are a preparation for our reward in heaven. We can not afford to give ourselves to any other human being. Our sole purpose is to live for God and save souls while saving our own.'

Frankie felt deflated. Did the nuns regard her friendship with Margaret as verging on being a particular friendship? She refrained from looking round to catch Margaret's attention.

6

ROUTINE

*W*hen Frankie entered the study she noticed that twenty-four aspirants were sitting in serried rows at school desks with flip-up lids, pencil rests and built-in ink wells. Sister Rita looked down at them from a small antique Victorian mahogany desk that had three drawers to each pedestal. The study was a fairly big square room with waist-level windows along one side and a picture of the Pope on the green painted wall on the opposite side. Green walls with brown paint work seemed to be the basic colours of the convent. A picture of the Order's Mother Foundress was displayed on the wall above Sister Rita's head and a statue of Mary Immaculate, with a vase of marigolds, sat on a mantelpiece behind the statue. No one moved except when they needed to go to the toilet. When this need occurred they were instructed to approach Sister's desk quietly so that they could barely be heard tiptoeing across the highly polished floorboards.

Frankie saw Sr Superior enter the study and whisper to Sr Rita who immediately announced.

'Frances, Sister Superior would like to speak to you.'

Why am I being summoned to Sister Superior's office? Frankie asked herself. *Was it because I laughed aloud?*

She had been thoroughly amused while she was reading Jerome K Jerome's 'Three Men in a Boat.' She could not contain herself especially when she reached the description of two of them trying to cope with Montmorency the dog, at the same time as stuffing a kettle with food.

Straight after laughing she called out, 'Sorry, everyone. I won't do that again.'

Sister Rita stared at her. Frankie looked around and saw that most of the other aspirants were smiling and nodding.

Frankie was still worrying if she was to be punished for this when she knocked at Sister Superior's door.

'Come in and sit down, Frances. You'll remember that at our meeting I said that we have decided that it is best for you to continue your schooling. Although you have the necessary doctrine examinations, you are to do a further course in Catholic philosophy as well as typing proficiency lessons. You are also to join the Beginners Italian language class.'

Philosophy? She must be joking. Sister can't have read my report, thought Frankie.

'Margaret will be with you initially but as she had passed many more exams at a higher level she will naturally move on more quickly.'

Frankie nodded.

Sister continued, 'As it is Mavis's second year in the Aspirantate, she will accompany you both to school tomorrow.'

Frankie tried not to show that she was glad that Margaret and Mavis would be with her.

Sister waved a finger at Frankie. 'I hope you do not need to be warned to behave as model students at all times. As aspirants, specially chosen by God, you will not mingle with either the boarders or the day girls. They live differently. They may discuss matters that are now extraneous to the life of an aspirant. When you have greeted them, you are to sit at the back of the class without drawing attention to yourself. As soon as a lesson has finished, either return to the convent or go to the chapel to pray until the next lesson begins.'

'Yes, Sister Superior.' responded Frankie as she tried to imagine how the other sixth formers might regard the aspirants. *Probably think we're very unfriendly... stand offish.*

Sister carried on issuing instructions, 'You will be pleased to learn that Sister Wilfred teaches typing. Later on, when you have mastered a little of the typing skills, you will be expected to consolidate what you have learnt by teaching some of the aspirants who will remain here in the convent and have not been as fortunate as you in attending school. Depending on your proficiency, the same may apply to Italian and perhaps even philosophy. Here is your timetable. Go to Sister Laura now. She will equip you with a school uniform.'

Typing? That could be useful, reflected Frankie. *If I left the convent I could get a job in an office.*

Aware that Sister Superior was watching to see if she remembered Sister Rita's instructions about opening and closing doors quietly, Frankie carefully eased the door handle into its socket as she left Sister Superior's office. Sr Laura was waiting for her outside.

'Vieni Francesca! Follow and we fit your uniform for school.'

Sister Laura led Frankie across the landing to the workroom.

'You like sewing Frances... Frankie?'

Frankie nodded.

Sister opened a large brown wardrobe. Frankie could

71

see lots of blue and white striped school uniforms on hangers. Sister handed her two of these. 'Try for size.' Then she pointed to a screen in the corner of the large square room.

'Try. Show me.'

Frankie chose the smaller of the two to try on first. When she looked closer at the dress, she realised that it was not new and that the sleeves were lengthened, supposedly in order to cover the whole arm.

Emerging from behind the screen Frankie declared, 'This one fits, Sister.'

'Now try other one, per favore.'

'It will be too big.'

'Si! More bigger. Try.'

Frankie felt that she had to do as she was instructed. As she expected, the larger size was longer too. Sister Laura said, 'Better you wear that one. We are fortunate. Students give back dresses when they leave school.'

As I suspected, thought Frankie. *Poor as we were, my mother would have preferred not to have sent me to school in cast-off clothes*. Frankie realised that she could do nothing. When Sister handed her a cardigan, that she guessed would also be too large, she thanked her.

Frankie looked at Sr Laura's face and was surprised to see her wink at her.

'Try this blazer, Frankie. It's a new one.'

'Thank you, Sister... '

Sister Laura stood back and looked at Frankie. Frankie saw her reflection in the glass window of a big book case. She was delighted to see how smart she looked. A door opened and Sr Maria emerged onto the landing. She looked displeased.

'Take that blazer off, Francesca! Take it off.'

Turning to Sr Laura she said, 'Sr Laura, you are meant to be teaching the aspirants to learn humility, not pride.'

'Scusi… sorry, Sister Maria. We were fitting for size.'

Frankie tugged the blazer off as she watched Sr Maria march across the landing and out into the corridor that led to a part of the house that the aspirants were forbidden to use.

'Lots of humility to learn, Frankie,' said Sr Laura as she shook her hand.

Frankie thought she saw a glimmer of a smile in Sr Laura's eyes. She wondered if Sr Laura was not as strict at keeping rules as Sr Maria.

The following morning Frankie felt that everyone was looking at her and her two fellow aspirants as they filed into the back of the school assembly wearing long versions of the school uniform.

Frankie whispered to Margaret, 'Everyone's looking at us.'

'Pretend you haven't noticed,' Margaret whispered through closed teeth.

Frankie wanted to run out of the hall but when she glanced at Margaret, she saw that she was standing tall and erect. Frankie sensed that her red cheeks were beginning to cool down. After the final hymn Margaret turned to Frankie, smiled and held out her arms and declared, 'We are sensational, Frankie.'

'Indeed. But for the wrong reasons. I've never felt so embarrassed.'

'Here come some of our class to escort us to the sixth form block,' said Mavis, as she turned to address Margaret and Frankie.

Mavis seems unfazed, thought Frankie. She wondered if she would be able to accept the fact that aspirants were accepted as being different.

A tall smiling girl dressed smartly in what looked like a new dress and blazer addressed the three aspirants, 'You know the way, Mavis. Welcome to your friends. I'm Joan.

Would you like me to lead the way?'

'Yes. Thank you,' chorused all three aspirants. Joan escorted them to the six form block. 'Sister Rose said that those places are reserved for you.' Joan pointed to three seats at the rear of a small room. She then went to her take her place nearer the front.

The other students turned and smiled. Frankie felt that although the girls seemed polite and chatted among themselves, they appeared to be keeping their distance from her and the other two aspirants.

Contrary to their expectations, before Sister Rose started her lesson, she smiled at the aspirants and called out, 'Girls, we have two new students joining us this year. Frankie and Margaret, please stand up so that we can all welcome you. Like Mavis, Frankie and Margaret are aspirants. Welcome, girls.'

Frankie sensed blood rushing to her cheeks as the class turned round and smiled at them. She also wondered if she had imagined that the class seemed to let out a sigh of relief. She was certain of that when she heard a positive reaction as Sister Rose held up a copy of Charles Darwin's *'On the Origin of Species by Means of Natural Selection'*.

A mighty discussion followed Sister Rose's lecture in which she touched on natural selection and referred to another of Darwin's books, *'Vestiges of the Natural History of Creation'*.

Sister Rose dismissed the class. As the aspirants were closing their files, putting them into their bags ready to slip out of the classroom quietly, Sister Rose called out to them, 'Aspirants. Please could you wait behind? I would like to have a word with you, if you don't mind.'

After the last girl departed, Sister Rose beckoned the aspirants.' Come nearer. Why don't you pull up chairs and sit round my desk?'

'Gosh! She's different,' observed Margaret.

'And the name suits her. Her tiny red lips look like a rose bud,' agreed Frankie.

'She's as petite as a rose too.' added Margaret.

She smiled at each of them as she put her hand up the back of her veil to scratch her head through her bonnet. She folded her arms and leant forward, 'I hope you are ready for this type of discussion, aspirants. As a result of the second Vatican Council, much controversy has ensued. We, as educators, must be informed and prepared to discuss these issues with the laity. I don't know if you are aware that Sister Patricia and I attend courses at Corpus Christi each Thursday in order to be kept up to date with the teachings of the Catholic Church. In these days of ecumenism, we have studied the beliefs of other denominations too. Have either of you heard of the Jesuit priest, Pierre Teilhard de Chardin?'

'Yes Sister. He was a French philosopher who trained as a paleontologist and geologist and died in 1955,' answered Margaret.

Sister Rose pursed her rose smile and said, 'Excellent Margaret. We will get on well.'

She continued, 'Perhaps it is better not to give an account of everything that is discussed during this philosophy class back in the convent. This is simply because while we are required to be accountable, belief systems spoken about here could lead to misunderstandings. Remember, even Sister Superior has yet to attend the lectures that Sister Patricia and I have been singled out to follow at Corpus Christi College and at other venues. As philosophy students, I would expect you to comprehend this reasoning. Have I made it clear? Do not mention these matters to others in the Aspirantade. Should you be asked, simply reply saying 'philosophy' comes from the Greek meaning 'love of wisdom.' You are intelligent girls. Use your discretion. You will see the reason as the discussions proceed. Is that alright?'

After they left the room, Mavis commented, 'Sister

Rose treats us like adults, doesn't she? That pleases and puzzles me at the same time.'

'How do you mean?' asked Frankie.

'I find it difficult. Maybe it's just me. I feel that while Sister Rose is encouraging me to listen, reflect and come to my own conclusions about different issues, Sister Rita and in particular, Sister Superior present us with conclusions and facts that we are obliged to accept without question.

Conscience. That's what we have to develop. That is difficult. The rights and wrongs of behaviour often have to be weighed up by each individual. That is going to be hard to do while we are being trained and given rules to obey.'

Frankie scratched her head and furrowed her brow. 'I'm lost! I only get glimpses of what you mean, Margaret. Could you please explain?'

'Sister Rose gave us a presentation of Darwin's theory of evolution and then the Catholic Church's teaching. While we have been informed of the thinking of both, we can come to our own conclusions.'

'But we can't choose to believe the bits we like, Margaret. Can we?'

'It won't be easy, Frankie. Did you have discussion groups at school?'

'Yes, of course we did. How do we apply this to what Sr Rose has said, though?'

'Okay. Take, for example, the fact that we have been warned several times that we are not to form special friendships yet you must have noticed that Sister Stephanie and Sister Wilfred nearly always go places together.'

'I've noticed that. Sister Breda and Sister Mary are often together too. They are nearly like twins, Margaret.'

'So you see, Frankie, although they have to keep the same rules about the particular friendship that we have to observe, they must think it is alright to have special friendships.'

'I can see what you mean, Margaret. Most of the time the nuns tell us what they think is right or wrong. I doubt though that they will be keen for us to make up our own minds.'

'That's what I think Sr Rose was encouraging us to do, Frankie.'

'Thanks, Margaret. That's cleared up some of my confusion. Have you noticed what Sister Maria gets up to? Apparently the other day a police car followed her to the front door of the convent because they had witnessed her driving under the railway barrier as it was about to go down.'

'Oh no!'

'Do you know what she said to the police?'

'Go on,' encouraged Mavis.

'Well, she retorted, 'You must have driven under it too to get here so quickly!''

'Oh! Sister Maria is hilarious. Her pupils love her. When she takes them away to our Hastings Convent, they all eagerly devour the lasagna that she prepares in those long school dinner tins. I wish all the nuns were as good humoured as she is.'

When they reached the main building of the school, Frankie asked, 'What's going on?'

'All that noise? All that clattering and banging?' added Margaret.

'Don't worry,' assured Mavis. 'That'll be the aspirants hauling brushes, buckets and other cleaning equipment from a cupboard ready to begin to clean the school.'

'The day girls are still here. They'll think we're cleaners,' remarked Frankie.

As they donned their big overalls, Sister Laura called them all together:

'Big clean... inspectors coming tomorrow. Up and down, in, out, getting rid of dust. All sparkle and shine.

Clean! Polish all that needs it. You understand. Inspectors see all ways. God sees you too.'

Frankie recalled that there were lots of posters with, *God sees you,* on walls in the convent and in school. She stood still and asked herself: Does the *God see you* sign imply that God is lovingly looking down from heaven approving of what I do or is He a demanding God ready to punish me if I don't work hard? She noticed that Sister Laura had finished. The other aspirants had gone off to the chores that they were allocated.

Frankie's job was to clean Catherine Foley's room. She was the aspirant who taught history. As Frankie arrived, her students were filing out to go home. She stood to one side and smiled as they passed her, totally ignoring her presence. When she caught sight of her reflection in the classroom door, she realised that with her denim wrap-around apron and broom, all she needed was to add a turban with a few curlers sticking out to make her resemble a housewife. Catherine seemed to forget who she was, when she issued instructions, 'Come in now,' she said. 'Start by washing down the blackboard.'

Before she bent down to dampen her sponge, Frankie felt that she should pretend to salute a sergeant major.

'Oh, you'd better go into the playground first. Bang the blackboard rubbers against a wall to make sure you remove every particle of chalk.'

As Frankie moved towards the door to the playground where she would be able to bang the rubbers. Catherine continued to issue commands, 'Then when you have swept and pushed the polisher over the floor, wash the bins inside and out.'

'Yes. I will.'

'Another thing. Arrange the desks back into straight rows.'

How demanding, thought Frankie. She had been told to

push a cloth under a broom so as to put a shine back on the worn part of the floor between the desks and also to dust around desks tops and the blackboard. She hoped it would not take more than the three quarters of an hour allotted because she was instructed to join the others walking back to the convent to recite the rosary at four o'clock.

Margaret appeared at the history classroom door. 'I've finished cleaning and tidying the headmistress's office. Sister Laura sent me to help someone else. Shall I dust the book shelves, Frankie?' asked Margaret.

'Oh great, Margaret. Thanks. What's all the fuss? Surely this type of inspection is routine. You'd think the Pope was coming, wouldn't you?'

'I've just overheard a conversation that explains everything, Frankie. Some of the nuns teaching in the school are not qualified teachers. Tomorrow they have to prove that they are up to the job or... If not, I suppose they don't know what will happen. Maybe they'll have to find qualified teachers.'

7

THE CHICKEN CHARGE

*F*rankie had fond memories of looking after her aunt's chickens when her family lived in Dingle. She was thrilled when at the end of the first week, the jobs, or as the nuns preferred to call them, the *charges* were changed. She was now assigned to looking after the chickens.

Second year aspirant, Mavis, was to be her instructor. 'Frankie, I have asked Sr Laura's permission to take you away from recreation so that I can show you the cupboard where we keep the clothes to be worn when we're on the chicken charge.'

'I was wondering about that, Mavis. It will be too late to get fitted up tomorrow morning.'

'Yes, we go there straight after Mass. Come on. I'll make sure you that we can find wellington boots that are nearest to your size.'

'Near my size? What do you mean?'

'There are four pairs that we share. Hopefully one of those will fit. Stop laughing, will you, Frankie?'

'Well… well, exactly what else have you lined up for

me that will nearly fit, Mavis? Is it any wonder that I'm laughing?'

'Wait until you lay your eyes on the fashionable overalls, Frankie!'

'Oh no! It looks like the one my old aunt back in Kerry wears.'

The boots were only one size too big but when she wrapped the big blue denim overall around her, they struggled to stop laughing.

'Ah, would you look at the auld woman, would you?' laughed Mavis.

'Will you stop, will you? Sure, you'll be no better in your outfit.'

Frankie pretended that she was walking down the cat walk, 'I'm now modelling this unique number only available here tonight ... so hurry... there are only two left!'

'I'm not quite sure. Could you turn around and walk back down without swaggering?' replied Mavis as she nearly doubled up from laughing, her hand crossed over her stomach.

'Oh no! There goes the end of recreation bell. Come on, Frankie.'

'Oh! I was enjoying myself... oh!'

'Quick. Hang up your apron on this peg with your name above it. Shove the wellingtons in the locker underneath. Thank goodness, you've got your veil with you. We'd better pull ourselves together and join the others in chapel, Frankie.'

'Okay, Mavis. I'll meet you here after Mass.'

Next morning.

'We were a long time in chapel, Mavis.'

'Nearly two hours. But then it is the 8th of September, the feast of the Birthday of the Blessed Virgin Mary. Mind you, that's a minor feast, Frankie.'

'Special morning prayers from the Divine Office.

Two scripture readings at Mass. The statue of Our Lady decorated. Blue candles lit in front of it. Lovely, Mavis.'

'*Where are you bound, Mary, Mary, where are you bound, mother of God?* Isn't that hymn set to a beautifully lilting melody, Frankie?'

Frankie began singing this hymn as they made their way down the path to the chicken run.

'Singing the hymn stopped you from laughing while you donned your apron but I'll have to switch you off before you reach full volume, Frankie,' joked Mavis.

'Oh I'm sorry. I forgot we are supposed to keep the silence, Mavis.'

'No, we'll have to talk while doing this job but there are no rules laid down for singing. Just the same, you'd better quieten down before we reach Sister Mary. She looks after the chickens as well as the garden.' Mavis smiled and added, 'Maybe the chickens won't appreciate your singing, anyway?'

'Sometimes Sister Mary isn't in chapel in the morning. She reappears later in the day.'

'Where does she go, Mavis?'

'Oh, she drives up to Covent Garden twice a week.'

'Covent Garden! Is that where all those bananas come from?'

'Yes and that Dutch chocolate that we are given at break time and lots of other food, too.'

'Does she beg, Mavis? I mean does she go round to each seller asking if they have anything to donate to the convent?'

'I expect so. All I know is that when she returns, we aspirants are often called to help unload her van. We carry in food and all sorts of goods. We store them down in the cellar beneath the refectory.'

'I saw the stairs going down but I never knew...'

'Yes. I think Sister distempered the walls and organised

the storage of whatever she brings back. She made shelves and there are fridges in the cellar. She's always busy.'

'That's Sr Mary coming down the path, isn't it?'

'Yes. Have you been introduced? You'll probably have seen Sister Mary in the garden.'

'Viva Gesu! Sister Mary.'

'Welcome aspirants. I've a head like a sieve. It's Mavis, isn't it?'

Mavis nodded.

'You must be Frances?'

Shaking hands with Sister Mary, Frankie had mixed feelings. She suspected that this smiling, middle-aged, rotund nun could be quite strict. Her firm handshake confirmed that judgement.

'Have you killed chickens before, Frances?'

'I'm afraid my uncle did the killing of our chickens, Sister Mary. I know what to do but well...'

'That's a start.' Sister Mary started gesticulating while she gave instructions, 'First you have to decide which chicken you want to kill. Then you chase it into a corner. You grab hold of it by the scruff of the neck and choke it. That's all there is to it, Frances.'

Frankie watched Sr Mary raise her hands in the air as if to emphasise how easy it was.

'I know... I can't...' confessed Frankie.

'The sooner you get used to this task the better.' Sister smiled beguilingly. 'After all, the three of us are Irish. We are used to farm life, aren't we?'

Frankie felt frightened and challenged. She rubbed her hands together:

'Okay. Let's target and corner one chicken. Which one would you like, Sister?'

'That brown one that is already in the corner over there,' replied Sister Mary.

'Let's go, Mavis!'

'Hold on now, Frances. We both can't charge at it or it will fly off.'

'Alright. Suppose I lure her with some seed and you creep round behind her and pounce?'

Frankie scattered a handful of seed and began calling out, 'Chick, chick, chick… come on chick, chick… I won't harm you.'

'Oh no! She's no eejit! Did you see that? I grabbed her but she flapped her wings so hard that I couldn't hold on, Frankie.'

Mavis called over to Sister Mary who was setting up a table, 'She's frightened off now, Sister Mary. We'll have to try another one.'

'Let's change roles this time, Mavis. You do the seed scattering and I'll come up from behind.'

'If these wellies weren't that little bit too big, Mavis, I could move faster!'

'Shish, will you?'

'I've got her! I'm holding her wings down.'

'Good Frances. Twist her neck now… go on… '

'Oh no! She's run off… she's run off without her head…'

'Oh that's cruel… but it's funny too. Catch her… you must, Frankie,' Mavis shouted.

The chicken with its head hanging off ran near Sister Mary. She reached down and grabbed it. The two aspirants clapped.

'Good. The next stage is the plucking and cleaning out. While we're waiting for one of the sisters to bring down a kettle of hot water, you'll need to catch four or maybe six more chickens. Off you go!'

'Uck! I'm not looking forward to that bit,' exclaimed Frankie, once they moved out of earshot from Sister Mary.

'Come on. Let's get this over with,' replied Mavis.

Keen to finish and get back to breakfast, Frankie moved quickly to catch and strangle two more chickens. Mavis had just finished killing another two when Sister Mary called, 'The hot water is here! We'll have to pluck straight away. Come.'

'At home in Kerry, my mammy refused to do the plucking and cleaning out of the chickens... '

'Ah now, that explains your reluctance, Frances,' interrupted Sr Mary.

'Mammy told us that whenever her uncle killed a chicken, he presented it to her when it was ready to be cooked.'

'You hold the chicken like this over the bowl and pour the water so that it loosens the feathers... Mavis, you know what to do. Show Frances. Is it Frankie you're called?'

'Yes Sister, Frankie.'

After a few minutes Frankie didn't mind the plucking but she dreaded cleaning out the inside of the chicken. She could smell the entrails that were being pulled out of the chicken that Sister Mary had in her hand.

'You two will need to be quicker or the water will go cold.'

Frankie started to calculate that at the rate Sister Mary was cleaning out the entrails of the chickens if she went slightly slower, Sister Mary would be almost finished while they were still plucking.

'Bring that chicken to this side of the table now, Frankie. Mavis can show you how to pull its entrails out.'

Frankie felt as though she was going to vomit but she knew that she couldn't on an empty stomach.

'You've gone white, Frankie. Don't faint. I can pull quickly. Don't... Look ... No, don't, I've finished.'

Frankie held on to the table. 'It stinks! Oh Mavis... Can we go now?'

Just then, the sister who had previously carried down the kettle of hot water arrived.

'Good, you two! Now you can look forward to enjoying

roast chicken for our feastday meal tonight. Off you go up to breakfast.'

Mavis winked at Frankie and put her hand on her stomach.

'We're late!'

'I'm dying to get out of these clothes, Mavis. Oh, for a good wash!'

'Let's run. We can wash our hands and wellies under the tap outside the hut.'

'That'll be cold. What about our clothes? Hot water and soap. I can take my cardigan off but what about the cuffs of my blouse, Mavis?'

'Sorry Frankie. Stick your wellingtons under the tap and rinse your hands. That's all we can do. Take off our aprons and off we go in to breakfast.'

'This is horrible. These smelly clothes make me feel sick.'

They arrived late at breakfast. When they finished praying the grace and slipped into their places at the table, Frankie noticed that it was boiled eggs for breakfast. She quickly put her hankie over her mouth as she heaved.

8

A PENNY FOR YOUR THOUGHTS

'*Y*ou look cold this morning, Frankie. Here, take this woolly shawl to wrap round you,' said Mavis.

'Thank you.'

'The chickens don't smell as much in this cold weather, Frankie,' added Mavis.

'That's true.'

'You're very quiet today. A penny for your thoughts, Frankie?'

'I was praying for Brenda. Is she ill? She wasn't in chapel.'

'You never know what others are going through, do you, Frankie?'

'You know something, Mavis?'

'I'm not sure, Frankie. Brenda may have left.'

'That's what I guessed, Mavis.'

'Everyone noticed that Brenda wasn't at supper last night. That's often the sign that someone's on their way home. Something similar happened last year when another aspirant left.'

'Maybe Brenda isn't well, Mavis?'

'I wish I hadn't gone up to the dormitory before supper last night, Frankie. I needed to take a hankie from my locker. I heard Catherine and Brenda arguing.'

'Oh?'

'I heard Brenda say, 'Just look at yourself, Catherine. Why do you ken we have no mirrors? If you could see yourself now, dressed in that stupid child's blazer and Tammy!' Catherine shouted, 'Stop this, Brenda. You're letting your anger rule you.'

The two of them obviously thought there was no one listening. I was too scared to make a noise. I sat quietly on my bed hoping that they would stop arguing, Frankie.'

'You should have coughed. That would have stopped them.'

'Perhaps. But I didn't. Then I heard Brenda again, 'We were told to line up like primary school children.' She imitated Sister Rita's voice, 'Stand next to your partner and form a crocodile!'

'Stop! screamed Catherine, but Brenda continued, 'It's a wonder we weren't instructed to hold hands. Oh no, I forgot we can't do that in case we fall in love with each other. What do the nuns call it?' Forming *particular friendships*.'

'That's enough!' shouted Catherine.' I'm going down to supper while you calm down.'

'Then there was sobbing. Catherine must have tried to console Brenda. Then I heard Brenda,

'For God's sake, remember who we are? I've a university degree. I'm a PE, physical education teacher. But I'm dressed like someone out of a mental health institute.''

'Did Brenda really say that?'

'She did. Catherine managed to calm her because everything went quiet again. I wondered how I was going to get down for supper without them hearing me. But as luck would have it, two younger aspirants came up to get something from their lockers. I managed to slip out of the dormitory with them.'

'Thank goodness for that, Mavis. I wonder what will happen now.'

'I wouldn't be surprised if Brenda's bags are packed.'

'Imagine that? But she's a teacher. She must have signed a contract.'

'The school is run by the nuns, so perhaps she didn't need to. I don't know?'

Frankie felt shaken and scared because of what Mavis had told her. Even though she sometimes found convent life hard, she preferred it to going home.

9

THEIR LITTLE SECRET

*W*hen the aspirants assembled for prayers after Mass on Saturday morning, Frankie noticed that Sr Rita was holding a sheet of paper.

'Aspirants, I have a list of new charges. Change is good. It helps us detach ourselves from earthly things so that we are free to concentrate on our heavenly goal.'

Just as I was getting used to the chicken charge and I'm getting along well with Mavis too, thought Frankie.

Sr Rita announced, 'Margaret, since you appear to have studied Latin, I have put you on the sacristy charge. The sacristan is guided by a book called the Ordo. Parts of it are written in Latin. If I put Frankie with you, you could translate that part where it lists the various colours of the vestments. You put the correct colour vestments out each night ready for the celebrant to wear at Mass the following morning.'

Frankie rolled her lips together to prevent a smile forming. She looked straight ahead instead of following her inclination to grin at Margaret, raise her hands and shout

out, *Hurrah! Margaret and I have been put together.*

Waiting for Margaret to join her in the chapel, Frankie faced the tabernacle and whispered, 'Thank you, Jesus.' Then she moved nearer and looked closer at the beautifully painted frescos that one of the Sisters had painted on the two wooden panels in the alcove around the altar.

The chapel door opened. 'Margaret, I can hardly believe that we have been put together to do the same charge.'

'It's wonderful, Margaret. Maybe, Sr Laura doesn't realise that we were friends before we entered...'

'Since we were warned about 'particular friendships', we must be careful not to be seen together too often, Frankie.'

'It's so lovely in here, isn't it, Margaret. I like the light-brown coloured woodwork and polished floors.'

'Those beautifully painted Fra Angelico frescos on the panels are so inspiring. Sister has used such wonderfully vibrant colours. The faces are so expressive. Look at those eyes. You'd think they could see us. Sister has copied them so well, Frankie.'

'I was just admiring them. I don't know anything about Fra Angelico. I am so pleased that I am standing here in this clean sacristy, ready to handle immaculately white, starched linen instead of treading muck and racing after dirty chickens.'

'This book. The Ordo. It's written in Latin?'

The sacristy door swung open and in waddled a middle-aged plump-looking nun.' Viva Gesu! I'm the other Sister Mary. You'll have seen me in the community and in school. Sr Laura has asked me to show you around the sacristy and explain what you will be expected to do on this charge. What are your names?'

'I'm Frankie. This is Margaret, Sister Mary.'

'Good. Shall we begin with this little book? The Ordo. If you opened it, you will have seen that some parts of it are written in Latin. The Ordo is a liturgical rule book published for use in sacristies. Essentially, you must familiarise yourselves with the names of the colours in Latin.'

'If it says *Alba*, lay out white Mass vestments. If it's an ordinary day. i.e. not a feast day, it'll say *Feria* and you put out green-coloured vestments. There are a relatively few other colours you need to know, Frankie,' said Sr Mary.

'So white, green, purple. Black, for a Mass for the dead. That's all, is it?'

'Rose pink for the fourth Sunday in Advent and Lent, Gaudete and Laetare Sunday. Should you get stuck, you can ask either Margaret or me, Frankie.'

'Can we? I thought we weren't permitted to speak to Sisters in the community, Sister?'

Frankie noticed that Sister Mary wheezed as though she was short of breath.

She continued, 'I know the rules state that aspirants are instructed that strictly speaking they are not to have dealings with Sisters other than their assistants and Sr Superior, but in this case, it should be fine.'

Sr Mary left them. They waited for Sr Laura to arrive and show them how to do the Saturday big clean.

Frankie said, 'I'm so glad we're working together, Margaret.'

Margaret clapped her hands. 'Yes, despite the warnings about particular friendships!'

Sr Laura arrived. 'Come!… you come with me. We clean the floor.'

'Lovely parquet flooring, Sister,' remarked Margaret.

'Si, Margaret. Remember silenzio in chapel… ma first, forse I explain.

'Insieme! Together we lift the benches. Then possible to polish.'

'Do we sweep first, Sister?'

'Brava, Frankie! You begin to sweep. Margaret, you

put polish on parts where people scraped off polish. Then Frankie, you help Margaret polish. While you two polish, I go to get *donkey*.'

'Donkey!' Frankie began to laugh. She thought that Sr Laura had used the wrong word.

'Sister is right, Frankie. I've seen a thing called a *donkey* being used in school, Sister Laura.'

'Sorry, Sister Laura. What's it like, Margaret?'

'It looks like a broom. The handle and the bottom part are made of heavy wood. The handle is screwed onto the heavy, oblong base. You move the handle backwards and forward to polish.'

'The floor... she becomes shiny. Molto ... very heavy... very good,' added Sr Laura.

'Precisely. The bottom part is very heavy. It needs to be heavy because it is used to take excess polish off and make the floor shine,' said Margaret. 'My mother has one.'

Sr Laura started to demonstrate. She moved an imaginary donkey back and forth, 'Now you push. Now you pull.'

'Oh, and you put a piece of a blanket or cloth underneath the base, too,' added Margaret.

'I can't wait to see it,' said Frankie.

Margaret laughed as Sr Laura went off to get the donkey. 'You can do the donkey work when Sister returns.'

Even though it was tiring, Frankie enjoyed being with Margaret polishing, shining the chapel floor and lifting the benches back into place. When Sr Laura had shown them what to do, she left them together while she went off to supervise the other aspirants. As soon as the door closed behind her, Frankie said, 'Remember one of the aspirants asked what a chemise looked like?'

'Yes. You were helping in the laundry. Have you seen one, Frankie?'

'Better than that, Margaret. I've seen the lot. What I

mean is, I happened to go into the laundry when one of the nuns was folding the Sisters' bundle of linen.'

'I don't understand... '

'Well, you know we find our clean underwear rolled up in a towel at the bottom of our beds? That's what I mean. Sister was putting the nuns' underwear into their towels ready to roll them up. She had laid about a dozen towels flat on the linen table and was about to put various pieces of underwear into each one.'

'I see. How were you able to have a good look at them?'

'I was sent down to the laundry to tell the Sister working there that Sr Superior wished to speak with her immediately.'

'So you stayed behind when she rushed up to Sr Superior?'

'And I held up a long, linen t-shirt-like garment with a three buttoned opening at the neck. I think that is what they call a chemise.'

'Ooo, ah! And what else did you see, nosey Frankie?'

'Long drawers, Margaret!'

'How long were the knickers?'

'As long as our school shorts had to be.'

'Down to the knee?'

'Exactly. They had slits from the waist to half way down on both sides. And two long white strings hanging from the waist bands. I suppose they were to tie round the waist to keep their knickers up.'

'Now we know, Frankie. Anything else?'

'Some had that rough towelling that is used for sanitary towels.'

'Oh don't remind me of that dreadful episode, Frankie.'

'Have you discovered anything of interest, Margaret?'

'Well it just so happens that I have...'

'Go on... '

'The other night the young aspirant sleeping next to

94

me began to talk in her sleep. I had left the curtain at the bottom of my bed a little open.'

'And?'

'And even though the lights were out as the moon was bright, I saw Sr Laura walking past with a white bonnet tied under her chin.'

'Was any hair visible?'

'Shh, I can hear Sr Laura returning... '

Sr Laura opened the chapel door. 'Good, aspirants. Now you take rest.'

'I feel thirsty and hot, Sister.' said Margaret, miming herself lifting a glass to her mouth.

'Bene. First you drink then go to the kitchen garden. Ask Sr Mary. We need flowers for...'

'The altar? Sister.'

Delighted that they had enjoyed chatting, they closed the French windows behind them and almost skipped down the path to the kitchen garden.

'Here comes Sr Mary, Margaret.'

'She looks friendly enough, Frankie.'

'Ah, come on over here 'til I show you what I've got in the way of blooms. Wasn't I hoping that one of ye would come down now while they are at their best.'

Sr Mary led the way under an arch that separated the vegetables from the flowers.

'You girls are far more educated than I was in my day. Ye most likely know heaps more than I ever did about plants.'

'Not me, Sister Mary. Maybe Margaret...'

'Nonetheless, let me tell you, modern chrysanthemums are much more showy than their wild relatives! How about that, eh?' She walked over to a huge bed of bright yellow flowers.

'Ah, Sr Mary,' assured Frankie, 'I might as well own up. I know next to nothing about flowers. All I know is that chrysanthemums are a golden colour.'

'Well Sr Mary,' admitted Margaret, 'I'll have to confess to knowing even less than that. Chrysanthemums remind me of pompoms or buttons. My father talked about 'herbaceous' and 'perennial'. He was always reading plant manuals.'

'Ye both know more than I expected ye to know. Did Sr Laura say how many flowers that she needs?'

'As many as you can spare, Sr Mary. She was talking about putting vases on the main altar and in front of the statues of Our Lady.'

'And St Joseph's statue too,' added Margaret.

'Alright. Wait here a minute 'til I get some get proper scissors to cut the flowers.'

'You were going to tell me something before Sr Laura returned, Frankie?'

'About hair. I asked one of the aspirants who has been here for two years. You know, Pauline? Well I asked Pauline who cut her hair.'

'It looks as though someone put a bowl on her head and cut round it!'

'It does. She told me that her father always wanted her to have long hair. He used to say that a woman's hair was her pride and glory.'

'My father says something similar. That green liquid that we are given to wash our hair doesn't even lather. I think it's damaging my hair, Frankie.'

'Mine's the same. It's all dry and split at the ends.'

'No creams, talc or proper shampoo…'

'… or mirrors. Just as well we can't see ourselves, Margaret. We must look like gypsies.'

'Another aspirant told me that earlier, the aspirants had to wash their hair in soda. You know the kind that gets lumpy. They had to break it down.'

'Frankie, I'm so glad that Peter can't see me like this.

What I'd give to see Peter, Frankie!'

'I sometimes image that John's kissing me.'

'I used to take such care of my appearance, Frankie. My mother used to love brushing my hair. I've always grown it shoulder length. Rosie's the same.'

'You're mother brushed it for you? Gosh, you were lucky, Margaret. Not my mam.'

'She used to rub Nivea cream into our skin, too. Now my skin's all dry.'

'Shish! I can hear Sr Mary's clop-clopping down the path.'

10

VISITING SUNDAY

*S*eated on a shoe locker to lace-up her plimsoles, Frankie was delighted that the aspirants were going to play hockey. Hilary called out, 'When you are ready, I'll give you a hockey stick. Join the others lining up to be given positions on the field.'

'Who's for hockey?'

'Ho! Ho! Margaret. You look just the part, smiling away. Twirling your hockey stick above your head. The well worn hockey stick shows you up though,' laughed Frankie.

'I love hockey but not in my Sunday uniform, Frankie. We're going to get all sweaty before our visitors arrive. I can't see us being given enough time to have a wash, can you?'

'I'm going to whip off my collar before we begin. Hopefully Sr Maria won't notice. What do you think, Mavis?'

'I love my Sunday dress,' remarked one of the other aspirants twisting around as she did.

Frankie looked down at her black serge dress. 'I like

98

the way it is drawn in at the waist with a narrow belt made from the same material.'

'And the white Peter Pan collar is detachable. I can take it off before it falls off, while we're playing.'

Frankie felt guilty, 'No, you are right. It is a lovely black dress. The three pearl buttons down the front of the bodice make it look pretty. If only my mother had bought finer material.' As she looked across at Mavis's dress, she realised that hers too was made from coarser serge.

Running up and down the hockey field appealed to Frankie. She could hear lots of comments from those around her, 'Fresh air. Fresh air. I love it!'

'We were a long time at Mass this morning. Two readings and then the conference.'

'The rosary, too. But it's only on Sunday and feast days.'

'I'm not complaining. We chose convent life, I'm surviving and it is visiting Sunday. So, heigh ho.'

Visiting Sunday was from two until four on the first Sunday of each month. The aspirants left the hockey field at half past one, changed their shoes, donned their mantillas and went into chapel to recite *Prayers before the Blessed Sacrament*.

Once they were all seated in the study, Margaret asked, 'Please Sister, may I be excused? I need to go to the bathroom.'

Frankie wished that she had thought of asking too because she wanted to splash water on her face before two o'clock when her mother was due to arrive.

Sister Rita rang a bell when Margaret returned from the bathroom. Everyone was seated in silence in the study.

'I see that some of you have already taken out your writing paper to write letters home. I remind you to be sensible about what you put in your letters. Remember that they will be read by Sr Maria before being posted. If you don't want to rewrite your letter, make sure that it is presentable. It would be sensible to omit comments or observations that may be misunderstood by people who are not aspirants.'

Frankie looked back at Margaret who was seated one row behind to the right. Frankie mouthed 'chickens.' Margaret winked back at her.

Sister continued, 'I realise that some aspirants may not wish to write to anyone. These aspirants can read some of the approved books from the shelf over there.'

Monique, the French aspirant, stood up. Sister waved her hand to show her to sit down.

'Wait until I have finished, before you choose a book. Only one aspirant at a time is allowed to do so.

'Let me explain what those of you, who will have visitors, must do. Sister Laura will come in here and inform me when a visitor arrives. I'll call out the person's name so that she can go down the stairs quietly to meet her visitors and lead them into the visitors' room. She will then form a circle of chairs that are needed for her visitors. You are then free to talk to your visitors until half past three. When the tea trolley is pushed into the visiting room, each aspirant is expected to serve tea and a piece of cake to each family member.'

One of the two twelve-year-old aspirants raised her hand, 'Sister, our Tommie's only three. Will there be orange juice too?'

'Yes. That reminds me. Don't allow youngsters to run around. The parquet floor is polished. It will be tempting for them to want to skate along it. Warn them that that is not allowed in the convent.'

'Are there any other question before I continue?' asked Sister Rita.

'Presents? I know my mother is going to bring me a bible. She said she would. Can I keep that? It is a holy book,' asked Stella, who was expecting her aunt.

'Good. I'm glad you asked that, Stella. The answer is 'no'. You cannot keep anything before Sister Superior has seen it and given permission. Even a bible has to be handed in after the visitors have gone home.'

'Why must bibles be handed in?' whispered Margaret.

'My mother said there are parts of the bible that should not be read. We never had one in our house. Come to think of it we only have the *Messenger* and The *Universe,'* replied Frankie.

I suppose that is why when I handed in the bible that my Mam gave me, I never got it back, reflected Frankie.

Frankie realised that the Scots, French Monique, Brigitte and Anna most likely would not have visitors.

I wonder if Anne Elizabeth's parents will visit her? I suppose not. She is older and a convert to Catholicism. I heard someone saying that they were not pleased with her decision to enter the aspirantade.

Sister Laura opened the study door, 'Mavis, come to meet your family.'

Earlier she told Frankie that she was expecting all five members of her family.

Frankie wondered if her mother and her twenty-four year old sister, Mary, would come to visit her. She suspected that if they did, they would arrive late. Her mother was a terrible time-keeper. She recalled the many times when her mother took her, her sister Mary, and older brother, Dominic, into Woolworth's on a Saturday evening as the staff were about to cash up. Often the staff had thrown white cloths over the tills and refused to serve her. Frankie hoped that she had changed her ways.

Just then Frankie's name was called out. Sister whispered to her that her visitors had been seen walking from the railway station by another visitor as they drove past. As they were going to arrive late Frankie was told to wait for them in the visitors' room. While seated there

Frankie noticed that two nuns were holding open the door of the visiting room. A woman pushing a wheel chair headed towards Margaret, seated near the bay window.

Margaret reached to hug and kiss the girl who looked similar to her. Frankie was wondering if this was Margaret's sister. Was she was mentally as well as physically disabled? A tall well groomed man, their father, entered carrying a big holdall. He patted Margaret's shoulder before sitting down and stroking her hand. Sister Laura brought the girl a glass of water.

As Frankie started to lift another chair into a ring that she had prepared, her mother and her sister, Mary, arrived. Her mother was mopping her forehead with a hankie. Her sister was flapping the bottom of her blouse in and out. They seemed all hot and bothered. She suspected that they would smell of cigarettes. Frankie was relieved that at least they had both made an effort to dress better than she expected. Her sister was wearing a navy-blue trouser suit and cream blouse. Her mother had a brown tweed costume and lemon jumper. Frankie remembered Mrs Kelly being dressed in the same costume at her grandson's christening. No doubt Mrs Kelly had loaned it to her mother. Not used to showing such signs of affection, they didn't kiss or hug Frankie. She pretended that she was not disappointed.

'Who's her nibs in the wheel chair? What ails her?' were Frankie's mother's first words whispered loud enough for all to hear as she approached the chairs that Frankie had put near her.

'That girl's sister, Mammy.'

Just then a little blonde child from Mavis's circle ran after a toy car heading for Margaret's visitors screeching 'Mi car... mi car.' Sr Laura took hold of him, the way that she have might have lifted a dog from the middle of its back. He was about to knock a flask from a tray attached to Margaret's sister's wheelchair. Sr Laura put the little fellow down near his relatives. Everyone simultaneously gasped a sigh of relief. The little child yelled and kicked. Mavis scooped him up in her arms and tickled him back to laughter in no time.

'Well, give an account of yourself, Frankie. What with no husband and all, it's not been easy at home, has it, Mary?'

Frankie surmised that Sister overheard how brusque her mother sounded because she came over to them, 'You welcome. Long journey here. You want better chair?'

Thanks to the mercy of God, we're all well, Sister.' Frankie's mother stood to shake hands with Sr Laura. 'Things could be much worse. I mean, at least we're not confined to a wheelchair. My three are well fed and sane, thanks to Him above.'

Frankie's mother blessed herself; glanced heavenwards and continued to air her opinion while looking in the direction of Margaret's family. 'What a misfortune to have an imbecile? What a cross that family has to bear?'

These comments silenced the room. Margaret's mother stared at Frankie's mother while her husband put his hand on her knee to comfort her. Frankie's mother waved back and said 'May God and his Blessed Mother reward ye all.'

Frankie felt so embarrassed that she wanted to shout out, 'Sorry!' She could feel blood rushing to her face. She muttered to herself under her breath: *She never lost it. She's programmed to create a scene.*

Frankie's sister must have been embarrassed because she immediately stood and moved the chairs nearer to the window.

Fortunately, Mavis's little brother, broke the silence by imitating car sounds as he rolled it round the floor. 'Rum! Rum!'

11

UNLOADING

Two-thirty. It was time for the Thursday walk. Sr Maria was standing on the first step of the stairs leading down to the hall. Frankie heard someone near her whisper, 'She looks happy.' Then Sister raised her arms and began to quote Keats: *Season of mists and mellow fruitfulness*.

'Praise God, as you walk through Richmond Park. Enjoy the glorious array of colours on the multiplicity of gorgeous autumn trees. Hopefully, you will see the red fallow deer. However, be warned that because of the November cull, there will most likely be restrictions along some pathways in the park.'

After the scene on visiting Sunday, Frankie hoped that she would be partnered with Margaret. She wanted to apologise for her mother's disgraceful comments about Margaret's handicapped twin sister. She was also curious about a letter that she had seen Margaret receive from a day pupil.

Sr Maria partnered four sets before she said, 'Now, let see... Frankie, maybe, if you walk with Margaret, you could discuss how you are coping in the sacristy.'

Frankie looked down at her shoes. When she sneaked a quick glance over at Margaret, she saw that she was shaking her head as if to signal that she would rather not have to accept Sr Maria's choice.

Outside the door Frankie wanted to punch the air and shout: We've done it! We've managed to be selected to walk together. Unsure of the response she might receive from Margaret, she kept silence.

They joined the walking line following along a lane that the Sisters called 'The Path of Perfection'. It led round to the front gate.

'Margaret, I am so sorry for what my mother said on Visiting Sunday. She's like that. It was appalling. I could not stop her. Everyone was shocked and... '

'You're right. Your mother spoke out of turn. Everyone heard her.'

'If only she could keep her mouth shut! She can be so embarrassing.'

'Most folk are probably too polite to say, 'Handicapped imbecile'. That's what she said.'

'If the ground could have opened up...'

'I'm responsible for her disability. I encouraged my sister to jump off the cliff at Hastings. It's my fault that she is in such a terrible state. She'd be better off dead. That's why I joined the convent, Frankie. I couldn't tell you before. I know I said that it was because I wanted to be a teacher.'

Stunned by this response, Frankie stuttered, 'Oh... ah... I would have thought I'd be the last person you would want to talk to about that, Margaret. How can you be totally responsible for your sister's ill health?'

'You don't know what happened, Frankie. It was my fault.'

'What happened, Margaret?'

'Oh Frankie. I think about it all the time. I'll be ill if I had to keep it to myself any longer.'

'Tell me, Margaret.'

'We were only eight years old. The nuns, who used to teach us in Battersea, took a group of thirty children to one of their other convents in Hastings for a week's holiday. Rosie and I loved swimming. We take after our mother. She is still a powerful swimmer. So is my dad. We were delighted when the nuns said that we were going to spend the afternoon near Firelight Glen where we had enjoyed such good times with our parents. Rosie and I had recently learnt how to dive but the nun in charge, Sr Elsie, had warned us to be very careful when we were on the beach. She warned us not to climb the cliffs. Not to be tempted to dive from there. There were strict rules about what we could and should not do.'

Margaret began to titter and then to giggle. 'Sr Elsie looked so funny, demonstrating how we were to get dressed... oh... we were to arrive at the beach with our swimming costumes under our clothes so there would be no problem putting on the costume. Before we left the convent Sr Elsie put a towel round herself. Of course she was still dressed in her long black habit. It was so funny. She pretended that she was pulling off her wet costume and putting on her knickers. She kept calling them underwear. The towel fell down and we all howled.'

'Modesty! Glad there was something to laugh about, Margaret.'

'No, but let me tell you. While Sr Elsie and Sr Susan were encouraging a small group of reluctant swimmers to at least paddle in the sea, Rose was desperate to dive off a rock jutting out just a few yards from where we were. We had been to this beach many times. We had dived from these rocks before. The nuns did not seem to be worried about us. They seemed to have decided to concentrate on the reluctant and more needy children. Rosie persuaded me that we should climb out on the rock and dive in. She went first. It all happened so quickly. Oh, I am sorry, Frankie... all I can see is Rosie and the ambulance. A man must have realised what had happened and ran to a phone box and the ambulance... the nuns... we never thought she would end up like she is...'

Tears trickled down Margaret's face. Frankie slipped her hankie into Margaret's hand. 'You need to cry, Margaret. I wish I could hug you ... but...'

'I'll never forgive myself, Frankie. Rose is paralysed and mentally damaged. Can... will God forgive me? Can I ever bring my twin back to how she was? After all these years I still cry. Often I can't sleep from crying, Frankie. I should have saved her.'

'Margaret, if you continue to blame yourself, you will make yourself ill.'

'I'm sorry, Frankie. I do blame myself. I realise that you are not your mother but you see I have always blamed myself for what happened to our Rose. It was my fault because I should have stopped her diving from that rock... oh, I am sorry.'

What can I say? worried Frankie

'Don't worry, Margaret. Maybe we've not had time to really know enough about our families yet.'

'Families always have secrets, don't they, Frankie?'

They walked in silence for a while. Frankie was desperately thinking of how she could distract Margaret.

'I'm a little puzzled, Margaret. I hope you won't mind me asking about the letter I saw you being handed from a day pupil? I thought it was from Peter? Your friend at the disco. Maybe it wasn't?'

'Oh if only, Frankie! No, it was from my brother, Peter.'

'I didn't know you have a brother, Margaret. He didn't come on visiting Sunday.'

'No. Mum said the nuns would prefer that boys didn't

visit. Like you I have a brother and sister. My brother, Peter, and his friend, Peter both used to attend the same grammar school in Wimbledon.'

'Love letters! Does John, the guy I danced with, go there too?'

'Yes, all three of them were in the same class. Maybe they're wandering around Wimbledon miserable without us? I couldn't tell Peter where I was going. I just wrote him a note saying I was beginning an apprenticeship and gave it to my brother to give him.'

'No last kiss, Margaret? I still dream about John.'

'Well, Frankie, the letter you spied me receiving from Pat Reilly, was from my brother.'

'I wasn't spying on you, Margaret. I was curious, a little jealous. I wondered if it was from your friend, Peter. Most of all, knowing how strict the nuns are about letters, I was frightened that you might get into trouble.'

'That's it, Frankie. Because the Sr Superior reads the letters coming in and out, I can't tell my brother how I am getting on in the convent. He can't keep me up-to-date with how my sister is. You must understand, Frankie, I am responsible for my sister being both paralysed and mentally ill.'

'You weren't to know what was to happen, Margaret. After all, you didn't push her. Stop thinking like that, especially now that you have time to examine your conscience.'

'Do you know, Frankie, you're a rock of common sense. I need some cheering up. Maybe having you around will help me put up with convent life.'

'Me, doing you good?'

'I admit that I ran away to the convent to suffer and do penance on behalf of my sister. To make amends for having ruined her life.'

'Margaret, you are not responsible for your sister.'

'But I feel that I am. I wonder if I am jealous of all the attention and care she gets. I know it's silly. She is so loved while I feel blamed in spite of the fact that my family continually reassures me that they do not hold me responsible.'

'Margaret, don't you think I wonder what my motives were for joining this order of nuns? You saw and worse still, heard my mother. I have run away from her. Wouldn't you?'

'We're a right pair, aren't we, Frankie? It might be easier to run away. Do we stay or leave the convent?'

'Wait until I tell you what Sr Rita did to me in the laundry, Frankie. You'll remember the incident of my period. No one will forget that. Well, it was my turn to help in the laundry that week. Sr Rita took great pleasure in telling me to wash the sanitary towels.'

'That's terrible. How can she be so thoughtless?'

'Worse than that... '

'Worse?'

'She actually held up my soiled and smelly towels for all to see. Then she said, 'Some towels even resist the heavy duty bleach. Look at this one, for example. Maybe you should give yours a good scrub then bleach them and after that put them out on the grass to see if the sun might work its magic.'

'I can't believe she'd be so cruel.'

'I think she is trying to get rid of me, Frankie. Perhaps she thinks I should be at home helping my parents to care for my sister. But do you know, the more she tries to send me away, the more I am determined to stay.'

'Why would she want to do that, Margaret?'

'You remember when I asked for an aspirin and a hot water bottle for you. Maybe she thinks I'm too outspoken. I hate injustice. Perhaps I feel hard done by.'

'I am grateful for all you've done for me, Frankie. No, the nuns wouldn't want to drive you away. They need vocations. Sr Rita is strange. Perhaps she's got a split personality? Remember, she sang that beautiful song about flowers, butterflies and friends?'

'Has she learnt to cover up her real feelings? Is that what nuns do and what we'll be expected to do?'

'Hope not. Listen to this. I have not told anyone about the incident with the squirrel. This may make you change your mind. Did you know that squirrels have been climbing up the ivy and into the first landing bathroom?'

'The one across from Sr Superior's office?'

'No, the one on our side of the building. Well, last Tuesday evening after taking my turn with the group washing the pots and pans I came up to go to the toilet. I was turning the door handle when Sr Mary came out holding a broom. She seemed glad to see me. She told me that a baby squirrel had jumped into the bathroom. She said that she was trying to get rid of it. She asked me to go in, trap the squirrel and kill it with the broom!'

'They're like rats, Margaret. What did you do?'

'It was no use arguing because I could see how determined she was. She was not going to change her mind. Even so, I didn't expect her to lock me in the bathroom and tell me that she would not let me out until I killed the squirrel.'

'That is awful, Margaret.'

'I know. Even though I screamed, she didn't open the door until I eventually killed it. I left it on the bathroom floor and ran out. Sr Mary just brushed past me, dropped it into a bucket, and said, 'well done' as I ran past her, crying. You won't be surprised to learn that I have had nightmares ever since.'

'That's sheer cruelty. I never imagined that Sr Rita was capable of that. Is she frustrated or something? Does she not suffer from guilt? She must be screwed-up inside.'

'Maybe?'

'And you? Someone complained about one of us making weird crying noises during the night. I didn't hear because, as you know, I'm down the other end of the dormitory. I never thought that you were having a nightmare.'

'Margaret, what are we to do? Parts of me wants to persevere and serve God and merit heaven. But bits of me tug at my heart and my beliefs.'

'What beliefs?'

'Well, all this fuss about *particular friendships*. What are the reasons for that, Margaret?'

'I don't know for certain, Frankie. We had two girls in our sixth form at school. They said they were 'in love' with each other.'

'Two girls?'

'Apparently it can happen. They said they were having a lesbian relationship.'

'Uck! That's surely not natural?'

'Well it happens. The nuns... maybe they form relationships.'

'Well then they can't be really be worried about any of us?'

'The nuns may have been told to watch out. We're a bunch of girls living very close to each other...'

'... cut off from our family and friends. Likely to get lonely.'

'We're good friends but do we have a *special relationship*?'

'We talked about this before. Remember when we spoke about some of the nuns who are always together because they work together?'

'Yes, Margaret. You said that we need to judge what is right and wrong for ourselves. We met before we joined the convent. I don't think that there is anything wrong with our being friendly. Do you?'

'Neither do I, Frankie. Jesus had friends. In the Gospel

he tells Peter that he loves him.'

'Whatever happens, Margaret. I don't want to end up like my mother. If I had had to suffer as much trouble as she had to put up with, maybe I wouldn't be any better.'

'Did your mother encourage you to become a nun, Frankie?'

'I've been thinking about that, Margaret. Perhaps she wants to prevent me from suffering from the loneliness that she suffers since my father died. I wonder. I also remember what she told me about her being with another man? I wonder who he was. I often think it might be the man I call my uncle.'

'We have good times too, don't we, Frankie? You were a howl in that amusing sketch you did with Mavis last Sunday when Mother Provincial's guest had to be entertained.'

'Oh yes! We were told to put on a show... a sketch to entertain some nuns who came from another community to visit our nuns.'

'You like acting, don't you? You acted out the changing of the guards at Buckingham Palace. You two were hilarious together. What was it you sang?'

'*They're changing guard at Buckingham Palace. Christopher Robin...* Shish... the aspirants walking behind us have started to laugh at my singing...'

'They enjoyed it when you were doing the sketch, didn't they?'

'Good, you two laugh. Perche?'

As usual Sr Laura was moving through the line of walking partners. Frankie was relieved that Sr Laura joined them when Margaret was laughing.

'Oh! It was something that I remembered happening when I was at school, Sister.' Trying to change the subject, Frankie pointed. 'Look at those deer. Aren't they beautiful creatures?'

'They are so elegant, lady-like, sprightly. Their

camouflage is brilliant, isn't it?'

Frankie noticed that Margaret gave her a sly smile.

'In the psalms, it says, *'Like the deer that leaps for running water.'* We need water. God is always looking after us.'

'That's a lovely image, Sister. Deer do leap gracefully.'

Sr Laura moved on to join the partners that were ahead of them. But she was still within earshot.

So Margaret nudged Frankie and quietly said, 'Sr Laura makes me smile. She's such a contrast to Sr Rita. She seems to be so genuine and full of enthusiasm. The other day she said: When make your bed in the morning, do not worry to keep head impression in pillow. Shake instead so that you can make one more mark of head following night! All she wanted to say was give your pillow a good shake when you make your bed.'

'She's a perfectionist,' replied Frankie.

'Ah but Margaret, she can be frightening. She told our group that when we go to bed, we should lay on our backs like a corpse, cross our arms over our chest and picture Jesus on the cross. Be prepared to die. No joke there, eh?'

'That's scary, Frankie.'

'I've hidden a photo of me and my Mam taken on my First Communion Day inside my pillowcase. I heard Sister telling Jeanette that aspirants are discouraged from keeping photos. She made her put her photo of her parents in her case.'

'There is nowhere to keep any personal things. Nothing displayed on our lockers. I've hidden a picture of my family in my prayer book.'

'Talking's good. It helps me feel that maybe I can cope. We'll have to find ways to get together.'

'The nuns might think we're... what did you say? Lesb...?'

'We're not lesbian. We're just good friends. Nothing's

wrong with lesbians anyway. I'll never forget the way you cared for me... or tried to, when I had my first period, Frankie.'

'We'll have think of some way to be with each other. The chances of us being partnered again for a few months is nil.'

12

AM I GOING TO DIE? THE FEAR OF GOD.

*I*t had been raining heavily. Frankie was disappointed that the aspirants had to spend their evening recreation indoors. One of the Scottish aspirants was asked to teach them a few dances.

'We'll end with the Gay Gordon's. Form a circle of eight. Again, boy, girl, boy, girl...'

'If only there were boys,' whispered Margaret as she held Frankie's hand.

'Just pretend I'm Peter. Grasp my hand tightly, Margaret.'

As the music was beginning, Sr Maria came into the refectory and clapped her hands to get the aspirant's attention.

'Oh, I was enjoying that, Frankie.'

'Me too. But not as much as the disco, Margaret.'

'It is two minutes past nine o'clock. Time for the Goodnight, aspirants. Carry the tables and chairs back into place for breakfast. Then you may be seated.'

'Here we go again, Frankie. Furniture removers.'

'If she's telling us to sit down, we must be going to have a long session.'

'I'm thirsty after all that dancing, Margaret.'

Sr Laura signalled to her and Margaret, 'Two more… help put table qui… more … more here.'

'No hope of a drink, Frankie.'

'No Margaret. Sr Maria looks serious. We'd better take a seat.'

'Aspirants, do I have to tell you everything. Turn your chairs to face me.'

Frankie grabbed a chair next to Margaret. She whispered, 'Something's happened?'

Sr Maria coughed, 'Aspirants, tomorrow is the first Saturday of the month. It is our retreat day. A day of silence. Reflection.'

Frankie thought, *how am I going to manage to keep silence all day*?

Careful not to be noticed, Frankie turned towards Margaret. She felt her shoulders rise as she turned the palms of her hands up and gestured a helpless shrug.

'The parish priest will celebrate Mass tomorrow morning. He will be in the confessional after breakfast.'

Frankie saw Margaret take a piece of paper and a pencil from her blouse pocket. Margaret passed Frankie a scribbled note: I'll be first! Lots to confess.

Frankie wondered if Margaret meant that she would have to confess that she had broken a rule by accepting a letter from her brother, that hadn't been seen by Sr Superior. Then she felt ashamed that she had been thinking about John and his kiss.

Sr Maria continued, 'Retreat days are days of prayer and reflection. Only essential manual work is permitted.'

Frankie was only half-listening to what Sr Maria was saying. She felt that she didn't want to hear more details.

Then she heard the chicken charge mentioned.

'Those in charge of looking after the chickens, will of course still have to attend to them as usual. Chickens still lay their eggs and need to be fed and watered.'

Someone in the front row giggled and then coughed.

Frankie was glad she that she was no longer on the chicken charge before she realised that as a sacristan, she would probably be busy looking after the chapel.

Frankie's mind wandered as she reflected on what she overheard Margaret saying to Mavis the previous day. They were standing by the staircase waiting for Frankie. She was sorting out the dusters in the cupboard under the stairs, 'You look all hot and bothered, Margaret.' remarked Mavis.

'Have you been doing the toilet charge?'

'Oh no, Margaret. I'd imagine that must be the worst charge. You've been looking upset lately. You've gone quiet.'

'I know. Brenda's leaving didn't help.'

'She just disappeared. Didn't she? No goodbyes.'

'Sr Norma, one of the nuns from the community, replaced her very quickly.'

When she was back in the study Frankie thought: *Life in the convent seems to be becoming stricter. Surely we should be able to say goodbye to people who leave.*

Frankie's reflections were interrupted when one of the aspirants accidentally let the lid of her desk bang down.

Sr Maria was issuing instructs: 'Those of you who already have a copy, open *The Imitation of Christ.*'

Sr Maria pointed to Mavis, 'Mavis, please hand out a copy to the new aspirants. While you are doing that I will explain:

'*Thomas* à *Kempis,* author of this precious book titled '*The Imitation of Christ*', lived from 1380 – 25 July, 1471. He was a medieval holy monk. I ask each one of you to treasure this book. When you receive your own copy, take a few minutes to open it at random and ponder on whatever words of wisdom you read.'

Margaret scribbled: He was buried alive. When his coffin was opened it was revealed that he had bitten his nails.

'Horrible. Dread that,' whispered Frankie, as she grimaced her face and opened her eyes wide.

When Mavis handed Frankie her copy, she realised that it had a sour smell. On examination, she guessed that the first page had been stuck to the plastic cover with glue. Feeling tired after the dancing and sensing the tense atmosphere created by Sr Maria, she decided not to ask for another copy.

Frankie opened it at Book I, Chapter 3. She read: *At the Day of Judgment we shall not be asked what we have read, but what we have done.*

Immediately, memories of her Grandma's wake flooded her memory. Tears trickled down her face. As she tugged her hankie from her sleeve, her arm accidentally hit against Margaret's. Margaret looked at her and mouthed, 'Why are you crying?'

Frankie put her hand to her face.

Margaret lifted her hands and looked puzzled.

Frankie wrote a note, 'Opened book … about 'Death'. Grandma's funeral was sad but I enjoyed the hooley.'

Margaret slid another note under the desk to Frankie.' Hooley?'

Frankie wrote: 'Hooley = singing + dancing. Irish fun. Family and neighbours talked about the good times, ate, drank and spoke about Granny's reward in heaven.'

Sr Maria must have seen Frankie writing. She called out, 'Are you taking notes, Frankie?' Frankie nodded and when Sister wasn't looking mouthed to Margaret, 'That was a close one.'

Sr Maria continued, 'Aspirants, on a retreat day, the Holy Rule reminds us that we will all die sooner or later.

We must be prepared to meet our master whenever He comes. We should be like the ten wise Virgins who took their lamps with them when they went out to meet the bridegroom. Remember that parable?'

Frankie wanted to call out: They were happy! Why are you telling us all this in such a gloomy voice? Instead she fingered her brow with one hand and rubbed the back of her neck with the other.

Frankie thought that Sr Maria's tone of voice sounded even more serious as she warned them, 'Our lives here on this earth are a preparation for our real life in Heaven. Whatever we do, or omit to do, will be rewarded or punished accordingly. Heaven is our goal and pleasing the Good Lord, is all that matters. The more we have to suffer here, the more we will merit and enjoy eternity.'

It's all doom and gloom. Not more suffering, please! Frankie sighed. A young aspirant sitting in the front row was swaying about and continually scratching her legs. On her left side Frankie saw that an older aspirant had her hankie over her mouth.

But Sister continued, 'That is why we must be detached from places, things and people. That is the reason that we possess nothing. That is why we are not attached to any other human being. We have left the world in order to concentrate on saving the world. We have abandoned the love of parents and husbands, family and friends.'

No friends? These nuns seem to be determined that we don't form friendships. Particular friendships again, puzzled Frankie

'We can be a constant reminder to our families and to everyone with whom we come in contact that there is a purpose in life. We love. Yes, we love but it is a superior, self-sacrificing love.'

In Frankie's head, the mention of love triggered visions of the Beatles singing, 'Love, love me do!' She felt a smile soften her face as she imagined them jigging about while the drums belted out lively rhythms.

'You're smiling, Frankie?' Sr Maria was looking at Frankie. Frankie was conscious of blood rushing to her cheeks. She rolled the smile off her lips. She felt embarrassed and guilty for privately indulging in sentiments of love.

Sister continued, 'We wear our religious dress; our holy habits, as a reminder, a pointer to heaven, much like the steeple of a church or cathedral does. Busy people can easily forget the higher values that they aspired to when they were baptised. We must become detached from the things of this world. We don't choose where we sit, sleep or work. We do not single out people to befriend. No special friends...'

Not again! thought Frankie. She dared not look towards Margaret.

'It's not that we can always negate our feelings. We will still be tempted. Jesus allowed himself to be tempted precisely in order to show us how difficult it is to resist the devil.'

Thank goodness! thought Frankie. She rubbed her brow. *I'm always being tempted by the devil.*

'If the Son of God was tempted, don't be surprised if you find yourself tempted. We do not look for temptations. We don't read the newspapers and certainly not novels, nor do we possess radios or even mirrors or have photographs, either taken or given. But we do have lovely awe-inspiring hymns. Take for instance this one.'

Surely she does not mean my photo of my mam? thought Frankie. *I hope not. Still, I'll keep it hidden, just in case.*

Frankie was surprised when Sr Maria seemed to become relaxed. She asked Sr Laura to accompany her on the guitar while she sang a beautiful hymn written by Gerald O'Mahony based on William Blake's words:

He who binds to himself a joy does the winged life destroy. He who binds to himself a friend lives to see the friendship end; he who suffers a friend to be free, will die to make the friendship be.

While Frankie marvelled at Sr Maria's fine soprano voice and Sr Laura gently plucking the guitar, she felt confused. She reflected: *I love the music, the caring sentiments, the strumming; the gentle tone of Sr Maria's seductive voice but why are friendships banned? One minute she's hard and serious and the next she's angelic. She seems to be a barrel of contradictions. Is this the result of suppressing her feelings? Is this what we are expected to do too?*

This question preoccupied Frankie as the aspirants filed out of the refectory. She went into chapel. Margaret was ahead of her. As soon as they pulled the sacristy door closed, Margaret threw her arms up in air exclaiming and echoing Frankie's frustration, said 'What's wrong with friends? I'd go mad if I didn't have friends.'

'Nothing. Jesus had his friends.'

'I desperately need to unload in confession...'

'Do!'

Later on when Frankie returned to chapel with the others aspirants she saw that a big crucifix had been placed on the altar in front of a red velvet background. Underneath, the words *My God, my God, why have you forsaken me?* were inscribed on a scroll. Two big candles were placed either side of the life-like crucifix. Jesus's head was bowed in death, his eyes closed and his side pierced by a lance. Blood was streaming down his side. There was blood seeping down his face from the crown of thorns on his head.

Frankie felt numbed into the silence.

For five minutes, that seemed like an hour, nothing moved. Silence reigned as they knelt in the chapel.

Tired and thirsty, Frankie nearly fell asleep. She jumped suddenly when someone began playing the organ. The sisters seated at the back of the chapel started singing:

Lord, have mercy. Christ have mercy...

Sr Maria spoke out, 'Please sit up and listen.' She then read the following meditation:

'Imagine yourself lying on your death bed. You are fully aware that you are about to meet your maker, your father and redeemer. You know that although you have tried your best throughout your life, you have sinned and have to suffer in order to purify yourself from sin and all earthly comforts and cravings.'

Her voice became more strident, 'You are covered in sweat and your hair is standing on end. Your eyes are in a fixed stare, you are gasping for breath as your entire body is writhing in pain.'

'No! No! Stop!' Frankie shouted out.

Sister did not stop. No one did anything. Sister Maria continued,

'Look at Jesus on the cross and hear him call out: *My God, my God, why have you abandoned me?*

Unlike Christ dying on the cross, you are not innocent and will not have the strength to cry out, so now say, '*My God, my God why have you abandoned me?*''

Frankie stood up. She was at the end of the bench. She took one step. She felt strong arms grasping her and forcing her back down onto to her seat. She called out, 'Let me go... I can't...'

Sr Maria continued, 'Then remember that Jesus died so that as long as each one of us sinners does our best in this life, we would not be abandoned.'

Frankie sobbed into her hands. Sr Maria continued, 'I want you to recall what happened when one of two the robbers who were to be crucified with our Saviour cried out, 'Jesus, remember me when you come into your kingdom' (Luke 23:42). Jesus responded, 'I tell you the truth, today you will be with me in paradise.'

On no! thought Frankie. *I can't take much more of this.*

Sr Maria said, 'All kneel down and we will conclude our service with the *'Jesus, Remember Me'* that comes from the Taizé community. Most of you will no doubt know that this is an ecumenical community in France. In the Taizé tradition, short meaningful sentences are sung repeatedly with various descants. Even if you are not familiar with this refrain, it is easy to join in and repeat it.'

Feeling herself tremble, Frankie removed her hands from her face and looked over to Margaret. She was not surprised to see that she was biting her nails. Margaret reached over and put her arm around Frankie.

Frankie stood and left the chapel. Margaret followed her out. With Margaret's arm supporting her, they went into the refectory.

'You're frightened, Frankie.'

Frankie nodded as she felt tears trickle down her cheeks. She smothered her face in her handkerchief. The door opened. Frankie shook as Sr Maria's voice bellowed:

'What a scene! Drama! You'll have to go home. Have your case packed by the morning.

As for you, Margaret. I credited you with more sense. Go straight to bed.'

Frankie watched Margaret leave her. She said, 'You frightened me, Sister.'

'Control. You are not able to control your feeling, Frances. Like mother, like daughter. You've proved that you do not have the qualities required. I mean what I said. Have your bags packed. Go to bed. No more wincing.'

After Frankie heard the door close, each time that she struggled to stand she collapsed onto her chair. She put her hands over her face and sobbed so loudly that she did not hear Sr Laura until she rested her hand on her shoulder and whispered, 'You tell me, Frankie what troubles you?'

Frankie looked up to see Sr Laura's kind face.' I see the boy.'

'The boy? What boy? Where, Frankie?'

Consoled by Sr Laura's kind voice and the fact that she had pulled a chair closer to her, Frankie began, 'His face was so cold, Sister. He was only five.'

'What happened? You tell me, Frankie.'

'Patrick Toomey. He lived next door. Oh Sister I can see him now lying in his little coffin. He was so small.'

'Don't cry again. You become sick, Frankie.'

'I can't help. I can't control… his face was so cold. My mother told me to kiss him. Everybody in the line did.'

'You were small too, Frankie? How old?'

'Same age… five, Sister.'

Frankie felt Sr Laura's arms round her as she drew her close to her. 'Cara Francesca... you not worry.'

The door was opened. Sr Laura dropped her arms. Frankie sat up straight. Sr Maria said,

'Frances Danivet, I told you to go to bed. Enough drama!'

She pointed at Sr Laura:'Make sure that she does not disturb the dormitory. She is to be ready to leave for home in the morning.'

When Sr Maria left the room, Sr Laura said, 'Come, Frankie. Come to bed. I will speak with Sr Maria. Not to worry. I explain.'

The lights were out. Frankie wondered why Margaret had left her to cry as she struggled to undress, go to the toilet, and crawl into bed blinded by her tears. Then she heard the curtains rustle and felt her forehead being stroked.

'Frankie. Oh Frankie… you're frightened. You won't die yet… well, not if you stop crying.'

'Sweating. No it's the coldness… skin like marble. Oh Margaret. I'm not afraid of dying.'

'Margaret, you go back to be… not disturb. I take care.'

Frankie noticed that Sr Laura was holding a cup. Her voice was caring and she was patting Margaret's hand.

'Try and sleep, Frankie,' whispered Margaret as she blew Frankie a kiss, lifted the curtain round Frankie's cubicle and left.

'Frankie, drink chamomile. Will help sleep. Not to worry,' whispered Sr Laura. She handed Frankie a mug with the hot drink and made the sign of the cross on her forehead before leaving her.

As Frankie sipped the chamomile, she kept hearing Sr Maria's words, 'Pack your case and be ready to leave.' She imagined her mother's face drop when she arrived back home. She'd shout: 'Even the nuns won't have you! What do you expect me to do with you? You're a disgrace!'

Frankie sipped some more and slid down the bed pulling the crackling polyester sheets right up to her head. She tossed and turned. She saw Patrick Toomey and screamed out, 'I don't want to kiss him! Eyes closed. Cold! Dead!'

'Shish! The dormitory lights went on. Frankie realised that she was sitting up in bed. She saw Sr Laura in her cubicle. She was saying: 'Frankie, lie down. Sleep!'

'Sister, I don't want to go home. Please? I prefer to die.'

'Die no! You sleep, Frankie. You scream... everyone wakens.'

'Sorry, Sister,' whispered Frankie as she lay down again.

When Sr Laura had gone, Frankie tried to sleep. She felt for the photo of her mother tucked inside her pillowcase. She imagined her mother telling her to get a job. She thought her mother was forcing her face nearer to Patrick Toomey's face.

Frankie heard someone call out, 'Shish! Go to sleep. Stop talking.'

When the bell rang and Sr Laura called out 'Benedicamus Domino' Frankie sat bolt upright in her bed awake wondering if she had dreamt that Sr Laura helped her to pack her case. *'My photo…the photo of me and Mammy. Did Sister see that?'*

She searched under pillow. *Oh Mammy. I love you.* She kissed her. She was about to get out of bed when Sr Laura lifted the curtain at the end of her bed and whispered, 'Va Bene, Francesca?' She smiled and added: 'Forget the case… I explain… normalmente… you well? Dress for chapel.'

Frankie watched as Sr Laura waved herself out of her cubicle. She remained seated in her bed still wondering if all her dreaded fears of death had been a horrid nightmare.

The others are getting ready for chapel. Should I do the same? She asked herself. She put the photo in her locker. She felt as though she was on automatic pilot making her bed and walking to go to the bathroom, cleaning her teeth etc. When she lined up outside chapel, Margaret crept up behind her and whispered, 'You're doing well. Carry on as though nothing has happened. You'll be okay.'

That is what happened. When Mass was over each aspirant went off to see to their charge and Frankie and Margaret tidied up the chapel and sacristy.

When the bell went for breakfast Margaret came behind Frankie as she hung up her veil on a hook in the corridor. She patted Frankie on her back, 'Well done, Frankie.'

13

BARMBRACK AND COKE

'*I* think I can hear Sr Maria and Sr Laura's voices. Yes, here they come. As usual, Sr Laura's waving her arms around. Typical Italian! They talk with their hands. I love the way they gesticulate. It's so expressive,' commented Frankie.

'Oh! About time! It's cold out here,' Frankie heard someone behind her moaning.

'We're not school children!' complained someone else.

'We look like a rent-a-crowd group from the scene of an industrial revolution', said Catherine, the history teacher.

Sr Rita clapped her hands.

'Thank goodness for that,' whispered Stella.

Sr Rita raised her hands ready to instruct the aspirants. She was standing next to Sr Laura on a step outside the French windows.

'Aspirants, just to remind you that it's 31st October. It's Hallowe'en this evening.'

I loved Hallowe'en when we kept it back in Kerry, thought Frankie. She touched Mavis's shoulder and whispered, 'Barmbrack round the bonfire and bobbing for apples. Remember that?'

'And the singing and ghost stories. I loved it all. They don't have barmbrack over here, in England, Frankie. I miss it. Delicious fruit cake with the ring and money hidden inside a piece of linen cloth.'

Sister Rita cleared her throat, 'Aspirants, this afternoon, we will have to split into more groups than usual. You will have noticed that the house is getting colder. Soon the heating will have to be switched on.'

'Getting colder? The bedroom window had ice patterns on it the other morning! She mustn't feel the cold,' whispered Frankie.

'Three of you will be allocated to pushing coke down into the furnace area. To do this you have to remove the cover over the manhole outside the kitchen. Then the coke will need to be raked from the pile down onto the furnace floor.'

'That will be dirty work, Frankie. I hope I don't get that job,' wished Margaret.

'Frankie, Mavis and Jeanette, pick up a rake and follow Sr Laura. The coke is piled over there.' Sr Rita pointed.

'Oh no! Why do I always get the mucky jobs? Is she punishing me for my outburst on retreat day?' whispered Frankie to Margaret.

'No, Frankie. Try and forget that. You promised.'

'Hilary, Margaret and Stella, your job is to trim back the hedges, remove the weeds and clean the dustbins at the back of the kitchen area.'

'Mucky and smelly. I've been given a hard task too. Whose job is the dirtiest?' asked Margaret.

'Bene! We enjoy,' said Sr Laura, as she folded her habit skirt in half and pinned it up with a big safety pin to waistline of her habit. She turned her modestina bib round so that the big part was on her back. She pulled on a denim overall and pinned back her veil. Taking up a rake, she signalled the three of them to follow her round to the pile of coke.

'Enjoy? More like endure,' laughed Hilary

'Vieni. Come. You'll see,' Sr Laura said as she smiled at Hilary.

Frankie admired Sr Laura's strength as she tugged up the heavy manhole cover.

When they peered down the hole to the floor of the cellar, she gauged that the job would require a lot of strength.

'Jeanette and Hilary, you stand at the top... push hard the coke down to Frankie. We two push down the hole,' instructed Sr Laura.

We're going to be covered in dust, reckoned Frankie.

'The coke is light! This is fun!' shouted Jeanette. 'When it gets high enough, we'll be able to jump on it.'

'No! No jump, Jeanette! You fall in hole,' warned Sr Laura waving her rake.

'Sorry, Sister,' responded a deflated Jeanette.

'The noise, plus the grit! Wait 'til I take put my glasses safely in my pocket,' said Hilary as she tugged up her overall and located her skirt pocket.

'My eyes, nose, mouth and even my wellingtons are full of coke dust, Sr Laura,' complained Frankie.

'Ecco fazz... hankie, you say? Take... wipe,' Sr Laura handed Frankie some tissues.

'Oh, Frankie! You look so funny. Your face is black... so's your hair, Frankie!' laughed Jeanette, as she pointed her finger.

'Just as well there are no mirrors, Jeanette.'

'Oh my leg, Sister! I think I ... it feels ... no, I think I'm okay.' said Jeanette

'Come here. I look... no... You hit with rake... go slower... look all time, Jeanette.' instructed Sr Laura.

Frankie was watching Jeanette when she heard a familiar voice.

'There's my daughter, Sister. I'd recognise her voice anywhere. In the name of... what have you got her doing? Those overalls! There's black dust flying all over the place.'

Frankie turned to see her mother accompanied by her friend, Moira, being escorted by Sr Rita.

Frankie gasped. 'Mammy it's not visiting... has something... ?'

'Come here, my girl. What a way to greet your own mother? And me, in my new rigout, having travelled all the way here to bring you barmbrack.'

'Sorry, Mammy. It's... your visit's so unexpected.'

Frankie looked round to see the reaction of Hilary, Jeanette and Sr Laura. Margaret and the others had stopped to look too. They were staring with their mouths wide open.

'It seems to me that it's just as well that we did arrive unannounced! What else are the nuns using you to do? Slave driving? ... and all the time I've been thinking that you're being educated. Education, my eye!'

Frankie was glad when she noticed Moira tugged her mother with one hand and put her finger to her lips with the other. Thank God she is trying to calm Mammy down.

Please God, prayed Frankie, *don't let her make a scene. I wonder where she got that lemon coloured twin-set and the green costume. The brown necklace and dangling earrings. The matching high heels, too. What is she up to? Surely she must realise that she is only permitted to visit on the first Sunday of each month.*

'You are very generous, Mrs Danivet, to think of bringing us cake to celebrate Hallowe'en.'

Frankie watched Sr Rita smile and placed her hand on her mother's arm.

'*You* might call it cake, Sister. We call it barmbrack. The dough is sweeter. It's a special recipe that has to be followed. Moira here, makes barmbracks for her Irish friends. It's up to us to keep the customs going,' replied Frankie's mother.

Frankie watched Moira rub her nose and put her hand over her mouth and cough: 'Sister, let me explain. Barmbrack is indeed a traditional Irish fruit loaf. If you follow the recipe properly you'll have a really beautiful, moist loaf, packed with flavour. You see it is full of mixed spice and dried fruit. You have to soak it overnight in cold tea and add a little whiskey. That's purely to bring out the goodness.'

'You'll have to tell them about the ring and stick.'

'Maybe we'll tell them all that later, Patsy.'

'Moira, may I ask, should we cut the loaf into slices?' enquired Sr Maria.

'Yes, a barmbrack is usually cut into long oblong thick even slices. You'll get a delicious fruity smell coming from the mixture. It comes from the oven looking a light brown colour with the currants poking through. Most folk spread butter on the slices. It's lovely with a hot cup of Barry's tea.'

'Thank you Moira,' replied Sr Maria.

'Frankie, get cleaned up. Then join your mother and her friend in the parlour as soon as you are ready,' instructed Sr Rita.

As Frankie went into the house through the kitchen door, she glimpsed Sr Rita gripping her mother's arm and turning her round towards the front entrance of the convent.

I hope Mammy calms down. I think she loves all the attention. Poor Mammy. She looks lovely in that outfit. I do love her. I wouldn't be surprised if she's up to something, though. Just as well Moira didn't tell the nuns the significance of the things we put in the barmbrack.

'You'll need these, said Sr Breda, handing Frankie a bar of carbolic soap, a piece of towelling, a white blouse and a clothes brush.' Go in there.' She opened the door. 'Strip off and wash yourself as best you can.'

'You heard my mother?' enquired Frankie.

'Couldn't help hearing, Frankie. Go in now. Close the

door. You'll have a job washing that coke dust off. If I were you, I'd step into the big basin on the floor. This is the only place in the convent where there's hot water.'

'Thank you, Sister.' She closed the door behind her and started taking off her overall. She shook and brushed her skirt and cardigan. *My knickers, stocking and petticoat are covered in coke dust too. I'll have to shake them and put them back on. Thank goodness, Sister has given me a blouse. I'll just have to strip and wash off as much as I can.*

After a while Frankie heard a knock on the door. 'Are you managing alright, Frankie?'

'I'm sorry I am taking so long, Sister. I've had to scrub my face and hands. The coke is so greasy. I'm nearly ready.'

'Good, Frankie. But hurry. Don't worry about tidying up. Sr Rita is with Sr Maria in the parlour. Your mother and her friend have drunk two pots of tea and four slices of apple tart already.'

'Sorry Mammy's causing so much trouble, Sister. She means well but...'

'She has come all this way, Frankie, to make sure that we all know about barmbrack. Maybe she just wants to check that you are okay.'

Frankie opened the door. 'Thank you for being so understanding, Sister.'

When Frankie reached the parlour, she saw Sr Maria breathing a sigh of relief.

'You look better. Sit over here next to your mother, Frankie.'

Frankie noticed that her mother seemed to be sliding around on an upright, straight-backed wooded chair. She had visions of her slouching about on her old sunken armchair at home. She guessed that she would be wishing that there were comfortable armchairs in the parlour.

'Have you no hair dryer?' asked Frankie's mother. She pointed to Frankie's damp hair.

Moira put her hand over her mouth and gasped.

'Ah now Mammy, we rub our hair dry with a towel in the convent. Besides, I was in a hurry to come and see you, Mammy and of course, you too, Moira. Thank you for coming all this way.'

'Much appreciated, Mrs Danivet. Mrs Kelly too,' said Sr Maria, offering more tea.

'Well, they know about our Irish customs now, Frankie. I've been telling them all about the pea, a stick, a silver sixpence. It used to be a thruppeny bit... and a ring wrapped separately in a piece of cloth. They're all put into the brack.'

Oh no! I wonder what explanation she has been giving to the nuns, thought Frankie as she scratched her forehead.

'That's good, Mammy. They'd need to be warned. Otherwise they might swallow them,' said Frankie.

'Frankie, it's nearly time for us to join the community in chapel for the recitation of the rosary. Sr Rita and I will leave you to enjoy your mother and her friend's company for a while.'

Frankie watched as the two Sisters shook hands with her mother and her friend. Each of them then picked up three barmbracks wrapped in grease proof paper as they left the room.

As soon as they closed the door, Moira handed Frankie a leaflet.

'Frankie, I persuaded your Mam that perhaps it was best not to give the nuns this leaflet.'

Frankie took the leaflet and saw a twinkle in their eyes. Then she read:

Each item, when received in the slice, carries a meaning to the person concerned: The pea means that the person would not marry that year; the stick means that the person would have an unhappy marriage or continually be engaged in disputes; those who got the cloth or rag, would have bad luck or be poor; instead those who pulled out the coin, would enjoy good fortune or be rich; and the person who got the ring, would be wed within the year.

Frankie felt them watching her reaction as she read. 'Hah! You two are always up to something! What would the nuns think if they read this? More to the point, what am I going to tell the aspirants when they find these things in the barmbrack?'

'Ah well, the important thing is that I wanted to visit you. I wanted to check that you are okay. There's not much we can say in our letters is there now that we know that the nuns read them?'

'I know that they read them alright because Sr Maria sometimes refers to something that you have written about, Mammy.'

'What did I tell you, Moira? By the way, Frankie, you haven't remarked on my lovely rigout. How do you like the costume?'

'You look grand, Mammy. You had your hair permed again? It suits you. No, the whole outfit looks so well on you. It's all matching and everything. You look lovely. You're a credit to old Ireland.'

'You can thank Moira. She saw the costume displayed in Oxfam. She said that bottle green would surely suit my tanned complexion.'

'It does too, Mammy. Thank you, Moira. What would Mammy do without a friend like you? Did you knit your gorgeous blue cardigan? It brings out the blue in your eyes. It really suits your colouring.'

Frankie beamed a smile at Moira. 'Thank you, Frankie. I knit when we chat. We enjoy putting the world to right, don't we, Patsy?'

'We do indeed, Moira.'

Frankie watched Moira tilt her head nearer to her mother's and place a chubby, clasped hand over her mother's hand which was stretched out on top of the polished table.

Thank goodness Mammy seems to have a friend that she can confide in. Moira's matronly figure seems to portray a warm-hearted woman. Dressed as she is, in a navy blue woollen dirndl skirt, the pale blue buttoned-up blouse and cardigan, she appears to be the type of person that Mammy needs.

'Your mother insisted in wearing the brown high heels today, Frankie.'

'Well you know on occasions, I love getting dolled up, Frankie. Mind you, I'll have to admit that Moira was right this time. I did have trouble going up and down the escalators to the tubes wearing high heels.'

Frankie was surprised when her mother stood up and embraced her.

'I miss you, Frankie. I do. Don't let the nuns make you work like you were today. Men should do that kind of work. I didn't send you to school to do manual work. You're not strong enough to be pushing filthy black coke down a hole. I told the nuns that you are not to do that kind of work anymore.'

'But Mammy, what are the nuns to do? We need to keep ourselves warm. Someone has to push the coke down the hole to the furnace. I don't want to do it either but who else will do it? We just have to take our turn.'

'Stand up for yourself, my girl. Blame me. I could appear unexpected on another day. I won't have you being treated like a slave. Remember you are my daughter. I love you, you know that, don't you, Frankie?'

'Oh Mammy, don't cry.' Frankie hugged her mother.

'No. You're right Frankie. You mustn't worry about anything. Try to let bygones be bygones.'

Moira shook Frankie's hand, 'When your mother told the nuns that you are not to push that coke down again, Sr Maria told us that Sr Laura will look out for you. Don't worry about the past, Frankie.'

Frankie wondered why Moira said that about Sr Laura and why her mother nodded in agreement. *What was all that about the past? What past?*

'Is that your coat, Moira? It looks lovely and warm. It's light too. It must be pure wool.'

'It is too, Frankie. Thank you.'

'Thank you both. I will take care of myself. Don't worry. Thank you very much for coming down. Did you use the barmbrack as an excuse to visit me?'

'I can't fool you!' said Frankie's mother as she winked and pinched Frankie's nose.

When Frankie closed the front door and turned round, she saw Margaret smiling as she walked towards her.

'You should have seen how dirty Stella and Jeanette were after pushing the coke down, Frankie.'

'I'm not surprised. It took a lot of scrubbing for me to remove the coke dust from my face, my hair and everywhere. You saw how filthy I was, Margaret.'

'Yes but after you were called away the other two filled up the hole. Then Sr Laura let Jeanette jump on the pile filling up the hole. You should have seen her skin, hair and clothes. She was covered in coke dust. She was black all over. She said it even blackened her underwear.'

'She must have enjoyed herself. She is really still a child. Did she complain about hurting her leg again?'

'She said it ached a bit but she was so excited that she persuaded Sr Laura that it was fine.'

'Was she allowed to get a bath?'

'She was allotted a half hour slot because it is a feast day. Oh, here comes Sister.'

'Francesca. Frankie. Your mamma... she is gone? Sr Superior like you to go to her office.'

Oh no! I'm going to be told off now. My mother always manages to cause trouble.

'Come in, Frankie. Sit down.' Sr Maria pulled a chair

nearer to her and signalled Frankie to sit.

'I am so sorry, Sr Superior, that my mother came to visit me on the wrong day.'

'That is why I have called you here, Frankie.'

I am going to be sent home, thought Frankie. *I thought that the way I behaved on retreat day would eventually be discussed. My mother's arrival on the wrong day has added to the fact that I am seen to be unsuitable.* Frankie was conscious that she was squeezing her fingers.

'You look frightened, Frankie. There is no need for you to be afraid. You remember how afraid you were when you recalled having to kiss that dead boy?'

Oh no! She is going to scold me. She will send me home.

'Frankie, your mother didn't turn up uninvited today. Sr Laura explained to me the reason why you were so frightened on retreat day. Sr Rita did not know the reason. I needed to speak with your mother. You understand we have to know the background of our candidates?'

Frankie felt tears beginning to run down her face. She wondered if her mother had been called to the convent to prepare her to take Frankie back home.

'Have you a handkerchief, Frankie?'

'No, Sister.'

'Here take this one. Wipe your eyes. Let me explain.'

'I know, Sr Superior. You are sending me home.'

'No, Frankie. At least not in this instance. Not because of what happened. No, we invited your mother to come here. Sr Laura was concerned. We were concerned.'

'So I am not being sent home? Mammy, my mother knows? You invited her?'

'Yes, Frankie. After the fear you showed as a result of being encouraged to kiss the forehead of your neighbour's dead five-year-old son, we felt that we should discuss this matter with your mother. Sr Laura was most concerned about you. At first your mother told us that this is what people did at that time in Ireland.'

'It is, Sr Superior. Home in Ireland we have the dead person in our homes until they are buried. During the Wake the coffin is open. I noticed here in England that dead persons are covered over. That doesn't mean we can't be frightened though.'

'Your mother wanted to make sure that you are alright. When she suggested that she would bring some what is it... barmbrack?'

'Yes Sister.'

'We thought it best to invite her to visit. Unfortunately she did not inform us when she intended coming. It would have been better had she not visited when you were engaged in pushing down the coke.'

'Mammy didn't think that I should be doing that, Sister. I tried to explain but... '

'It's only natural, Frankie. Your mother loves you, Frankie. She made that quite clear today. She also suggested that maybe we might think of another way of getting that coke down into the cellar. Perhaps we could have the manhole already off so that the man who delivers the coke could put it straight into the cellar.'

'That's a good solution, Sister. Thank you.'

My mammy has forced the nuns not to make us push coal down into the furnace. Now I know why Mammy said 'let bygones be bygones' and Moira assured me that Sr Laura would look after me, reflected Frankie as she closed the door to Sr Superior's office behind her.

'Oh, Sr Laura! I didn't see you sitting there.'

'I want to speak with you, Francesca... Frankie. It is better we speak now.'

'Thank you for explaining everything to Sr Maria, Sister.'

'Vieni. Sit. I explain what happens tomorrow night.'

'Tonight is Hallowe'en, Sister?'

'Si! First vig... day before feast of all Saints... questa sera.'

'This evening is the vigil of All Saints. The vigil of the Feast of All Saints. Tomorrow evening we begin to get ready for feast of All Souls which is on the following day. Is that correct?'

'Si! Si! You must not get afraid, Frankie. Tomorrow evening on the vigil of the feast of All Souls, we have a big blackboard outside the chapel. Piena... full of shape of hearts. Represent souls in Purgatorio. You pray merit grace... favour. You know?'

'I understand, Sr Laura. Sr Rita explained. Every time we go into chapel to pray we help a soul out of Purgatory. Then we come out and rub out one of the heart shapes on the blackboard. Our prayers help a soul who is in purgatory to go to heaven. Have I understood correctly, Sr Laura?'

'Ma che brave, Frankie. Ma but you not have paura... Fear. Not worry you, Frankie, cara.'

When Sr Laura traced the sign of the cross on Frankie's forehead, she became conscious of a warm current of love surge throughout her body. *Sr Laura loves me, she thought. I love her too. Is it alright to love a nun? She's a holy woman... but she is still a woman? Sr Maria knows that Sr Laura is looking after me. This is so confusing. We've been told not to have particular friendships. Oh God help me!*

At the end of the reading at supper that evening when Sr Rita asked Frankie to explain to the others the significance of the barmbrack, Frankie felt that Sr Rita seemed to speak in a gentler tone of voice.

'My mother brought six fruit cakes that Irish people call *báirín breac* or barmbracks. She hopes that these will help us to celebrate Hallowe'en or Holy evening. Watch out for the coins wrapped in cloth and the stick, pea and ring.'

Frankie noticed that Mavis put her hand in front of

her mouth. Then she winked when she saw that Frankie sat down without explaining the significance of the various things put in the barmbrack.

Frankie thought it inappropriate to give the explanation that she read on the leaflet. She knew Mavis would understand. The barmbrack was cut and and a slice was passed round to everyone. Frankie felt embarrassed but delighted when they all clapped her. Then Sr Rita rang the bell. Sr Maria arrived in the refectory.

'Aspirants, let me remind you why we celebrate the two feast days. We will enjoy the barmbrack so kindly given by Frankie's mother tonight on the eve of the feast of all Saints. We will eat cake even though it is Friday. As you know we normally do penance by not eating a dessert on Friday. Later we will play games, dance and duck for apples and enjoy ourselves.'

'Thank you, Sr Maria,' shouted out Pauline, a young aspirant.

Friday was not a day when we did penance in our house, thought Frankie. *It was the end of the week so Mammy got paid. She bought lots of sweets for us to enjoy before she went off to the pub to kick-start the weekend.*

'Tomorrow you will wear your black Sunday and feast-day dresses because it is a special feast day. It is a national holiday in Catholic countries. The Catholic Church commemorates and prays for the faithful departed who have not yet been purified before they can enter heaven. Christians who celebrate All Saints' Day and All Souls' Day do so in the fundamental belief that there is a prayerful spiritual bond between those in heaven in the Church triumphant and us living here on earth that are referred to as the 'Church militant.'

'Thought we were going to have fun? Not another lecture. We know all that,' whispered someone behind Frankie.

14

CHRISTMAS

*F*rankie felt hot and exhausted after scrubbing the kitchen floor. Longing for fresh air, she rushed out to join the others at recreation. After that exertion she was not sure that she needed the thick cardigan that Sr Laura had given her from the lost property box.

Jeanette called out to her, 'Thank goodness you've finished. Sr Rita's carrying a bundle of letters. She's waiting until everybody has finished their charges.'

'Thanks Jeanette, I hope there's one for me.'

'If there's one with blue crossed over it'll be a registered letter from my Mum. She always sends the nuns money,' said Jeanette

'Oh, I always recognise my mother's envelope. Woolworth's best, purchased a very long time ago, going yellow. There must have been a sale or a clear out back then. Mam got a job-lot.

She keeps them in a shoe box on a shelf next to our radio. They're oblong and smell of cigarettes.'

'I think I saw two airmail envelopes. They'll most

likely be for Monique and Stella,' added Jeanette.

As soon as Frankie joined the aspirants walking up and down the garden path, Sr Rita announced, 'The following aspirants, come to me to collect your letters: Monique, Hilary, Frankie, Jeanette and Margaret.'

Frankie couldn't recognise her mother's envelope among the pile in Sister's hands.

'Sister did call out my name, didn't she, Margaret?' Frankie whispered.

Before Margaret answered Sr Rita said, 'Yes Frankie, there's a letter for you too. It's the last one. Come.'

Oh Lord, what is the matter now? Has my mammy put swear words in the letter?

'Frankie, I've had to put a sheet of paper around your mother's envelope. She must smoke a lot. The letter reeks of cigarettes.'

Frankie could feel blood rushing to her cheeks but she was glad that there was a letter from her mother. She hoped that she was not still complaining about how hard life was for her.

'I think my mother wants the nuns to sell off the church silver in order to help her out, Margaret,' sighed Frankie.

'Frankie, I recognise this writing! Oh no… I hope… '

'Who do you think your letter's from, Margaret?'

'Shish, Frankie… I don't want Sr Rita to hear.'

'But that letter... all our letters have been read. They're all opened, Margaret.'

'Be careful, Frankie. I could be in trouble if Sr Rita was to find out who I think it's from. Of course I know that the letter has been read but Sr Maria may not realise…'

'Realise what? You've got me curious. Read it. Tell me. Who is it from, Margaret?'

'I am trying to read it without anyone noticing me.'

Frankie watched Margaret slip the letter into her blouse pocket.

'Go back and join Sr Rita walking up and down the path with the others. I'll find somewhere safe to open it.'

'Okay, Margaret, but let me know, won't you? I'm going to read my letter now. I feel so guilty when I read my mother's list of complaints.'

Frankie slipped to the back of the group of aspirants walking along the path and read her letter:

Dear Frankie, You need not worry about me over Christmas. I realised that I would miss you. I'd be on my own. I wrote to a friend that I've known for many years. A near relative. Anyway he has invited me over to Kerry. He's paying. I'm going. It's for the best. You have the nuns and your new friends. I sail from Holyhead on 16th December. I miss you.
Love from your Mammy

Who is this man? Is it my Uncle Brendan's friend, Louis? Why doesn't she name him? She has not been back to Ireland for years. Why is she going now? Maybe she really does miss me. If he is paying her fare over... She'll be delighted if he is. Is she leaving our flat? Supposing I decide to leave the convent I'll have no where to live. Frankie wondered what was behind her mother's decision.

Frankie saw that Margaret was in the middle of the group of aspirants walking towards the door leading into the convent. Her hands were clasped. There was no sign of the letter.

'Choir practice in five minutes. Make sure that you have seen to all your needs, aspirants. Those of you who are in the choir, be back here ready to familiarise yourselves with the music for the coming feast days. The rest of you will be preparing the vegetables or be helping in the workroom,' announced Sr Rita.

'Oh no! More buckets of spuds. All the eyes have to be taken out. The water will be cold. My hands will be freezing,' moaned Pauline.

'I'm useless at sewing but I bet I'll be sent to the workroom again,' said Anne. 'I hate mending sheets. Cut them down the middle and join edges. Who wants a sheet with a seam down the centre? So uncomfortable. Blame me!'

'Praise be to God that I can sing!' exclaimed Hilary.

'Remember your voice is God-given, Hilary,' retorted Sr Rita.

As they queued for the toilets, Frankie tried to move near to Margaret. She wanted to share her news about her mother and find out who had written to Margaret. She didn't succeed.

'Silence, aspirants! I can hear your choir teacher's footsteps,' said Sr Rita.

Frankie was standing at the back of the choir. She was delighted when the door opened and Sr Stephanie walked in. The aspirants clapped spontaneously.

'Grand! We're in for a good time,' exclaimed Mavis.

'Thank you, girls... aspirants. You're not in school. I'll have to be a little stricter with you here in the Aspirantade. Besides we have a lot to learn.' Sr Stephanie smiled and waved sheets of music.

Frankie heard Catherine remark, 'The pupils love Sr Stephanie. She seems to ooze music. She's very enthusiastic and relaxed at the same time.'

'You're going to enjoy the new music I've got for the feast of the Immaculate Conception. The Advent music is beautiful too. Wait 'til you hear it. Then there are all the carols! Come on. Let's start!' enthused Sr Stephanie as she reached over to touch the piano.' Stand on two legs. Find your balance. Breathe in and fill your lungs with air. Allow your breath to be released slowly. You'll know that this note is middle C. We'll begin with the scales.'

As Frankie loosened her vocal chords, she relaxed

144

remembering that Sr Stephanie usually gave the choir a break midway though their allotted time.

'You've mastered *'Tell forth my soul.'* Isn't it a lovely version of the Magnificat? Well done. Now we'll have a five minute break.'

'Thank you, Sister. It's really lovely,' complimented Margaret. 'I can play it on my clarinet.'

'Bring your clarinet next time, Margaret,' encouraged Sr Stephanie.

Frankie followed Margaret as she signalled her to join her near the bay window.

'Over here, Frankie.' Looking round to make sure that no one was watching, Margaret pulled a folded letter out of her blouse pocket.

'Peter has taken a huge risk, Frankie. You won't...'

'Your brother, Peter?'

'That's who he is pretending to be, Frankie.'

'Really, Margaret? Surely he'll be ...'

'I can't believe it. I read and re-read his letter. The nuns know I have a brother, Peter, so they let it pass.'

'Well whatever he wrote must be alright if it got past Sr Maria's scrutiny, Margaret?'

'Listen to this bit, *'I miss you very much, Margaret. Did I tell you that I love you?'*'

'Oh no, Margaret! I see what you mean... okay coming from your brother, but your boyfriend Peter saying that?'

'I love him. I miss him. I want to hug Peter. I want to kiss him. Oh Frankie, he even said that he will try to come here next visiting Sunday. Can you believe that? '

'How can he visit? He'd have to come with your family.'

'He must know that. But he said it. I can picture him winking as he wrote that. I love him. I miss him. I want to run all the way home, Frankie.'

'No letter. Not even a note from John, Margaret? I bet he has forgotten all about me. I feel jealous. I don't mind admitting it, Margaret.'

'Sorry, Frankie. I didn't mean to make you feel jealous. I've known Peter for a long time. He was often in our house. He attends the same school as my brother.'

'I know, Margaret. I feel lonely sometimes. When I feel miserable, I re-live that night when John kissed me. Oh, I'm in his arms again. He's hugging me tightly. That was so wonderful.'

'The dancing at the club that night was... I feel all tingly and oh... I wish we were there again. I want to be held tightly. I want to be tossed up in the air and be loved just for myself, Margaret.'

'So do I. Just imagine we're there. Stop twirling around and hugging yourself. Be careful, Anne Elizabeth's looking over at us. Stop. Okay she's smiling... we need to join the others..'

'My head's spinning... my heart's thumping. My imagination is running wild, Frankie.'

'So is mine. But let's pretend we're... keep walking. Keep talking.'

'Sr Stephanie is good. I love all the music. The Latin intro for the Mass for Our Lady in Gregorian Chant is so haunting and different. I just love it.'

'The notation is not like anything else. Heavy dots. I can imagine monks with those... what do you call them? Quills?... penning these Latin words onto parchment. Can you see them, Margaret?'

'When we sing in Latin, I feel a part of the nuns... actually the monks from long ago, Frankie.'

'Yes, I do too. Then *'Eagles Wings', 'Laudato Si'* and that hymn that we have just learnt are a complete contrast. So powerful. I enjoy them so much.''

'Tell out my soul, too.'

'Yes, Frankie, but all this talk about sublimating our feelings. I'm not so sure about that. I don't want to hide my feelings. It's so unnatural.'

'What exactly is meant by *sublimating feelings*, Margaret?'

'What I understand is that each time we want to be loved by a human, we're supposed to transfer our love for them to love Jesus or Our Lady instead. Sr Rita says that hymns and sacred music can help us to do that.'

'Margaret, what is wrong with loving another human being... especially John or Peter? What's wrong with kissing? It feels great!'

'Sr Stephanie is back at the piano. We'd better move to the choir, Frankie.'

'This time next year on the feast of the Immaculate Conception, some of you will be preparing to become novices. Once you have completed your two years as a novice you will make your vows and become professed members of our Order. You'll be nuns like me.' Sr Stephanie clasped her hands together and smiled.

'I won't even become a postulant on 11th February, the feast of Our Lady of Lourdes, Sister,' interjected Jeanette.

'I keep saying that she is too young to be here,' Frankie heard one of the teachers behind her whisper.

'That is true, Jeanette. You will become a postulant when you are sixteen and a novice six months later. You will know all of the hymns very well by that time. You'll be my right hand woman. I'll be able to depend on you.'

Frankie wondered what it must be like for Jeanette and Pauline to go to the same school as their friends and not be allowed to speak to them or join in their fun.

In the refectory when the reading from the scripture and a continuation of the life of the Foundress had been read, Frankie was surprised when Stella asked those at her table, 'How many of us sitting at this table do you think will persevere... stick it out... not go home?'

Frankie felt that she couldn't answer that question. She

felt so muddled. She longed to be hugged and loved. *Does one kiss mean that John loves me? Is it wicked to be hugged tightly? I probably would find other boyfriends. Maybe I could get a job in some shop. My mother has gone off to Ireland with someone I can't remember meeting. I hardly ever see my sister. Besides, she is married and has her own worries. My brother is in Australia. Perhaps I should stick it out.*

Frankie was struggling to find the right answer when she heard Sr Rita, 'God has called each one of us here. We pray every day that He will help us to persevere in doing His work here on earth. We are His hands and feet, His eyes and ears. Isn't that right, aspirants?' she asked from her seat at the top of the table.

Frankie winked at Margaret sitting opposite her. Mavis scratched her head, turned to Frankie and said, 'I keep praying.'

Frankie thought that it was just as well that Sr Rita could not read her thoughts.

'It's my turn to help washing the pots and pans tonight, Mavis.'

'Never mind, Frankie. When Sr Joan is in charge, we have great fun. She's a rebel. She says whatever comes into her head.'

'I know. What was it that she was singing last week when we were on the same charge?'

'*John Brown's body...* wasn't it? She said that she wants that sung at her funeral. She's a howl. Sometimes she sings Irish rebel songs like '*A Nation Once Again*' and the one about Bobby Sands... she's a scream!'

'Another announcement, Frankie. Sr Maria has arrived with the bell,' warned Mavis.

'I hope that you were all able to enter into the spirit of the feast of the Immaculate Conception today, aspirants. The singing was inspirational. In a few days time we will begin the season of Advent. Four weeks in preparation for Christmas and the celebration of the birth of our Saviour, Jesus Christ. We use this period to render an account of ourselves to God and of course to those of us who hold responsibility for each one of you.'

'What does that entail?' enquired Hilary.

'Good you asked. Let me explain, Hilary. There is nothing to be frightened about. I will sit in my office and each of you will come and tell me how well you are progressing as aspirants. Then I will be able to inform you what opinions assistants Sr Rita and Sr Laura have formed about you. It will be as simple as that.'

'I'm glad that she cannot see inside my head. If my head was a television, she'd turn it off,' whispered Margaret.

'You and Peter? Love films are forbidden!'

When Sr Maria left the refectory Frankie overheard one of the aspirants exclaim, 'I think that I have pleaded guilty to offending God by misusing every one of my senses at least four times during this last year.'

Frankie thought that Sr Rita must have heard the same comment and seen Frankie's puzzled face because she rang the bell again to say, 'Aspirants, let me explain that when you go to speak privately to Sr Maria what passes between the two of you is confidential. You examine your conscience and truthfully explain how you see yourself before God.'

Frankie leaned closer to Margaret to whisper, 'Should I tell Sr Maria about Peter?'

'Don't you dare, Frankie!' responded Margaret, pinching Frankie's arm.

'Live with your guilty conscience then, Margaret,' teased Frankie.

'Peter told me that the Beatles are bringing out an upbeat version of King Wenceslas.'

'Too upbeat for here, though,' laughed Frankie.

The next evening when the nuns intoned the Advent hymn:

O come o come Emmanuel. O come, thou Wisdom from on high... Frankie thought, we are singing O'come' just when my mother is leaving. I wonder why she is going over to Ireland.

'That was a cheerful sermon, Frankie, wasn't it? Fr O'Connor has a face like a cherub,' remarked Mavis as the aspirants filed out of chapel.

'Rejoice in the Lord always; again I say, rejoice. That's so encouraging,' joined in Catherine.

'I'm looking forward to the third Sunday of Advent, Gaudete Sunday, when the priest wears rose-coloured vestments,' added another aspirant.

'I need cheering up. I hope my mother is okay,' whispered Frankie to Margaret.

'Sr Maria is going into our refectory. She must be about to make another announcement, Frankie.'

As soon as the aspirants were seated, Sr Maria rang her bell, cleared her throat and said, 'Sr Stephanie told me that you have already prepared Christmas carols. I'm delighted because the parish priest has asked if you can sing them in church. The headmistress of the primary school has also invited you, aspirants, to take part in the school children's carol concert. She is keen to help the children to imbibe the true meaning of Christmas and to remember that God gave us the best present of all when he gave us His son, Jesus.'

'I'm sure the aspirants will enjoy that. Thank you, Sr Maria, said Sr Rita.'

'My sister is singing too. She's in the top class, Sr Maria,' called out Pauline.

'I can't wait to have my first mince pie. I love the marzipan under the icing on the Christmas cake too,' exclaimed Jeanette.

'I'm glad we're going to the parish church, Margaret. We'll be able to mingle with outsiders,' whispered Frankie.

'On occasions like these, remember aspirants, that there is to be no idle chatting with mums and other family members. We will keep together and act with decorum,' declared Sr Rita.

'Spoil sport again!' sighed Margaret.' What does she think we'll say?'

'There is something else that I wish to tell you. As well as preparing ourselves spiritually for the great feast of Christmas, we also need to prepare our convent. We will clean, dust and polish the entire house. While you are engaged in tasks such as cleaning out drains, unscrewing the pipes underneath sinks, scrubbing or polishing floors, helping in the laundry or chopping the vegetables, you'll have an opportunity to examine your conscience.'

'We'll be exhausted once school breaks up. I usually go away for a holiday,' Frankie heard teacher, Anne Elizabeth, say.

'More drudgery, Frankie,' whispered Margaret.

'I've had enough cleaning to last a life time!'

On the 16th of December when we begin the novena leading up to Christmas, I will also hand out Christmas cards signed by me. Each one of you will add your wishes to this card. This will be our combined card to your parents and loved ones.'

My Mam goes to Ireland on the day we get our signed Christmas card. Where do I send it? I hope she didn't give up her flat. I'll have nowhere to go, worried Frankie.

Frankie was surprised the following evening when Sr Rita announced, 'Since we have a mix of aspirants from different nationalities, Sr Maria suggested that we try to observe some of their customs.'

'The feast of St Nicholas is celebrated in two days time, Sr Rita,' called out Brigitte.

'Yes, Brigitte. I'm glad that you suggested this idea to Sr Maria.'

Frankie began trying to recall any Irish customs.

'Perhaps we should start with Brigitte explaining Dutch customs,' announced Hilary.

'In my country children prepare for the big feast of St Nicholas on 5th December by putting their shoes in front of the chimney.'

'What happens if your house hasn't got a chimney? Ours hasn't,' asked one of the group.

'I know. I was going to explain that that doesn't matter nowadays. We choose somewhere central in our home as the spot where we place one shoe. Often we put a carrot or some hay in the shoes, as a gift to St. Nicholas' horse.'

'It's lovely to observe old customs, Brigitte,' said Stella.

'Anything else, Brigitte?' enquired someone else.

'On the eve of the feast the family sings *Sinterklaas* songs. We have St Nicholas instead of Father Christmas.'

'What kind of presents do they receive, Brigitte?'

'Small presents. Well that is how it used to be. We receive anything such as sweets, marbles or some other small toys.'

Sr Laura and Stella started singing:

Santa Lucia! Santa Lucia!
Venite all'agile barchetta mia,
Santa Lucia! Santa Lucia!

Frankie automatically started clapping and soon realised that everyone else seemed to be familiar with this tuneful song.

'I know the tune... but the words... What do they mean?' asked Monique.

'You've both sang it as though you already knew it. I thought you were Maltese, Stella?' questioned another aspirant.

'Many Maltese speak Italian. I'm of Italian extract,'

explained Stella.

'Saint Lucia... luce... light? Dicembre she is dark month. Lucia bring light, correct Stella?' Sr Laura turned to Stella for confirmation.

'Yes on 12th December we welcome the light. Saint Lucy was a wealthy young Christian martyr. From the third century, I think? It's a traditional Neapolitan song, isn't it, Sr Laura?' checked Stella.

Frankie watched as Sr Laura began to make wavy movement with her hand and say; 'Vieni, Lucia.'

'Barca... boat.' Sr Laura outlined the shape of a boat.' *barchetta mia,* how you say? Come, my little boat. Come light.' Sr Lucia tried to explain.

Sr Stephanie popped her head round the door of the music room. Sr Rita rang a bell, 'Second year aspirants, gather round the piano and sing our special Advent hymn. The rest of you bring your chairs nearer. Could one of you dim the lights? Yes, light the candle on the piano, Anna, please.'

They had only sung the first line of the hymn and Frankie felt transported to a peaceful place:

A shoot shall spring from the Root of Jesse
A king shall be born of David's line
And the wolf and the lamb will lie down together
And a little child will lead you
The Lord himself will give you a sign:
A maiden you will find with child
She will soon give birth and the Son she bears
She will name him Emmanuel
On Him will rest the Spirit of the Lord and the fear of Yahweh, his breath
And the land will be filled with the knowledge of the Lord
And the waters swell the sea

No one clapped. Frankie sensed that the melody and theme of this hymn had transfixed all those present.

'I can see that you each appreciated that lovely hymn. We sing it often throughout the Advent season. With the rich liturgy of the Christmas novena, confession and eventually midnight Mass, we will prepare well for Christmas,' concluded Sr Rita.

'Thank you. Beautiful! A haunting melody,' Anna addressed Sr Rita and the second year aspirants.

'Thank you, Anna. The bell will ring for supper in five minutes. Off you go now, aspirants,' instructed Sr Rita.

Frankie noticed that Pauline took her mantilla from her peg and went into chapel. Suspecting that she must be lonely too she decided to do the same a few minutes later. In the dim light of the chapel crumpled on a pew, Frankie found her sobbing. While Frankie hugged Pauline, she hoped that her own mother was safe wherever she was in Ireland.

As the aspirants gathered together before going to bed that night, Sr Laura asked Frankie if there were any Irish Christmas traditions. Frankie was delighted and looked over at Mavis. Mavis nodded. They both stood up and began by reciting:

The wren, the wren, the king of all birds,
On St. Stephen's Day was caught in the furze;
Up with the kettle and down with the pan,
Pray give us a penny to bury the wran.

'Oh that's an old tradition, isn't it Frankie. It goes back a long time. Back to even before my mother's time. On what you call Boxing Day, we celebrate St. Stephen's Day,' explained Mavis.

'It's great fun. When I was small we still had bands of so-called Wren Boys. They blackened their faces with shoe polish or wore masks so that nobody would know who they were. '

154

'Sometimes they made their masks out of calico, didn't they? They painted these with shoe polish or some kind of black paint that could be washed off.'

'They cut holes in the masks for the nose and eyes.'

'They'd be about ten or twelve boys dressed in old trousers made of calico or curtain cloth. Their coats were made of the same material.'

'How would you describe their hats, Frankie?' asked Mavis.

'The ones in our area wore hats decorated with feathers. Sometimes they'd attach horse hair to these hats.'

'Or as whiskers onto their masks.'

'Anyway there was a great splash of colour about them.'

'Don't forget to mention that there would be dancers and musicians, who played the fiddle, flute, melodeon or bodhran. They were often accompanied by at least one good singer.'

'And sometimes they'd cycle to neighbouring towns.'

'It was great fun watching them sing, dance and play as they travelled from house to house. Sometimes we'd join in...'

'Collecting money as they went.'

'Where did this tradition come from?' enquired Hilary.

'Some say that a wren betrayed the Christian martyr, St Stephen's hiding place. Others say that the wren was responsible for revealing where the Irish soldiers were hiding when they fought the Viking invaders,' added Frankie.

'You are both avoiding or denying to inform us all about the disgusting part of this tradition. These so call Wren-Boys hunt and kill wrens and carry the dead wren around in a casket! It's a pagan sacrificial tradition from pre-Christian times! You should be ashamed of yourselves!' screamed out Catherine, their history teacher.

Frankie felt tears trickling down her cheeks. She heard Mavis sigh, 'Oh no!' No one spoke. No one moved.

'Anger is a sin. No matter what the facts are or what you think, there is no excuse for such outbursts, Catherine,' reprimanded Sr Rita.

'I apologise for my angry outburst, Sister but…'

'No *buts,* Catherine. I'll speak to you in my office tomorrow morning. You should know better than most that many of the traditions that we celebrate have dubious origins. Take bonfire night, for example.'

Frankie stretched out to touch Mavis's hand before they both returned to sit in their places. She was pleased that Mavis squeezed her hand and that Sr Rita had reprimanded Catherine.

At school the next day, Frankie discussed this incident with Mavis who was sitting at the desk next to her. The class was waiting for Sr Rose, their Religious Education teacher, to arrive.

'The prefect in our class is making a collection for a present for Sr Rose, Mavis. I'd love to contribute. Sr Rose has been so understanding and kind to us.'

'I know what you mean, Frankie. But we don't have any money. You'll have to accept that we can't contribute to this.'

'What are we going to tell the girl who's collecting, Mavis? Here she comes.'

'Leave it to me.'

'Sorry Sarah! We'd love to join in. Sr Rose is so good. But we don't have any money.'

'No money at all? You don't have any money. Oh well.'

Just as she turned away carrying the collection tin, Frankie had an idea. 'Come back in a minute, Sarah, and I'll see what I can do.'

'Okay!'

'Don't look, Mavis. I know I have a lovely medal in my piety bag.'

'A medal, Frankie!' exclaimed Mavis.

'Mavis, it's difficult enough losing the button on my crocheted piety bag. Just as well my Postulant's cape makes it a little easier to reach into my chemise.'

'Spare us the details. You'll make a show of us. You can't give a medal instead of a coin. Have you finished probing inside your chemise pocket to find a medal? The girl's going to think we're weird. Sarah's on her way back.'

'Here you are, Sarah. Take that for Sr Rose instead. Do you like the blue glass over the top?'

'Frankie, what are the girls going to think of you now? They ask for money and you give them a medal!'

'It won't make much difference. The girls already regard us as different.'

'I'm not surprised, Frankie.'

'I hate it when they see us in our overalls getting ready to clean the school just as they are preparing to go home, Mavis. They must think of us as cleaners.'

'I know, Frankie. That is the sacrifice we have to make. You wait until school breaks up and the big clean begins. All the aspirants come over here to scour the place from top to bottom.'

'Oh I'm dreading that, Mavis. The skin on my hands is already red raw after washing the pots and pans. It's the soda that rips the skin off. My hair is straggly too. Sr Laura just cropped it. When I caught sight of myself in the mirror in the girls' washroom I looked like a roundhead!'

'Well Frankie, you're going to have to put up with lots more visions of yourself because you and I are on the team cleaning all the washrooms in the school. Toilets, unscrewing pipes under sinks to clean out and drain the pipes. Using Vim to remove marks from the floors and...'

'Stop! I hate all this cleaning, Mavis. I detest looking like Mrs. Mop. I had to do all the cleaning at home but I didn't expect we'll have to do the same in the convent. I entered the convent to go out to other countries and...'

'spread the Word of God. To teach people how to live better lives?'

'D'you know what kept me going, Frankie? Last year when this big clean began, I started singing all those lovely hymns and carols that we rehearse for Christmas.'

'But don't you miss all the Beatles songs? I'd love to hear their version of Good King Wenceslas. It'll take more than singing in my head to keep me sane, Mavis. I've had enough cleaning. Besides I bet we'll have to hand over any presents that anyone gives us to Sr Maria.'

'We're allowed phone calls over Christmas though, Frankie.'

'No consolation for me, Mavis. My mother has sailed to Ireland.'

Back in the study Frankie heard Margaret practising Christmas carols on her clarinet. The places were changed in the refectory. She was no longer seated near her. At recreation she chatted to another aspirant. Frankie felt lonely and very tired.

'Cara Francesca, you are sad?' Sr Laura placed her arm on Frankie's shoulder as the aspirants gathered round Sr Rita to listen to the customary 'Good Night talk' given before the aspirants went into chapel to say their night prayers.

'I feel so tired, Sister. Thank you.'

'You are lonely, perhaps?'

Frankie blinked tears away. 'My mother is in Ireland, Sister.'

She felt Sr Laura squeezing her arm. The warmth spread joy through her body. Once in the chapel she put her head into her hands and let the tears flow so much so that when the prayers were over she could barely see the steps on the way up to the dormitory. As she twisted and turned in bed and struggling to find dry parts of her handkerchief to mop up her tears, the lights were switched off.

Where is my mother now? I am all alone. Margaret must be so happy playing her clarinet. She doesn't even notice that I am sad. No one really cares about me, thought Frankie. *Margaret doesn't love me yet I love her.*

Suddenly the curtains round the bottom of her bed were parted. Sr Laura came near and drew a cross on her forehead.

'Cara figlia, dormi. Non ha paura! Sleep... no fear.'

While Sr Laura's hand rested on her forehead a surge of love continued to flow through her whole body. She thought, *Sr Laura loves me. What kind of love is this? Sisterly love?*

'I'm looking forward to our choir practice, Frankie. I can put up with all the scrubbing and cleaning when I know that I will enjoy playing my clarinet at the practice,' said Margaret at breakfast.

She's so happy with that blinking clarinet that she doesn't see that I'm feeling low. She is bouncing about full of life. Well I can do that too. My Mam's in Ireland. So what? I'm determined that I won't be dragged down.

Frankie replied, 'Good for you, Margaret.'

When Frankie looked toward the end of the table, her eyes met those of Sr Laura. Sister smiled and then winked.

Thank God for Sr Laura, sighed Frankie.

Frankie turned to look towards the top table where Sisters Maria and Rita were seated. Sr Maria tinkled a bell to gain attention:

'Well done, aspirants. You have cleaned the school and the convent. All that remains to be done is collecting wood for the fire and shovelling coke down for the furnace. Of course you will need to practice the music and prepare the vegetables,' announced Sr Maria.

While they were all still listening, Sr Rita turned to Sr Maria to say: 'You asked me to remind you to explain about Christmas cards and presents, Sr Maria.'

'Thank you, Sr Rita. Yes of course. When each of you

come speak to me in my office, I will give you the cards. Those of you who are fortunate enough to have parcels sent to you will be notified individually. This is to prevent anyone who does not receive a parcel from feeling left out. What is given to one will be shared by all. The same will apply to the Christmas cards. We will display a few of these here in the refectory.'

'But what about personal things like underwear?' enquired Pauline.

'Of course, Pauline, remember that each of you have been allocated a part of a shelf in the linen cupboard on the landing. Personal items like that are stored there until you need them. You only require one change of underwear in your locker,' replied Sr Maria.

I wonder if Mammy's pub friends will send me something, thought Frankie.

'Sr Maria, forgive me for interrupting you again but have all the aspirants been to speak with you individually?' enquired Sr Rita.

'I'm very grateful to you, Sr Rita. I still have to see Frankie and Mavis. Would you two come with me straight after breakfast? I have a few matters to sort out with each of you. Sit at the table on the landing until I call you in.'

I don't want to be sent home, thought Frankie. *There is no one there. I'd better stick it out at least until Christmas is over. I wonder if my sister would let me stay at her place. But there's such an age gap between us. We're different in so many other ways, too.*

'Mavis, what am I suppose to confess when I speak to Sr Maria? Would it be okay to say that I am dreading Christmas?'

'You'd be a strange individual if you weren't, Frankie. Sure, didn't I hear you say that your mammy's in Ireland? To top that, doesn't everyone feel nostalgic and lonely at this time of year?'

'Margaret doesn't seem to be feeling that way. She's smiling and bouncing around.'

'Mark my words, Frankie. She may be engrossed in her music now but there will come a time during this season when loneliness will hit her too. The nuns will do their best to cheer us up but...'

'They must miss their families too, Mavis.'

'Ah now, sure they have their own means of coping. We'll be reminded to walk with Mary and Joseph on their journey to Bethlehem. How could you grumble when you recall how poor and needy they were.'

'Frankie, please come in now?' announced Sr Maria as she held open the door to her office and beckoned Frankie to sit opposite her on an upright wooden chair. Frankie noticed that she had a small opened parcel on her desk.

'I have a little surprise for you, Frankie. A group of your mother's friends must have been concerned that you might be feeling lonely over this holy season of Christmastide. They knew that your mother is in Ireland so they have clubbed together to send you two parcels.'

Frankie couldn't believe it. *I haven't been forgotten after all. My poor Mammy must have told them to send me a parcel. She does love me. Why did I doubt that?*

'Here, take some tissues, Frankie. You see your mother is thinking about you and so are her good friends,' consoled Sr Maria.

'Thank you, Sister.'

'Move nearer so that you can see what they have sent you, Frankie.'

'A watch! Like a nurse wears... upside down... a fob watch!'

'Yes precisely. A fob watch. Of course you don't need that now so have a good look and I will keep it safely until it becomes necessary for you to use, Frankie.'

Frankie pursed her lips. She wanted to say, *I could wear*

it. The aspirants who are teachers keep theirs. Granted that Sr Rita stores them in her desk overnight but they retrieve them each morning to wear at school. Margaret has her clarinet. Why can't I have this watch?

Too frightened to dare to utter this, instead she said, 'Thank you, Sr Maria,' and smiled as Sister put the lovely silver watch back in its box. A drawer of her desk was opened and the watch disappeared from sight.

'Remember that I told that you have received two presents, Frankie. The other is a lovely big Christmas pudding. Sister has that safely stored in the kitchen. On Christmas day I will make sure that it's you who carry it into the refectory.'

Frankie rolled her lips to prevent a smile forming. *Knowing those friends of Mammy's, I bet it is laced with whiskey and port. Maybe I will be helped to forget my loneliness. We can all drown our sorrow and toast my mammy.*

'I'm glad to see you looking a little happier now, Frankie. Sr Laura told me that you seem to have been downcast lately. This of course is understandable. I want to assure you that we are all very pleased with the progress that you have been making. Keep it up. Remember to pray to Jesus and His Mother, Mary. Life was not easy for them either. At this time of the year we recall how difficult it must have been for them when they left their home in Nazareth to travel to Bethlehem. Mary must have found that journey particularly difficult.'

'Yes, I will pray, Sister. Thank you,' said Frankie as she stood empty-handed and walked toward the door of Sr Maria's office.

The back of the watch was engraved with my name so one day it will be mine, thought Frankie. *I'll just have to put on a brave face and try and enjoy Christmas. I can't wait until they taste that Christmas pudding.*

On Christmas day when the community of aspirants stood around the decorated tables ready to commence their Christmas meal Sr Rita reminded everyone: 'Before we pray Grace let us bow our heads and remember poor starving people all over the world. While we feast ourselves they have very little or nothing to eat.'

'Why do nuns always trot out this reminder?' whispered someone near Frankie.

'Happy Christmas, Frankie! Colour has come back into your cheeks at last,' said Margaret while she shook hands with Frankie.

'So you did notice that I was not myself, Margaret?' replied Frankie.

'Oh of course I did, Frankie. But I wasn't worried because I heard Sr Laura going into your cubicle each evening. She smiles at you a lot.'

I can't tell even Margaret how much I have grown to love Sr Laura, reflected Frankie. I can't help it that's how I feel. Each evening when she pats my head and draws the sign of the cross on my forehead, my body trembles with a lovely, loving feeling.

'You were so absorbed in your clarinet playing that it's a wonder you saw anything else, Margaret,' teased Frankie.

'Oh come on now, Frankie. I didn't want to make you jealous... shish.'

Margaret leaned nearer to Frankie and whispered, 'It's Peter's clarinet and he rolled another love note inside it.'

'Risky! Supposing it was found?'

'If music be the food of love, play on. Give me excess of it... He's a clever lad,' smiled Margaret.

'Twelfth Night? No one would suspect. Quoting Shakespeare is a smart ruse, Margaret.'

'Have you been up to anything secretive, Frankie? Maybe you might want to confess to me?' joked Margaret.

'Wait until you taste the Christmas pud. Ask for a

second helping, Margaret. My mother's pub friends made it.'

Sr Rita invited Frankie to fetch the pudding: 'Frankie, would you like to go out to the kitchen and carry in the special Christmas pudding that your mother sent?'

It was Sr Mary's turn to prepare the Christmas meal. She welcomed Frankie: 'Let's light the holly and … oh it's …'

Frankie could not believe her eyes when the whoosh of the flame soared up from the pudding. Then Sister dropped the pudding.

'Don't worry, Sister. I'll pick it up. Put it on another … but the glass, Sister?'

'No one will know, Frankie. Let's just push it all together into shape. Look here's another plate. Sure we can pat it back together. Here we are. Now it looks fine. I'll stick this spring of holly on top and light it again then you can carry it in,' assured Sister as she almost shoved Frankie into the refectory.

While everyone was clapping, Frankie held the pudding aloft, hiding the fact that she was worried that someone might end up in hospital with shards of splintered glass from the broken bowl in their throat. However soon all fear disappeared when she consumed a big cut of whiskey-laced Christmas pudding.

'Frankie, is this whiskey?' enquired Margaret as she nudged her.

'Who knows, Margaret? I'd say it was whatever and as much as my mother's friends could get their hands on. They sure want me to be happy, Margaret.'

Frankie was relieved that no glass was found by anyone on Christmas day or the following day either. She felt that whatever alcohol there was in the pudding helped her to drown her sorrows. The other aspirants looked jolly too.

Two days later on the eve of the 27th December, Sr

Rita stood on the second to last step of the stairs leading down into the entrance hall and clapped her hands, Frankie hoped that the good feeling she was experiencing would not be spoilt.

'Aspirants, I want to explain a custom that we follow each year on 27th of December. I'm sure that you will all enjoy hearing about the *Lord of Misrule* who turns the world upside.'

'Upside down, Sister?' asked Jeanette.

'Thank goodness this lasts just for a day. Let me explain for those who don't already know.'

'Do you want me to explain, Sister?' interjected Catherine.

'No, Catherine. I'm aware you teach history but I'll do the explaining.'

It was Catherine who lost her temper when we were told about St Stephen's Day, remembered Frankie.

Sister continued, 'We are told that long ago on 28th of January following an old custom kings and those in authority, changed places with the poor. For one whole day, folk with responsibilities were encouraged to leave them aside and behave as carefree people and ordinary folk while simple folk borrowed their crowns, wigs, capes, gowns and behaved like kings, queens and judges. Added to that during the time that those pretending to be royalty could issue rules that everyone had to obey throughout that day. Fun ensued throughout.'

'Can we really make others do as we say too, Sister,' asked Pauline.

'Yes, just for the day. You could elect the youngest aspirant as queen for the day and she could lay down a rule for example, requesting the oldest aspirant to carry her mantilla , or... you'll have your own ideas. So, how about that? Now you can all go into the dining room and decide how you are going carry this out.'

'Oh Boyoo! This is good fun,' exclaimed Mavis. 'We had a great time last year, didn't we, second years?'

'Isn't 'Misrule' associated with disorder, lawless confusion, ineptitude, unwise rule and misgovernment?' asked Hilary.

'Come on! Let's go into the dining room and get started,' invited Catherine as she waved her hands and took control.

Frankie noticed that Sr Rita raised her eyebrows and scratched her head through her veil.

'This is so uncharacteristic of Sr Rita,' observed Margaret.

'Is it a trick?' asked Stella.

'I can't believe that Sr Rita is handing the aspirants control of events all day.'

Frankie overheard Catherine whispering, 'This is our chance to turn the tables on that control freak, Sr Rita.'

'Sr Laura and Sr Rita look as though they intend observing us, Catherine. If you start organising the group, they may well stop you. Let me do the explaining, Catherine. Is that okay?' asked Hilary.

Frankie watched Catherine purse her lips and eventually nod in agreement.

Hilary beckoned everyone to sit. She stood at the front to address the aspirants.

'Before we start would you mind me giving you a little bit of background to this?'

It seemed to Frankie that both Sr Rita and Sr Laura were taken aback when Hilary made that announcement but nevertheless they nodded their consent.

'The Lord of Misrule is one of the lost characters of the riotous Medieval Christmas celebration. Sometime in November, it was customary among the European peasantry to draw lots for the title of Lord of Misrule.'

'Is this going to be a history lesson, Catherine? I thought

it was to be fun,' commented Stella.

'It is fun. Wait until I explain. You see, the Lord of Misrule wears a paper crown and a mixture of regal clothes. He changes or abandons the rules to be obeyed,' responded Catherine.

'That will result in chaos. Folk will do what they like,' retorted Anna.

'Perhaps it might be best not to imagine what kind of fun will be engaged in, once they have had a drink,' warned Hilary.

'Of course, we won't do that,' Hilary interrupted Catherine. 'It's good to know the background of Misrule, isn't it?'

Catherine glanced at Sr Rita. Sr Rita coughed. When Frankie looked over at her she was screwing up her forehead and squeezing her hands together.

'The most sacrificial elements were removed or replaced by the less barbarous practice of burning the god in effigy.'

'Sounds gruesome, Hilary?' called out Anna.

'Yes it was.'

At this point Sr Rita intervened with, 'All this explanation is beginning to be too pagan. Remember that although we plan to have fun, it is also the feast of the Holy Innocent that we are keeping. Why are you providing the aspirants with this ancient history, Catherine? I expected you to know better.'

'I'm sorry, Sister. I felt it necessary to remind everyone of the background to this feast.'

'I'm not so sure that all that is necessary. Aspirants, if you consult the Ordo or look in the Divine Office books and of course refer to the Holy Gospel according to St Matthew where it is recounted that 28th January is the day on which we, as Catholics, remember that the Holy Innocents merited the martyr's crown. *On the lips of children and of babes you have found praise to foil your enemy.*

If you read St Matthews's account, King Herod orders the execution of all young male children in the village of Bethlehem, to avoid the loss of his throne to a newborn.

Frankie blocked this counter explanation out. She began scratching the back of her neck. She looked around and saw others yawning and moving from one foot to the other. She noticed that Sr Rita was tugging at her veil and adjusting her bonnet. Sr Laura must have realised that things could only get worse because she stood up, 'Si! Importante remember gli innocenti, poveri babini... babies. Herod is bad king. Ma in Casa Generalizia... our Mother home, they have fun too. For esempio madre... mother? Even she's not in charge on this day. We laugh a lot...'

Frankie thought that this must have been too much for Sr Rita because she stepped down from the rostrum and left the aspirants to continue to prepare for a mixture of the Lord of Misrule and the feast of the Holy Innocents.

Hilary appeared undeterred. As soon as Sr Rita had gone, Catherine stepped up to the rostrum.

'Catherine looks scary. What do you think, Frankie,' remarked Margaret.

'I bet she wants to get her revenge from being told off...'

'... and she hopes Sr Laura won't understand her,' added Frankie.

Catherine started, 'I am merely going to tell you about tomorrow's feast. Some of you will know already. In the Middle Ages, on December 28th, the Feast of the Holy Innocents, following the customs of Misrule that had become widespread in Europe, a boy was chosen to act as bishop.'

'Stop! We've had enough explanations, Catherine,' shouted out Stella.

'Phew! What is she trying to prove?' whispered Margaret.

'I don't know but I saw Sr Laura signalling her to

stop, too. I suppose she didn't want her to give any other opinions on the background to these feasts. Watch, Sr Laura is mounting the rostrum now,' added Frankie.

'Aspirants! Not to worry much. Forse... maybe youngest aspirant, Jeanette, become Sr Superior... Sister in charge for the day?' announced St Laura.

Delighted that there seemed to be a light-hearted approach, Frankie joined in the clapping as Jeanette walked up to join Sr Laura.

'Do you accept, Jeanette?' asked Sr Laura.

'Yes, but only if we can raid the dressing-up box and we make our own rules,' answered Jeanette.

Frankie noticed that everyone seemed to be relieved.

Jeanette addressed the aspirants to ask: 'What rule shall we make first?'

'I suggest talking. We can talk all day,' said Pauline.

'Choose our own partners when we go for the walk in the afternoon,' said Stella.

'Agreed?' said Jeanette.

'Great, Margaret,' said Frankie as she nudged Margaret.

The next day the aspirants set out for a walk in Richmond Park and Margaret partnered Frankie. They chose to walk near the back of the line. As soon as they thought that they were out of earshot of the two behind them in the line, Margaret asked Frankie if she had noticed that Jeanette was not at breakfast.

'She seemed tearful yesterday but I thought that like most of us she was homesick. So what do you think? Surely she can't have gone home so soon after Christmas, Margaret?'

'Well she was sleeping next to me in the dormitory. Her bed was left undone this morning. When we were at Mass I heard a car driving away from the convent. I presume that she has gone home for good. Of course I don't know for certain but that's how the nuns seem to send people home.'

'Oh Margaret, if only we could say goodbye and better still, if we were able to ask why she went. Do they ask to go home or are they sent home?'

'I think that I know the reason why she decided to leave, Frankie. It's not good.'

'Oh Lord! What now, Margaret?'

'I can't quite fathom it out myself but I'll tell you. See what you think, Frankie.'

'Oh Margaret. Please tell me.'

'Do you remember, Frankie, when we were in the study last Sunday and Sr Maria popped her head round the door to ask if anyone would mind running over to school to bring her back a small pile of books that she wanted to mark for the following day?'

'Sr Laura chose you, Margaret. She handed you a bunch of keys.'

'Yes and holding the keys to the school, I ran as quickly as I could and opened up what I thought was an empty school. When I got to the top floor and was about to turn right into her room I saw Sr Wilfred and Sr Stephanie standing next to a table on which young Jeanette was standing.'

'What was Jeanette doing there? Why was she standing on a table, Margaret?'

'Well that's what I don't understand. You see she was only wearing her vest and knickers. Sr Wilfred was rubbing her hands up and down her legs. Why would she be doing that, Frankie?'

'Oh my God, you don't think? Oh no. There must be some explanation, Margaret. Surely... ?'

'The only reasonable explanation is that perhaps there is going to be a play and they were measuring her for an outfit?'

'Yes, she needed a costume for the play. But remember what happened when she was larking about and jumping on the coke? She hurt her leg so maybe the nuns were looking at the bruises.'

Just then their conversation was interrupted, 'You two have decided to sing on the stage tonight and maybe you play clarinet, Margaret?'

'Oh, Sr Laura! You have come to join us?' exclaimed Margaret.

'You two learn Italian. I ask if you help prepare.. tell aspirants about Befana?'

'Of course we will, won't we, Frankie?' replied Margaret.

'Yes, Sr Laura. She is the Italian Father Christmas, isn't she?'

'Puts fruit, sweets in shoes children leave out for her. Three Wise Men, *re magi*, stopped at *Befana*'s asked directions on way to Bethlehem. She joined them,' explained Sr Laura.

Frankie started singing Santa Lucia.

'Can I butt in? When I heard you singing I thought you might be planning another concert?'

'Correct! We are, Agnes,' Frankie responded.

'Ye canna omit Hogmanay, surely?' said Agnes McInes.

'You don't miss much,' replied Margaret. 'Were you listening in there while you were walking behind of us?'

'Now you two, are ye aware that the Scots celebrate Hogmanay? Christmas was not celebrated as a festival and was banned in Scotland for around 400 years. Really from the end of the 17th century.'

'That was only because the Kirk portrayed Christmas as a Popish or Catholic feast and therefore had to be banned,' replied Margaret.

'Och! Never ye mind about all that. So long as we have the first footing, we'll be happy,' responded Agnes.

'First footing? What's that?'

''First Footing' it's the *first foot* that steps into the house after midnight! To ensure good luck, a first footer should be a dark-haired male.'

'Tall, dark and handsome!'

'Fair-haired first footers were not particularly welcome because folk still recalled the fair headed Viking who invaded Britain way back in ancient times.'

'Do you have to bring a bottle?'

'Yes, of course. Whiskey to toast the New Year. Traditional gifts include a lump of coal to be lovingly placed on the host's fire.'

Soon the walk finished and the aspirants were back in the convent. As they were about to enter the refectory for tea Sr Maria came in and beckoned Margaret to come with her. As she followed her she wondered why she was being called out. A few minutes later she returned and Margaret looked very downcast.

'Bad news, Margaret?' enquired Frankie.

'It's my twin sister. Rose was rushed into hospital with an attack of asthma on Christmas Day. Even worse, that must have been at the same time that I was tucking into our Christmas dinner.'

'Is Rose alright now, Margaret?' asked Frankie.

'Fortunately, she is okay now. I feel so guilty, you know. I was enjoying myself while she must have been so frightened.'

15

POSTULANTS

*F*rankie was not sure if it was she that Sr Rita was signalling. Just after the aspirants sat down to breakfast, Sister seemed to be indicating that she should go up to the top of table to speak to her.

'Yes, you, Frankie, and Margaret. Come nearer, I want to speak to you both,' called out Sr Rita.

'Coming, Sister.'

'Sr Rose informed me that the sixth former's Religious Education class starts at 10 this morning. I think I can trust you both to go over earlier. You don't need to wait to join the rest of aspirants. It won't be necessary for you to help clearing up after breakfast either. Use the time gained to study,' Sr Rita instructed.

Frankie was surprised that Sr Rita was allowing them both to walk over the hockey field together instead of following the usual routine of walking with the other aspirants. However, she felt it was safer to refrain from expressing her delight.

Frankie heard Margaret say, 'Thank you, Sister,' as she

walked back to her seat.

It was only when she and Margaret arrived in the study that Frankie felt safe enough to clap her hands and exclaim, 'We're trusted, Margaret! I can't believe it! Can you?'

'Do you think it is some kind of test we have to pass to see if we are fit to become postulants, Frankie?'

'Maybe, but it will be great to chat. We've not been able to do that for a while, Margaret. If we set off earlier, we can take our time. I saw Sr Rita getting into the convent car with Sr Maria. Why don't we start off immediately?'

'Good! Off we go.'

'I see you're carrying your Mac. I've got mine too. Sr Mary said that weather forecast for February is unsettled, changeable and freezing at night, Margaret.'

'I suppose after years spent in the garden, she's as good a judge of the weather, Frankie.'

'She gets her information from the newspaper.'

'I thought the nuns weren't allowed to read newspapers.'

'No, they're not but surely you've seen the weather information displayed on the notice board near the nun's ref? Apparently, the headmistress, Sr Alicia, cuts out the information from a newspaper that she deems appropriate and pins it on the board for the Sisters to read.'

'What did you say the weather is going to be? Unsettled, changeable and freezing at night? Sounds like how I feel, Margaret. I was counting the days until I would become a postulant. We've only a few days to go. I realise that I am being trusted today but sometimes I still doubt if I'll be accepted. Maybe I am still under observation.'

'I know how you feel, Frankie. When Catherine left, that was the fourth aspirant that has gone home or maybe, has been asked to leave, since our group began six months ago.'

'Margaret, I want to tell you what has happened to me, but I feel so embarrassed.'

174

'I heard your name being called out when we were in the study. Sr Rita said that Sr Maria wanted to see you in her room. I thought she might have received a letter from your mother. Is she back from Ireland?'

'My mother's back. I didn't tell you. I thought you might not want to talk to me if...'

'Why? Is it about your mother, Frankie?'

'Not about my mother. Margaret, I think I am lesbian! There now. I have said it!'

'Lesbian? How did you jump to that conclusion, Frankie?'

'I've fallen in love with Sr Laura! I can't help it. I just love her and want to be with her. What am I going to do? Sr Maria will tell Mother Provincial when she comes to interview us in order to determine if we are to be accepted as postulants.'

'Oh Frankie, don't be daft!'

'You're laughing. This is not a laughing matter, Margaret. I'll be sent home. I know I will.'

'No, you won't. You probably have a crush on Sr Laura. She was kind to you most likely because you were lonely over Christmas. Lots of people have crushes, especially when they are cooped up with a lot of females, Frankie.'

'But why was Sr Maria so strict? I didn't tell you that I wrote notes to Sr Laura. That's serious, isn't it?'

'What kind of notes did you write to her?'

'Just little notes: *Thank you, Sr Laura, for being so kind to me. I really appreciate the care you give me.* Then I put three kisses. I shouldn't have done that, should I?'

'Did you hand it to Sister?'

'No... this is even... I crept into her cubicle where she sleeps and put it on her pillow. During the day, of course. Oh, I shouldn't... '

'Did she say anything to you? She must have found it there.'

'No. She hasn't said anything.'

'She mustn't be worried about it. She would have told you if she was, Frankie.'

'I wonder. Maybe she will, though.'

'Frankie, Sr Maria like all the other nuns in this convent and probably in lots of other convents too, seems to be frightened that we will form 'particular friendships'.'

'There you are... you've admitted it, Margaret. Aren't the nuns trying to prevent us from doing exactly what I have done?'

'Mother Provincial goes around all the houses in our province. It's her job to see what is going on in all the houses of the Province. She must come in contact with some nuns who are friendlier towards each other than others. Look at Sr Stephanie and Sr Wilfred? They're always in each other's company.'

'When I told the priest in confession that I longed for Sr Laura to come and pat my forehead at night before I go to sleep, he gave me a penance. It must be a sin, Margaret.'

'Frankie, it's a sin because you think it's a sin. It isn't really a sin. Most folk would not regard waiting for a nun to pat their head before they go to sleep to be a sin. Most people would not feel guilty.'

'I'm confused, Margaret.'

'Well take it from me that you are to stop yourself from worrying. You're perfectly normal, as far as I can see. What I'm worried about is that once we become postulants, we'll have to wear a chemise, Frankie.'

'Oh that's nothing to worry about, Margaret. A chemise is just a long cotton T-shirt.'

'If that's all it is I wouldn't worry, Frankie. The fact is that we are supposed to wear this three quarter length garment at all times... even in bed. Worse still, when we go for a bath, we have to wear it in the bath! We've been told that we have to put a clean chemise over our heads as we pull off the dirty, soggy, wet one.'

'Sr Rita said that we have to do this so that we do not look at our bodies!'

'Precisely, Frankie! What is wrong with the body God gave me, I ask?'

'Well I suppose we have been growing into adults... you know, with all our bits changing. If we keep looking well...'

'Well what, Frankie? I have feelings and mood swings and longings so I don't have to look at my body to know that.'

'Oh, here comes Sr Stephanie walking over to school with Sr Wilfred.'

'Good morning, Sisters,' hailed Frankie.

'What did I tell you, Frankie? You need not worry. Talk to you later.'

Frankie did not mind sitting at the back of the class next to Margaret. She recalled that a few nights previously, Sr Maria instructed them that they were not to encourage conversations with either the day girls or the boarders. Her advice was: *As aspirants, you have chosen a different way of life. In order to prevent yourselves from becoming distracted from attaining the goal that you have set yourselves, it is better that you do not mingle with the pupils in your class.*

'I think we'll form a circle today, girls. Push the desks back to the wall and carry your chairs forward.'

'What are we to do now, Margaret? We've been told not to familiarise with the girls.'

'Yes, Frankie. Postulants join the circle here,' Sr Rose pointed to the end of the row.

'Come on, Margaret. Let's be brave and look normal,' whispered Frankie.

'Oh Suzanne... you had better rub that eye shadow off! You've traces of lipstick too. How did you manage to get past Sr Alicia this morning? Off you toddle to the cloakroom,' said Sr Rose as she pointed her finger at Suzanne.

'She wouldn't dare do that in our French class,' Frankie heard another girl whisper.

'No, but Sr Rose is human. She knows what we get up to, thank goodness,' Frankie heard another girl whisper.

Hopefully, Sr Rose realises that Margaret and I find it difficult to act naturally when seated so close to the girls in our class. Why do I feel this way? I suppose I know the answer. While they're putting on make-up and fashionable clothes, we're doing the opposite. What would they think about our chemise?

As they walked back over the hockey fields after a lively discussion on the role laity play in the Catholic Church, Frankie felt befuddled by all the opinions that had been given during Sr Rose's class.

'Sr Rose is very subtle in the topics she selects for our discussion groups, isn't she, Frankie?'

'Subtle? I say she's anything but subtle, Margaret. There we were discussing the vital role that lay folk contribute to the church, just as we are about to enrol as postulants.'

'And she pointed out that the number of young people entering religious life to become nuns and priests is declining, Frankie.'

'Well that could be taken two ways, Margaret. She could actually be encouraging the girls to swell the numbers of those choosing to become religious, couldn't she?'

'I wonder what the girls in our class would think about the talk that Sr Maria gave to those of us who want to become postulants, Frankie.'

'Yes. Sr Maria looked very serious when she read the rules about the Postulancy. The three 'Ds': dedication, detachment and doctrinal preparation.'

'Wasn't the detachment to do with how Jesus shows us to not to be worried about money. How the lilies of the field grow and are beautiful without any effort on their part. Why we shouldn't worry about money?'

'We'll have eight days retreat before we become novices. How am I going to cope with the silence and the sermons, confession and one-to ones with Mother Provincial?'

'Getting to know more about what motivated the Saint Maria Alberi, Foundress of the Order, too. Most of what Sr Maria said, I agree with, Frankie. We have to choose freely and be informed about the life that we are choosing to live. That part is necessary and sensible. It's having to wear a chemise and a cape. All this covering over my body. I'm not really sure of the reasons for that.'

'I like the look of the black cape. It's got a little stand-up collar and covers my shoulders to my waist. It looks smart. Sr Laura found me a black pleated shirt. With the black stockings and shoes, we'll look as though we have a definite purpose in mind. Don't you agree, Margaret?'

'Yes I do, Frankie. We'll have a lovely silver medal with Our Lady on one side and Saint Maria, our Foundress on the other. I have finished making the cord for it to hang from. My father will be very proud of me.'

'We're going to have to get up at the same time as the nuns. Their bell goes at 5.30. They are in chapel by 6 o'clock to start a half an hour's meditation, Margaret.'

'I'll probably be half-asleep. It's too early. I don't know if I'll get the hang of meditation either. How am I going to manage to keep still, Margaret?'

'I'll be meditating on my breakfast. Better still, I'll be thinking of the Beatles!'

'Or Peter? Just as well the nuns can't see through your veil and inside your brain, Margaret.'

16

IN THE WAY OF TEMPTATION

'*I* can't wait to meet the parish folk group, Margaret! I bet you're excited. You'll be able to play your clarinet. I need to learn a few more chords on my guitar.'

'Frankie, I've not had a chance to tell you. I've had another note from Peter, *not my brother.*'

'Gosh! He's missing you. How did it get past Sr Maria?'

'Same as last time. In with my mother's letter. Sister must assume that it is from my brother, Peter. The envelope had been opened and sealed again.'

'Your brother's in on this.'

'He must be. I'm assuming that he offered to post Mum's letter.'

'And popped Peter's in. What did he write this time, Margaret?'

'*I'm delighted to hear that you are still playing your clarinet. I'm playing mine. How about playing a duet?*'

'Oh Margaret, do you think he'll risk turning up at the folk group?'

'I hope he does! I know... I should have '*washed that*

man right out of my hair...' but I haven't. No matter how hard I try, I still long to be in his arms.'

'Maybe when he sees you dressed in your postulant's uniform, he might realise that you are seriously thinking of ... '

'That's just it, Frankie. I am trying but I'm not sure. Perhaps seeing him again might help me to decide.'

'Shish! I can hear footsteps. That's probably Sr Maria coming. She's most likely called Mavis out of the study to join us.'

'Frankie, don't tell Mavis. Don't tell anyone. Please?'

'Of course I won't, Margaret. It could spoil our fun!'

Still smiling, Frankie opened the parlour door for Sr Maria who was followed by Mavis.

'Thank you, Frankie. *Viva Gesu!* Postulants! Come and sit round this little table. What a lovely magnolia bud on the coffee table. Praise be to our Creator.'

Frankie remembered that Margaret told her that she felt annoyed every time that the magnolia was mentioned, 'That's the one thing I resent Frankie, about being sacristan. Every evening after I have laid the vestments out for Mass the following morning, I have to cut a fresh blossom. I miss some recreation time just to put a flower on the breakfast table for the priest to admire as he eats his breakfast.'

Frankie felt privileged to be among the three chosen by Sr Maria the previous evening to become members of a new parish liturgy group.

'I'm sure you have each been wondering what will be involved in helping with the music for the 9.30 Sunday Mass in the Parish,' began Sr Maria.

'Do they play folk music at that Mass, Sister?' asked Mavis.

'Yes, the Parish Priest, Fr Derek, is trying to involve the youth of the parish. He thought folk music might entice them. Let me explain. Father Derek asked me if someone from our community would consider helping with some of the pastoral duties and liturgical services. You may know that three of our Sisters teach in the secondary school, but as yet we have no direct links with the parish.'

'Will primary school children be invited into the music group too, Sr Maria?' enquired Margaret.

'The 9.30 Mass is a family Mass. Our aim is to involve as many young people as possible. Remember our mission, our raison d'être, is to educate young people and draw them to know and love Jesus, our Saviour.'

'Sister Maria, you said last night that you selected the three of us because we have passed our religious education examination. Will we be involved with catechetical teaching too?' asked Frankie.

'Let's not be too ambitious, postulants. At present we are delighted that Fr Derek has asked us to help prepare the music for the 9.30 Sunday Mass. Of course we are hoping we will eventually become involved in teaching children who attend non-Catholic schools. We have chosen the three of you to enable us to take our first steps towards our goal.'

'Thank you, Sr Maria. When do we start?'

'Tonight at 5:30. Each Friday you will meet with Fr John. He is the other priest in the parish. He has also invited some parishioners who are musicians to help prepare the liturgy for Sunday Mass.'

'Will they bring their instruments?' asked Margaret.

'Of course, Margaret. You will play your clarinet. Frankie, I hope you will be able to strum along on your guitar. Mavis, you will help to select hymns appropriate to the liturgy of the Sunday Mass. We are fortunate that we are to initiate our parish work at the beginning of Lent. Remember that during the forty days of Lent through prayer, penance, repentance, almsgiving, and self-denial, we prepare for Easter.'

Oh no! thought Frankie, *Lent, fasting and penance,*

that brings back memories of Mammy telling me how lax she found Lent being observed by churches when she arrived in England. She remembered her saying, 'English people think Lent means fish on Fridays and eating a little less on other days. Sure, they even think they can eat as much as they like on Sundays and feast days.' Tis we Irish, who do penance and keep the fast. *De hAoine is* Gaelic for Friday and Friday is always a day of fast. Jesus died on Good Friday.'

As soon as Sr Maria closed the parlour door, Margaret clapped her hands and exclaimed, 'Great. Freedom at last!'

'I can't believe this is happening! Unbelievable!' joined in Mavis.

'We've only an hour to go. Whippee! Are we actually being allowed to walk out the front door together and walk down to the parish church on our own?' said Frankie, smiling as she twirled round with her hands above her head.

'Let's see what time it is now. Just enough time for you to find your guitar, Frankie. I'll collect my clarinet. Shall we meet at the front door at twenty past five? Is that okay, Mavis?'

Frankie stood at the door carrying a child's sized guitar and was soon joined by Margaret.

'You do look the business clutching that clarinet, Margaret,' said Mavis when she arrived.

'I have not practised lately. Let's hope I'll be okay. The reed is worn. I need a new one.'

'A, D and G. They're the chords I know. I find it hard to play F, C or B. I really need to learn how to play more chords. Look at the size of my guitar, will ye? I think it came from the junior school.'

'What about me? With no instrument I'm in danger of ending up just handing out hymn books,' added Mavis.

'Count your lucky stars! We're free! Perhaps we're the first aspirants let out on our very own,' observed Margaret.

'I feel like singing '*Climb every mountain.*' I've been inside a whole year longer than you two… inside?… inside?… am I serving time in prison? Since I entered, fifteen months ago, I have not walked these few hundreds yards from the convent to the church without being chaperoned by one of the nuns,' marvelled Mavis.

As they opened the door leading into the church, Frankie counted about a dozen teenagers, seven girls, five boys. There were a few parents and the young curate, Fr John, waiting for them.

'Good evening, everybody. Thank you very much for coming. I'm Fr John. I hope you will all help to prepare the music for Sunday Mass. Fr Derek suggests that we use the room off the sacristy to practice. Would you like to follow me? We'll get to know each other in there.'

He is young and good looking, thought Frankie. She heard Margaret gasp and saw her putting her hand over her mouth. She nudged her and nearly knocked the guitar from her hand. 'He's here!'

Frankie found it hard to believe that Peter was already positioned at the edge of a circle of chairs and was grinning at them.

As soon as they were all seated, Fr John began, 'First, let me introduce Peter who has travelled from Balham to help us out.'

He looks like the cat that has got the cream, thought Frankie as she watched him stand, smile and bow to everyone.

'Welcome, Peter,' praised Fr John as he clapped his hands while nodding towards Peter.

Fr John continued, 'As soon as Peter heard that we are going to form a parish music group, he volunteered to come and help us. Would you like to explain about tuning to the pitch of the clarinet, Peter?' invited Fr John.

'Yes, Father. When we started our parish music group

we had two clarinet players. At first we didn't realise that the clarinet players need to make sure that they are in tune before everyone else tunes up. That's because clarinet players tune to B flat,' said Peter.

'Oh… just as well he came. I see that one of the postulants is carrying a clarinet,' said Fr John.

He's so devious, thought Frankie. *Margaret has her head down and is showing no sign of recognition.*

'Good thinking, Peter. Margaret. Your name is Margaret, isn't it?' Margaret must have nodded, thought Frankie. She dared not look straight at Peter. 'Perhaps you should tune up with Peter?

Unaware of Peter's subterfuge, Fr John continued, 'Now Sarah, you are a plucker and strummer on the guitar. May I introduce you to Frankie and Jackie? I play the guitar too. I hope to play along with you.'

Good, thought Frankie. *I'll be playing with Fr John. Maybe I will enjoy myself too.*

'We are fortunate to have Mrs Black, her daughter, Cecilia and young Dominic as our flautists and you three, Angela, Jane and Andrew on the descant recorders. Of course, Joe is on percussion,' added Fr John.

Great. If I make a few mistakes, it may not be noticed when the recorders and percussion join in, reflected Frankie.

'Now Mavis, I presume you have already looked up the liturgy. Keeping in mind the theme of the Mass for Sunday, would you select appropriate hymns?' said Fr John.

Mavis, who was standing next to Frankie, leaned towards her to ask her, 'I chose *My God Loves me: Plaisir d'Amour*' in the key of F# with the guitar chords G, D7, C and G7. Can you manage these chords?'

Frankie was watching Peter walking into a corner of the sacristy with Margaret. Mavis had to repeat her question before Frankie replied, 'Yes, Mavis I can play G and D7 and hopefully Fr John might teach me the fingering for G7. I find it hard to play the chord of C, but I'll practise.'

As Frankie spoke to Mavis, she continued to watch Margaret and Peter. She noticed Peter smiling. Margaret had her back turned towards her. Frankie imagined that Margaret was enjoying being close to Peter.

After a few minutes Fr John called out, 'Are you two clarinettists in tune yet?'

'Oh yes!' replied Peter.

In more ways than one, laughed Frankie to herself.

'Good. Can you help tune the guitars?' invited Fr John.

Frankie was glad that Margaret came immediately to her.

'I bet you enjoyed that, Margaret, you lucky thing. Peter is so cheeky,' commented Frankie as she plucked the G string on her guitar.

'So tempting! We were so close. I just wanted to fling myself into his arms, Frankie,' sighed Margaret.

'I'm so jealous, Margaret! Go and tune someone else. I know what I'll do. I'll get Fr John to tune my guitar.'

'Fr John. Please would you help me? My guitar is old and completely out of tune,' called out Frankie.

'Certainly, Frankie. Just coming.'

'Thank you, Father. I find the fingering for G7 difficult.'

'If I stand in front of you, can you mirror my fingering, Frankie?'

'I'll have to do the opposite to you, if I try to mirror you, won't I, Father?'

'Oh! Of course... you're right. Would it be better if I stood behind you and placed my hands over your hand and eased your fingers onto the correct strings?'

As Fr John leant over her shoulders and put his hands on hers, Frankie felt her body throb. Fr John was so close that she could feel him breathing. Her hands began to perspire. She wanted to lean back and let him embrace her. Instead she managed to say, 'Thank you, Fr John. I think that I know what to do now.'

As the music practice finished, Frankie sat at the back of the church waiting for Mavis to collect all the hymn books. She was wondering where Margaret had gone. Suddenly she rushed into the chapel and sat beside her.

'I bet you kissed Peter goodbye, Margaret? You did? You're blushing.'

'Frankie, I can't tell you... oh!'

'Well Margaret, I had a good time too.'

'I know. I spied Fr John leaning over you. I bet you enjoyed that. You naughty postulant.'

'Careful. Mavis is coming out of the sacristy, Margaret.'

'Fr John said that he is very pleased with our first music practice. He asked if you both could wait until he has said goodbye to the others,' said Mavis.

'Oh here you are, postulants. I'm delighted for your contribution to the liturgy. Please thank Sr Maria. Tell her that with your support I envisage that we will be able to draw the youth of the parish together.'

'We're glad we can help, Father. I hope the clarinet kept us in tune. That chap, Peter, is very helpful at tuning us all up,' replied Margaret.

Frankie rolled her lips to prevent them breaking into a huge grin at Margaret's comment. *She wants to make sure that she will be able to enjoy Peter's company every week*, reflected Frankie.

When Sr Maria came into the refectory that evening, Frankie saw that she was smiling. Sister rang the bell to gain attention, 'I want to congratulate the three postulants for their contribution to the parish liturgy. Fr Derek phoned to say that he has great hopes for the support of the newly formed liturgical group. Because we started at the beginning of Lent, hopefully our Easter celebrations will be even more meaningful this year. Well done, postulants.'

'Thank you, Sr Maria, for permitting us to contribute. It was a very meaningful experience,' called out Margaret.

'Yes, very meaningful,' whispered Frankie as she kicked Margaret under the refectory table.

'Would you be able to introduce the same music to the liturgy here in the convent, postulants?' asked Sr Maria.

'Yes, I think we might but we would have to practise, Sr Maria,' answered Margaret.

'Perhaps you may succeed better if Sr Stephanie helps you out. We'll see, postulants,' replied Sr Maria.

'Oh blow! I thought we could get time alone,' whispered Margaret.

'I'm sure Sr Stephanie will be too busy to join us very often,' remarked Frankie.

When Frankie tried to go to sleep that night she tossed and turned. Eventually she prayed, *Forgive me, God my father, for the pleasure I enjoyed today when Fr John came close to me. Did you allow my body to go into a spasm to remind me of your great love for me? Or should I feel guilty even though I did not cause this to happen?*

The following morning at breakfast Frankie leaned nearer to Margaret, 'Did you dream last night?'

'Better than ever, Frankie. I think I need to go to confession though.'

'If your dream was like mine I don't know how you are going to explain it to the priest, Margaret.'

'I know, Frankie. How am I going to live with the guilt?'

As Lent progressed towards Easter and the folk group flourished, they were appreciated even by the more traditional church choir and organist. Frankie felt that maybe it was not necessary to confess her sinful feelings.

'Frankie, do you think the others in the choir have noticed that Peter and I get on so well? Does anyone notice that we love being together?' asked Margaret.

'I don't think so, Margaret. No one said anything to me. Not even Mavis.'

'I'm glad Mavis has gone down to the parish before us tonight. I've wanted to tell you that I have cleared my conscience.'

'Have you been to confession, Frankie?'

'No, Margaret. But I've prayed a lot. I've come to a conclusion.'

'You sound contented. What's the solution, Frankie?'

'Sr Maria sent us down to the parish to help bring young people closer to God and we are succeeding.'

'How can you be sure of that, Frankie?'

'Because everyone seems to be happy. The group has grown. Fr Derek... everyone. They all keep congratulating us. God must be happy too?'

'You're right, Frankie. Fr Derek has even bought you a bigger guitar.'

'Yes, Margaret. God might want to test us. He has put us into temptation to see if we want to continue in our vocation.'

'Gold tested in the fire?'

'Something like that, Margaret. We're both still here, aren't we?'

On Easter Monday Frankie became even more secure in her belief that God was pleased with her when she was partnered with Margaret when they went for their walk.

'Don't look too excited, Frankie,' said Margaret after Sr Stephanie partnered them.

Thank goodness Sr Rita, Sr Laura and Sister Maria have gone on retreat,' whispered Frankie.

Before they started off Sr Stephanie said: 'I have decided to take you on the same river walk that I took some of the geography students last week. We'll go along by the River Wandle. It's a beautiful riverside setting,'

'You know that I said that I have been praying, Margaret. Well, I've thought of how we can help each other,' said Frankie.

'Good. I agree that we're in this together. What do you suggest?'

'You will not believe this at first but I think my crazy mother gave me the solution!'

'What? She who called my twin an imbecile. That same mother?'

'You'll never forgive her for that... but listen to me, Margaret.'

'It's not a question of forgiveness... it's just... ?'

'I know, Margaret. Let me explain: When we were little... in fact, all through my early years my mother had only one solution for everything. It was devotion to the miraculous medal.'

'My parents were the same, Frankie.'

'You might want to laugh, Margaret, but on Saturday night she would undo the safety pin on last week's soiled vest and transfer the miraculous medal onto the clean Sunday vest. She believed that Our Lady would protect us from harm if we wore the miraculous medal.'

'I firmly believe in this devotion, Frankie. I have a miraculous medal on me now. Sr Laura helped us make piety bags when it was our turn in the sewing room. I love the little crochet bag that I have attached to my vest.'

'We are being tested and protected, Margaret!'

'When we were in second year at school the nuns took us to the Rue du Bac, Paris, where it is claimed ... I still remember it... *on the night of July 18, 1830 Saint Catherine Labouré heard the Blessed Virgin Mary say to her, God wishes to charge you with a mission. You will be contradicted, but do not fear; you will have the grace to do what is necessary.* It's all coming back to me, Frankie.'

'You see, Margaret, we were meant to fall into

temptation so that we can repent and be saved. I think we must be strong. We'll have to stop putting ourselves in the way of temptation.'

'I had already concluded that meeting Peter is not helping me settle. I hate to admit that, Frankie.'

'You're brave, Margaret. Maybe just give it a try?'

'I know I'll struggle. What should we do?'

'How about making a pact with Our Lady? I wear my medal too. We could compose a prayer and organise a place and time. I don't know how... but...'

'I've got an idea, Frankie. You know that on retreat days we are sometimes sent down to the kitchen garden to cut flowers for the altar. There's a sta...'

'A statue of Mary Immaculate there! Yes, an old one, near the end of the garden. That's the one, Margaret.'

'Well, let's compose the prayer. Make a pledge? On the next opportunity we could promise to... well, be faithful and keep out of harm. What shall we pledge, Frankie?'

'Shall we make up a prayer first?'

'How shall we start it?'

'If we're going to be standing in front of the statue of Our Lady, shall we start with: In your presence, Mary ... Our Lady? Better still... Mary Immaculate...'

'... wearing our miraculous medals we, Margaret Blackburn and Frances Danivet, do solemnly promise?'

'We can't write it down now, but when we get back, we can each scribble what we remember down on paper, Frankie.'

Frankie was delighted that after spending the next few days struggling to compose the prayer when they had a chance to meet they joined their efforts together and eventually managed to form their prayer:

In your presence, dear Mary Immaculate, Mother of God, wearing our miraculous medals we, Margaret Blackburn and Frances Danivet do solemnly promise that from this day forward 27th March 1967 we vow to avoid any circumstances where we might be tempted to sin against purity either in thought, word or deed. We acknowledge that during these past few months we have been severely tried and have failed to curb our inclinations. To prove that we are sincere I, Margaret will no longer meet Peter at the folk group. I will inform Fr John that I am able to tune my clarinet. Consequently, there will therefore be no further need for Peter to travel from Tooting Bec each week to join us.

Likewise I, Frances Danivet, will tell Fr John that I have learnt to tune my guitar and should I need further help, I will ask Sr Stephanie.

With immediate effect from today, Easter Monday, we will repent for past failings by not eating chocolate for a month. This will form part of our penance. We will be steadfast in our resolve even when when Lent ends we will continue to abstain from sweets and chocolate.

Should one of us be tempted again we will pray the fifteen mysteries of the rosary. We have also devised a signal indicating that we would like to meet: Crossing our second and third finger and tap them three times on our foreheads. We also vow to continue to wear our miraculous medal. Amen.

As the days went by, Frankie feared that she and Margaret might not be able to meet. However, when Sr Laura came into the sacristy to say, 'Suor Mary... she is late from the market... the flowers on the altar must be changed. You and Margaret, you cut some in the garden?'

'Certainly, Sr Laura. I'll tell Margaret. We'll go to the kitchen garden immediately. Don't worry,' Sr Laura assured Frankie.

Frankie felt like skipping into chapel to tell Margaret the good news, 'Sr Laura needs us to bring her some flowers from the garden, Margaret! Have you got the prayer with you?'

'Oh Frankie... at last! Yes, I have our prayer in my pocket.'

'Let's go down to the statue as quickly as we can.'

'I'd love to hold a few lilies, Margaret. I had a bunch of lilies on my First Communion day. There are some lily-of-the-valley out over there.'

'You can smell them from here. Let's each pick a bunch.'

Frankie stood next to Margaret in front of the statue of Mary Immaculate, each of them holding a freshly picked bunch of lily-of-the-valley flowers while they recited their prayer.

'Thank you, Frankie. I find all this very meaningful. I feel overwhelmed. The strong fragrance, the perfect bell-shaped lily and the purity of its whiteness against their dark green leaves.'

'I think it's you that's making the biggest sacrifice, Margaret. I've fallen in love with Fr John but he's not my boyfriend. You... well, you love Peter. It won't be easy for you.'

'I realise that, Frankie. But I know I have to do something drastic. I have to try my hardest to see if I have a vocation.'

'Margaret, did you hear that bird singing? Is it a robin? Listen: *twiddle-oo, twiddle-eedee, twiddle-oo twiddle*.

'If I am not mistaken that is a robin warbling. Can you see him, Frankie? Bright orange-red breast, face, throat and cheeks edged with grey.'

'Oh Margaret. Robins mean a lot in my family. They appear at special times.'

'You're crying? Come here 'til I hug you.'

Snug in Margaret's arms, Frankie felt relieved, loved and satisfied that they had fervently pledged themselves to

God that day.

'Shall we hide our prayer underneath a heavy stone behind the statue, Frankie?'

'Good idea, Margaret. How about here at the back near the forget-me-nots?

17

UNFAIR TREATMENT

'*W*hy are you two not disappointed that Sr Maria won't let us go to the seaside with the choir?' Mavis enquired.

Frankie wondered how Margaret would reply.

'We'd love to join the others, Mavis, but we're postulants. We didn't expect to be rewarded for our part in the choir.'

'Besides you can't go to the seaside without going for a swim, Mavis, can you? Imagine trying to put on our swimming costumes in front of all those people. What would they think about our chemises?'

'I suppose so. We'd attract lots of attention. It's just as well. I was very excited when Fr Derek told us that's how he intended to reward us,' accepted Mavis.

When Mavis walked ahead of them, Frankie exclaimed, 'Thank goodness, Mavis accepted our explanation, Margaret.'

'I think even Sr Maria looked a little surprised when we seemed to be content to refuse Fr Derek's reward.'

'It's going to be hard keeping the promises that we

made, Margaret, but I am determined to repent. Let's say our prayer: *In your presence... dear Mary Immaculate, Mother of God,.......*'

'I recite this prayer every morning when we are lined up outside the chapel waiting to go in. I wish I felt as strong as you, Frankie. I long to strip off, jump over the waves and swim far out to sea.'

'Oh, that would be wonderful. Salt water. Freedom. There's nothing quite like stretching out and splashing through the waves.'

'We would be a laughing-stock on the beach anyway, struggling to take off those long, buttoned-up to-the neck linen chemises... we'd look ridiculous, Frankie.'

'Has Mavis noticed that you don't tune your clarinet with Peter any more?'

'After we made our promises and resolved to keep our distance from Peter and Fr John, I told Fr John that I no longer needed Peter's help. He comes less frequently now. I do miss being near him, Frankie.'

'I saw him winking at you though, Margaret! A promise is a promise.'

'Did you see the notice in the Parish newsletter about the HCPT pilgrimage to Lourdes, Frankie?'

'Is that the Pilgrimage Trust? Did it used to be known as the Handicapped Children Pilgrimage Trust?'

'Folk who are handicapped are referred to as having disabilities, now. They take people with disabilities on a pilgrimage holiday to Lourdes.'

'You must have gone there with your sister?'

'Yes, we... Oh, we're nearly back at the convent already. Pity that the distance from Church to convent is so short.'

'Hello you two! Fr John has asked some of the choir if you would be willing to join the group going to Lourdes.'

Frankie looked back to see one of the parents from the group calling out as she ran to catch up with them.

'Thank you, Mrs. Black. I was just enquiring about that pilgrimage,' said Frankie.

'We'll ask Sr Maria. She's in charge. We will ask her if she approves.'

'Good. Maybe you could give her this leaflet.'

Frankie began to read:

Every Easter, 1,000 disabled and disadvantaged children and young people enjoy a life changing pilgrimage holiday in Lourdes in the south of France. Children from the UK and Ireland travel there. The total size of the Easter Pilgrimage is around 5000, which includes all helpers, nurses, doctors and chaplains. The trips usually lasts a week and takes place over Easter.

However, it has been decided to postpone the Pilgrimage from Easter week to the week following Pentecost Sunday 14th May this year because:...

'The printing is so small that I can hardly read it,' said Frankie, pointing to the leaflet.

'My parents are taking my sister, Rosie, on this pilgrimage. As I've told you, I have been several times with them.'

'Oh Margaret, if we go, maybe we'll see her.'

Margaret and Frankie waved goodbye to Mrs. Black and closed the garden gate behind them and walked to the convent door. They heard Fr John call out, 'I'm glad I caught up with you both before you go into the convent. Fr Derek was wondering if you two musicians would be able to join the HCPT pilgrimage to Lourdes.'

'Mrs. Black has just handed us the leaflet about it, Father,' answered Margaret.

'Good. One of the party has had to drop out at the last minute. We leave next Monday!'

'How much is the fare, Father?'

'The fare has been paid. All you will need is £40 each for expenses.'

'Oh! Thank you, Father John. We will ask Sr Maria and let you know as soon as possible,' answered Margaret.

'I doubt if Sister will allow us to go to Lourdes, Margaret.'

'Now that they are two short, maybe we have a chance? Where can we get the £40?'

'Do you recall reading the *Mary Strand* column in *The Universe* Catholic paper, Margaret?'

'Yes. They support worthwhile causes, don't they?'

'Exactly! If we were granted the money from Mary Strand, the convent would not need to worry about the cost.'

'As we'd be looking after needy children, we'd qualify,' added Margaret. 'Shall we go upstairs and knock at Sr Maria's office door, straightaway?'

'Yes. Fr Derek will be waiting for an answer. Let's go immediately, Margaret.'

Sr Maria answered:'Come in! Viva Gesu! Oh, two of you have come together!'

As Frankie listened to Margaret explain their request, she scrutinised Sr Maria's face. Her piercing eyes relaxed. Initially Sister had appeared reluctant to allow either of them to go to Lourdes. But gradually she seemed to be changing her mind.

'Let me pray and consult on this matter, Postulants. You say that your parents are taking your sister, Rosie, Margaret and that you are the only flautist from the parish. Do you possess a valid and up-to-date passport?'

'Yes, Sister', responded Margaret.

'Fr Derek said that we need to bring £40 each to cover other expenses. Could we write to Mary Strand for that, Sr Maria?'

'Certainly not, Frankie!' Her voice was strident.' Although we are always short of funds, we are not as much in need as the people who merit to obtain support from that source.'

'My parents would pay if you agree that it would be helpful for me to go to Lourdes, Sr Maria,' said Margaret.

'Frankie, you didn't answer me when I asked if you have an up-to-date passport?'

'No, Sister. I didn't need a passport travelling from Eire. I haven't been anywhere else.'

I can only strum a few chords on the guitar. I haven't a passport. It's unlikely that I will be permitted to go to Lourdes, thought Frankie.

'I will pray and consult the community and let you know the decision, Postulants. Frankie, even if it is agreed that you could go to Lourdes, there will be very little time for you to obtain a passport.'

'I'd love to go. I hope they will help you to go too, Frankie.'

After they left Sr Maria Frankie told Margaret:

'No. No, I understand, Margaret, but that does not stop me from being jealous. I'm sorry, Margaret that you have a handicapped sister. You deserve to go.'

Frankie was not surprised when they were both called to Sr Maria's office the next day to be informed that only Margaret would be going to Lourdes.

'It's alright, Margaret. I guessed that you would be going. Your parents will be very proud to have you on the same pilgrimage.'

'I am delighted to be going. I really wish that you were joining me, Frankie. You heard Sr Maria say that I will be accompanied by a nun from one of the other convents. I don't know who she is yet.'

'It will all be lovely, Margaret! Is Lourdes near Paris? I'd love to go to Paris. Film stars go there. It's all so romantic. I can see myself walking down the Champs-Élysées.'

When Frankie waved Margaret off to Lourdes, she saw that an old nun was already seated in the car waiting to accompany her to meet up with HCPT group 44.

'Goodbye everyone! I'll pray for each of you at the Grotto,' said Margaret.

It did not take Frankie long to realise that she missed Margaret, especially on Friday when she went to join the parish music group. As many of the members had also departed for Lourdes, they were only required to prepare a hymn at the beginning and close of Sunday Mass. Since many prominent parishioners had gone to Lourdes, she knew that numbers in the congregation would be depleted.

After tea on Friday evening Mavis called out to Frankie, 'Meet you at the front door at five-thirty, Frankie.'

'No Mavis. We're only playing two hymns. There is no need to start off 'til 5.45.'

'Alright, Frankie, but remember that I still have to put the music and the stands in place.'

If looks could kill, I'd be dead, thought Frankie as she noticed Mavis' face grow red.

Frankie walked the short distance down to church carrying her guitar. Mavis walked in silence beside her. Frankie let Mavis hold the door open for her. She sat, leaving Mavis to put the stands and music out ready for the other musicians to arrive. Frankie tuned her guitar and practiced some chords.

'Here we are, Frankie. I have chosen number 81 from the blue folk group to play at the beginning of Mass. Maybe you can practise that until the others arrive.'

'Mavis! Have you looked at the chords for that hymn? C, F and G7. You know I struggle to play those chords. Besides, it's Trinity Sunday. That hymn only mentions Jesus, the second person of the Blessed Trinity.'

'What do you suggest, Frankie? I did try to choose hymns that echoed the themes set by the liturgy.'

'Think again, Mavis, this hymn fails to do that. It obvious that you don't play an instrument. We need hymns that have easy tunes. There are only a handful of us this week. Use your common sense.'

'No need to shout at me, Frankie. We don't have to be limited by the chords that you have mastered. Okay! Tell me what can you play?'

'Number 10 from the blue folk book. The chorus is *'Glory to the Trinity. The undivided unity...'* etc. You know the words. For the final hymn number 40, *'Go, the Mass is ended.'*

As they walked back to the convent after Mass, Frankie said, 'The choir was delighted with the hymns that I choose, Mavis.'

When Mavis didn't answer, Frankie asked, 'Are you angry with me, Mavis?'

Mavis didn't answer. They walked home in silence.

They parted in silence.

After supper Frankie was summoned to Sr Maria's office.

'Pride comes before a fall. You have become domineering, Frances. Mavis has been an aspirant a year longer than you and is older too. Why are you behaving in such a superior manner towards her?'

'I'm sorry... I ... '

Frankie felt tears trickling down her cheeks. She pulled out her hankie to mop them up.

'Think. Reflect. Examine your conscience, Frances. You come from a poor background and have few qualifications. What right have you to think you are better than anyone else?'

Frankie felt humiliated and angry, but she knew that it would be better not to show this.

She reflected: *I have made a huge effort to improve myself. I am not bossy. But maybe it's better to plead guilty and say sorry.*

She cleared her throat, 'Sister Superior, I am very sorry

that I have upset Mavis. I truly had no intention of been domineering. I will apologise to her.'

'You will do more than apologise. From now on, Mavis is to be consulted in all matters while working in the folk group. If I find that you do not adhere, you will no longer be trusted to take part in that group. Do I make myself very clear? You will also pray a decade of the rosary while contemplating the humility of Our Lady.'

This does not seem fair. Sr Superior does not know that I overheard Mavis telling Stella that she was going to tell those left in the choir that I can only play a limited number of chords. She'll say 'Frankie's such a show-off. Wait 'til the others are in Lourdes. I'll expose her. I'll choose the hymns! She thinks that she is better than me.'

Frankie wished that she could tell Margaret. She was disappointed that Mavis was so peevish when they had been friends.

Frankie thought: *She's jealous and calculating. What can I do?*

She decided to go into the garden and stand in front of the statue of Mary Immaculate. She clutched her miraculous medal but she was so angry that she couldn't pray. She stamped around the statue. Then she took hold of a rake that lay there. She plunged it into the ground several times. *I'm so angry... angry ... angry! It's so unfair. Mavis planned to rile me. If only I had a passport, I could have gone to France. I feel so closed in. We meet so few people. I want to break out of this place... Oh, it feels like a prison!*

After a while Frankie slumped onto a boulder and faced the statue of Our Lady. She prayed, *Mary, my heavenly mother, please help me. I feel lonely and angry. Is it wrong to want to have fun or even just to want to meet other people? If I'd gone to Lourdes I could have seen some of the outside world... that's while I was helping handicapped people. I'm even angry with your son Jesus! Why couldn't*

I go to Lourdes?

I shouldn't be angry with you, Jesus. You know what's best for me.

Mavis shouldn't have annoyed me. Maybe I should forgive her?

Jesus, I am sorry. Please bless Margaret and her twin, Rosie and Mavis.

18

LIFE AFTER LOURDES

*F*rankie was taken aback as she watched Margaret emerge from the car on her return from Lourdes. She didn't search for her in the group waiting for them in front of the convent. Instead, she went straight to embrace Sr Maria. Everyone clapped. Sr Maria and Margaret walked into the convent without turning round.

Frankie used their special signal to attract Margaret. I'll try again. She crossed her finger and tapped her forehead. Margaret didn't look in her direction.

How could Margaret have forgotten me? Maybe she is tired. Perhaps she does not want to let others know that we are friends. She is probably saving her news to share with me in private, Frankie reasoned.

'Announcement.' Sr Maria drew everyone to attention.

'It is good to have Margaret back in community. She will rest a while. However, she has asked me for permission to speak to all of you. We will assemble in the study at 3.30.'

Margaret is going to speak to all of us? I wonder why?

What has she to tell us that is so important?' Frankie puzzled.

At the allotted time, the aspirants and postulants filed into the study and were seated. Frankie watched Sr Maria enter the study with Margaret by her side. She was smiling radiantly. They sat side by side at the study desk at the front of the study facing everyone.'You can see for yourselves one of the miracles of Lourdes. Our postulant, Margaret, has been blessed on her pilgrimage to Lourdes. When I met her at the airport she explained what she wanted to tell us. I feel that Jesus and His Holy Mother Mary are speaking through her to each one of us.'

Goodness! So that's how Margaret managed to gain permission from Sr Maria to address us. Has her sister, Rose, been cured? She must have witnessed some miracle, reflected Frankie.

'Let us pray,' invited Sr Maria.

Once the prayer was said, Frankie watched expectantly as Margaret stood and adjusted her mantilla, making sure that only as few as possible of her auburn curls peeped out. Her hazel eyes shining from an angelically pale face, she looked demure, fragile yet confident as she began to address everyone:

'Miracles really do happen at Lourdes. I saw crutches left near the shrine. We were told that sometimes deaf people begin to hear. Others, who have been blind, recover their eyesight. I actually met a man from Manchester who arrived in Lourdes with sight in one eye but after bathing in special baths, he recovered his sight. Many pilgrims say that they benefit by giving themselves time to stop and reflect on their lives. A young woman called Angela told me that Lourdes gave her time to take stock of her life. She said that that as a result she decided to change certain aspects. I suppose you might be wondering if any miracle happened to me. Maybe if I retell you a story that a priest told us while we there, you will understand. It's about a man complaining to God about the cross that he has been given to carry in life. He prayed, *This cross is too heavy for me, Lord. I envy others whose crosses seem lighter than mine. I wish that I could change my cross for a lighter one.*

Then he had a dream. In the dream, he saw a cross that he preferred. It was beautifully fashioned with pearls, diamonds and gems that were precious and rare. When he tried to carry it, the weight of the jewels and the gold made it heavy. He put it back in the pile. Then he saw a cross covered in red roses. He was delighted. He thought that cross would be better. It is so dainty and fragile, lovely and light. He didn't notice the thorns on it until they started to pierce his skin. He searched for another cross. He saw a cross that was rugged, old and plain. So he tried it for size. It fitted comfortably. He decided that one would be best for him. As he was about to carry it, he heard God say, 'I made that cross especially for you'. It was then that he realised that this was the cross that he had originally carried.

'Aspirants and postulants, this man learnt his lesson. God helped him to understand that often the loveliest crosses are the heaviest crosses to bear. Only God is wise enough to choose a cross that is right for each one of us.

'The message is that we should never complain about the cross that God has given each one of us to carry. God made our cross to fit our shoulders.'

'Margaret has been inspirational. Each of us needs to reflect on how we accept the cross that He has chosen for us to carry. Let's take a few minutes of silence.'

Frankie felt her eyes moisten. She felt proud of Margaret as she wiped tears from her eyes. After a poignant pause Margaret began again, 'You may not know that I have a mentally and physically disabled twin sister, called Rosie. She was taken on this pilgrimage by my parents. I want to confess that initially when I watched my parents love and care for her, instead of feeling grateful that I am healthy, I felt jealous of the attention they gave her. I actually wanted her cross instead of mine.

I have made a resolution to …'

'That's enough, Margaret,' interrupted Sr Maria. She waved her hand.

'But Sister…'

'No more! Sit! Thank you,' Sr Maria pointed to Margaret's chair.

Looking exhausted Margaret slumped onto the chair.

Frankie felt very sorry for Margaret as she dabbed her eyes. Sr Maria leaned over and tapped her on her back. The aspirants clapped.

Sr Maria concluded the talk with, 'You see… another miracle.'

Frankie waved at Margaret. Margaret didn't respond.

Frankie reflected on how much she envied her tall, slim, intelligent Margaret. She felt a certain delight that she had also witnessed her fragility and humility.

When Sr Maria left the room, Frankie watched as the others gathered round Margaret. It seemed to her that they regarded her as their heroine. She listened as Margaret began to share information that up until now only she, Frankie, had been privy to.

Feeling upset, Frankie moved closer to listen.

'I did enter the convent to repent for not saving my twin from drowning. I feel guilty because if I had dived into the sea first, I might be the one that is handicapped now instead of my sister.'

Hmm, thought Frankie. *She is telling everyone everything. She might begin to confess her love for Peter. I hope she won't tell anyone any of my secrets. She has not even tried to talk to me. So much for friendship! We needn't worry about particular friendships anymore.* Frankie was confused.

Dear God, she thought, what was she to do? Should she confess these feelings to Sr Maria? That would be tantamount to proving that Margaret is important in her life. *I could be accused of Margaret being my special friend.*

Frankie quietly stepped through the French doors and sat on the doorstep.

Dear Mother Mary, what am I to do in my dilemma? While I admire Margaret, I also envy her. I feel guilty. I need to confess my anger, jealousy. I know what I'll do. Thank you, God and Mary. I'll go to confession. That will be safer. Because of the seal of confession, the priest will not be able to tell anyone what I have disclosed.

When Sr Rita announced the name of the priest who would be coming to the convent the following morning, Frankie was disappointed to learn that it would be Fr John.

I want to believe in the seal of confession but I am reluctant to unburden myself to Fr John. I love him. I also do not want him to learn that Margaret and I used to confide in each other.

After breakfast Sr Rita tapped Frankie on her shoulder. 'Some aspirants have told me that you are tossing and turning and disturbing the other aspirants in the dormitory. Have you a guilty conscience? Is something worrying you?'

Frankie knew that she went to bed rehearsing how she would confess her jealousy without mentioning Margaret's name. She woke feeling as though she had a heavy brick weighing down her stomach. She did not think Sr Rita would be sympathetic. Eventually she asked, 'Sr Rita, would it be possible for me to speak to the parish priest, Fr Derek?'

'Why do you want to speak to Fr Derek when you have Sr Maria or me to consult? If you feel you would prefer to talk to a priest, Fr John is in the confessional.'

Frankie noticed that Sr Laura was folding linen near enough to overhear this conversation. As soon as Sr Rita left Frankie, Sr Laura moved nearer and placing her hand on Frankie's shoulder said, 'Povera Francesca. No need to concern yourself, this night I go to the Parish church to bring clean linen and I choose you to accompany me. There we find Fr Derek before he leave after cena... supper.'

What a relief, thought Frankie.

19

IS IT SINFUL TO FALL IN LOVE?

*F*rankie was delighted when Sr Laura nudged her. She was carrying a pile of dinner plates out of the refectory. Sister had promised to take Frankie to Fr Derek after supper.

'Frankie, five minutes, you meet me, back door. Help me carry linen to parish church?'

'Of course I'll help, Sr Laura. Thank you.'

Frankie noticed that Margaret was leaning over the sink washing the dishes. Frankie saw her turn round. She thought that she must have heard her voice. Frankie thought it was a questioning kind of look.

Maybe, I was wrong in my judgement of Margaret. Perhaps she is struggling too. *Am I betraying her by confessing my jealousy of her,* wondered Frankie?

'Put your hands come... like this... porta... carry...'

Frankie started to laugh as she watched rotund Sister Laura, struggling to support two long parcels of church linen across her arms.

'Oh, Sr Laura, you're so funny. I'll be careful. Put the

linen over my outstretched arms. Don't worry. It's a starched altar cloth, isn't it?'

Frankie was pleased to meet Fr Derek when he opened the door of the parish house to them.

'Sisters, you're carrying awkward loads. He smiled. 'Follow me. You can lay them on the table. What would I do without you, Sisters? Thank you.'

'Bene, Father Derek! I take the place Suor Joan. She is on retreat. Frankie comes for confession. I go church, e poi... wash dishes.'

As Sr Laura waved goodbye and closed the door, Frankie felt apprehensive. Fr Derek beckoned her to sit on an armchair opposite his.

'Well now. May I call you Frankie?'

Frankie nodded.

'I am told that you enjoy being in the music group. Lovely group. So pleased to involve the youth of the parish in the liturgy.'

'Yes, Father. My guitar playing is improving. They are a talented group.'

'Do you mind me asking how you find community life? I see you're wearing the postulant uniform. You must have settled in. Have you?'

Frankie began to reflect: *I thought confessing my sins to the priest face-to-face would be preferable to being in a confessional box. It is better than having to speak to him through a grill. Being able to sit is better than kneeling while the priest sits. But now I'm not sure. How am I going to tell him that I love Fr John and that I'm jealous of my friend?*

'I have settled in, Father. I've been in the convent nine months now.'

'You look happy, Frankie. You seem a little shy, too. Is there something troubling you?'

'I asked if I could speak to you because there is something that ... well, that perhaps is sinful, Father.'

'Frankie, do you wish all we discuss to be kept under the seal of confession in the sacrament of Penance?'

'Yes, I do, Father.'

'Good. Then I'll begin… In the name of the Father and the Son …'

While the priest prayed, Frankie tried to think how best to tell Fr Derek that she had asked to speak to him instead of Fr John, because when Fr John was near her, she wanted him to hold her tightly and kiss her. How was she going to say that? If she did, would Fr Derek say that she could no longer be in the choir? Would Fr Derek have to tell Sr Maria? Would she be sent home?

What am I going to say about my friendship for Margaret? Why am I jealous of her? Does Fr Derek know what the nuns call 'particular friendships?'

Frankie raised her eyes. Fr Derek was looking at her. He smiled.

'Frankie, am I right in thinking that you find it difficult to say what you would like to say?'

Frankie nodded.

'Take your time. Imagine that Jesus is sitting here instead of me. Tell Him what you want to say. He knows everything. He can see into your soul. He already knows what is troubling you.'

Frankie felt herself raising her praying hands under her chin. She squeezed them together. Then she interlaced and flicked them backwards and forward.

'Father sometimes I feel… sometimes I feel lonely and … yes… I want to be loved.'

'You are young. Do you mind me asking how old are you, Frankie?'

'I was 17 in May, Father.'

'17? Did you have a good time on your birthday, Frankie? Presents? Birthday cake?'

'No, the nuns told us that we don't keep birthdays in

the convent. We celebrate feast days instead. Mine is in October. The feast of St Francis of Assisi. I was given a holy picture last year.'

My mammy has never given me a birthday card. We don't give cards in our family. I would like to have had a present though. Just something small to prove that she loves me. I wish the nuns had not instructed us to tell our parents that we keep feast day instead of birthdays. Maybe she would have written to me.

'Oh I see. You don't keep birthdays in the convent.'

Frankie watched Fr Derek raise his joined hands over his lips, frown and look into the distance.

'Frankie, I'm not surprised that you feel lonely. I'm sure many 17-year-old girls who have not entered the convent are not lonely. They will be loved and hugged by their parents, their families and maybe their boyfriends. On their birthdays they'll most likely receive lots of presents.'

Frankie's hands rested on her lap. She felt that perhaps Fr Derek understood why she felt the way she did. She looked at him. He looked at her. She took a deep breath.

'Father Derek, I love Fr John. I enjoy being friends with Margaret yet I am jealous of her.'

Fr Derek clapped his hands. 'Good, Frankie. You're normal.'

Fr Derek leaned forward.

Frankie could feel his eyes penetrate deep inside her. He smiled.

'Frankie, most teenagers fall in love. Especially when they are about your age. God made us in a way that we would be attracted to one another. We're human beings. If your mother didn't fall in love with your father perhaps you would not be sitting here talking to me. Do you understand what I am saying, Frankie?'

'Yes I do, Father. But I should not love Fr John. He is a priest.'

'Frankie, your feelings are natural and normal. However, it is advisable not to let them rule your life. You have to control and channel these feelings. There are people who hug everyone that they see. Well, you know what can happen if … well…'

'So it's not sinful to love Fr John?'

'You have chosen to make promises, vows, Frankie. You are only at the early stages of your formation. Feelings, longings, urges will probably be strong. Your imagination may wander. Will you be able to curb your imagination and control your feelings? Accept and acknowledge your feelings and see if you think that you can make and keep the vow of chastity? That's what you have to find out. The great St Augustine struggled. He prayed, *Too late have I loved you, Lord.*'

'Thank you, Fr Derek. You have been very understanding.'

'Why do I know about these feelings and about jealousy, too? Because we all struggle. Love is a very strong emotion. There are all kinds of love: Love for parents and children. Adolescent love. Love for each other. We become jealous because certain people matter to us. We sometimes want to be like them.'

'Yes. Margaret and I are friends. We care about each other, Father.'

'Shall I give you absolution now, Frankie?'

'Yes, please, Father. Shall I say the Act of Contrition?'

Fr Derek prayed the words of absolution as Frankie recited the act of sorrow.

I have a lot to ponder, she thought. She slept well that night.

The next morning, when Frankie knelt in chapel, she noticed that Brigitte's place was empty.

Maybe she is not well. She must be really unwell otherwise the nuns would not have allowed her to miss

Mass. Perhaps she will join us after morning prayers.

Frankie noticed that Brigitte had not come to Mass.

'Frankie, would you sweep and dust the study after you have swept and tidied the landing and office?'

'Is Brigitte not well, Sr Rita?'

'Brigitte will no longer be doing this charge.'

Frankie noticed that Brigitte's place at table in the refectory was empty.

Once Grace was said and they were seated for breakfast, Frankie whispered to Margaret, 'Brigitte was not at Mass. I was asked to do her charge. Where is she?'

'Didn't you hear a car rev up while we were singing the hymn before Mass?'

'She can't be gone, Margaret. She didn't say goodbye, did she? We weren't told.'

'She had an enormous spot on her face...'

'and her breath smelt. Do you think convent life was too much for her, Margaret?'

'Shish, Frankie! We weren't told. Mavis, Catherine and Sr Rita are looking this way.'

Why do aspirants disappear without trace? Why are we not given any explanation? We are left to guess what has happened when there is an empty space at table or when someone who had been kneeling near us in chapel is no longer there.

'Sister Laura, why didn't we say goodbye to Brigitte?'

Frankie couldn't believe that Stella questioned Sr Laura about Brigitte's disappearance while everyone was listening,. Everybody stopped talking at her table.

Frankie watched Sr Laura gasp and wipe her lips with her serviette. She moved about in her chair, looked pleadingly at Stella and said, 'Pray for Brigitte. I speak with you later, Stella.'

Frankie watched Sr Laura glance over to the table where Sr Rita was seated. They both nodded to each other.

Everybody started talking again. Stella shook her head. She whispered, 'We should be told. We should say goodbye.'

'It's nearly holiday time!' said Margaret.

'We've still got our Italian oral exam, Margaret. Once that's over I'll feel better.'

Frankie looked at Sr Laura. Sr Laura smiled back. 'Allora, dimmi un pensiero dalla meditazione, Francesca.'

'Please translate, Frankie,' pleaded Hilary.

'Sr Laura wants me to give her a thought from the meditation we pondered in chapel this morning. Let me think... *Amatevi come vi ho amato!*'

'Ma che brave, Francesca!' Sr Laura clapped her hands.

'Something about 'love'?' queried Anne.

'I guess it's from John's gospel, *'Love one another as I have loved you'*. Am I right?' asked Hilary.

'Correct!' said Margaret.

'Tut! Can be *I loved... liked... cared for,* Brigitte. So much for love!' whispered Stella.

When breakfast was over Frankie saw Sr Laura beckon Stella to follow her.

'Cloak and dagger! That's not right. We're all owed an explanation about Brigitte's disappearance,' complained Brenda as she ran the water ready to wash the crockery.

'*God sees you*' Brenda! Look at the notice Sr Rita has put up there above the sink,' teased Agnes as she pointed.

There's a lot of grumbling going on today. The nuns must have noticed. I agree with the postulants' criticism. What is wrong with saying goodbye to people we have lived with for these last few months, puzzled Frankie. *Was there something to hide?*

Sr Rita tinkled her bell. 'Once you have cleared up after breakfast, be quick going up to the study for the Sunday conference. No dilly dallying. The devil finds work for idle hands.'

More orders, thought Frankie, as she cleared the dishes.

'Good on you, Stella! Sr Rita's going to tell us where Brigitte is,' congratulated Anne.

'I wouldn't count on that, Anne. I've been warned. Enough said,' replied Stella.

'Did you hear those two, Margaret? I wonder what'll happen.'

'Where were you last night, Frankie? I saw you slink out with Sr Laura.'

'Confession in the parish. I feel so relieved now Margaret. I'll tell you when we get a chance.'

'Don't pull your chair in like that, Hilary. You'll take all the polish off the floor. You should have learnt how to lift it up properly by now,' reprimanded Sr Rita as she adjusted the long sleeves of her habit.

'What's rocked her boat, Margaret?'

'We're going to be lectured,' replied Frankie.

Sr Rita began, 'Each of us has a conscience. Each of us has an inner voice that tells us the difference between right and wrong. We can choose whether to listen to God and our guardian angel or to the devil. God sees you! God sees your innermost thoughts and feelings...'

'What did I tell you? She's off on a rant, Frankie,' whispered Margaret.

'There is no need to gossip or complain. If you have something to say you can tell either Sr Laura or me. You can speak to Sr Maria. Confession is available for you anytime you feel the need...'

'To be reprimanded and silenced!' whispered Stella sitting behind Frankie.

'Once the exams are over and school finishes for the holidays, the rising bell will be rung half an hour later...'

'Half an hour! Big deal!' Margaret slid a note over to Frankie.

'We can relax while we do some gardening and cleaning. We'll be able to go for a walk twice a week. On occasions I will dispense with the silence…'

'Thank you, Sr Rita,' called out Hilary.

'What's happened to her? She must have a hidden agenda,' whispered Stella.

'Wait for it. I bet she is going to ask for something,' commented Margaret.

'Sr Rita, it seems that you wish us to be more relaxed so I wonder if we could form prayer groups. Perhaps you could guide one group and Sr Laura, the other?'

'I knew it. What did I tell you, Frankie?'

Frankie watched Sr Rita. She rolled her lips and straightened her veil.

'We have set prayers, Hilary. We pray together as a community. What do you have in mind?'

'We have learnt inspirational hymns and liturgical songs. Margaret and Frankie have learnt other folk hymns in the parish choir. Perhaps it would help us to sing or listen and reflect, helped by the music… we could meditate…'

Frankie clapped. Margaret joined in. Many more clapped. Frankie checked to see if Sr Laura was clapping. She was clapping and beaming a big smile.

'Maybe a good idea, Hilary. I will consult Sr Maria. Please stand. I will leave you now to either write your letters home, study or read.'

Sr Rita left the study. Sr Laura followed her.

'No explanation about Brigitte, Frankie. That is sad.'

'We were not told the reason why any of the others left either, Margaret.'

'Stella, why do you think Brigitte left? What did Sr Rita tell you? asked Frankie.

'Maybe, while the nuns are out of the room, I should tell everybody, Frankie.'

Stella clapped her hands. She stood at the front of the room facing everyone.

'I'm sure that you would like to hear what Sr Rita said

when I asked her about Brigitte's disappearance?'

'Yes, please,' called out Anne.

'Sr Rita said that she could not reveal confidential information specifically about Brigitte...'

'I knew it. I knew she wouldn't tell us.' said Hilary.

'Of course she did say that the discussion with Brigitte was confidential...'

'See!' said someone else.

Stella banged on a desk and continued, 'But... but... listen. Apparently, as days near for postulants to become novices, we will have to prove that we are able to keep the rules set out by this religious Order.'

'What does that mean? How can we prove that we are suitable candidates?' asked Hilary.

'Wasn't Brigitte a suitable candidate?'

'That's what Sr Rita was telling us about when she spoke just now. Telling us about all the cleaning and gardening. She'll be looking assessing our attitude, our prayers life etc.'

'I hate all the cleaning. Nuns expect perfection. We never did all that scrubbing and rubbing in our house,' retorted Frankie. 'We enjoyed the dust!'

'The slightest sign of a cobweb is removed. Poor spider doesn't stand a chance of even beginning to spin a web.'

'Have you ever cleaned the drains outside your house? If it's hot and they begin to stink my mother sometimes threw a bucket of water with disinfectant down the drain.'

'We're cut off from the outside world... no newspapers or radios, no TV's. Not even photos allowed,' said Stella with her hands on her slim hips.

Frankie was surprised by the remarks that ensued. Then she remembered the photo that her mother had given her. 'I have a photo of my mam. But I've hidden that. I hope that is not confiscated.'

'Have any of you cleaned the gutters round your house?

We did this yesterday with Sr Laura. We live in a flat. I don't know if we have any.'

'It's stricter than the army in here! Up at 6. Lights out at 9.30!'

'Have you realised that although we're rubbing shoulders... living cheek by jowl with each other, this is the first time we've been able to voice our opinions freely.'

'It's good to air our concerns.'

'Ye... what about books? We are only allowed to read books approved by the nuns.'

'Our letters going in and out are censored.'

'We can only see our relatives on the first Sunday of the month from two to four...'

'During which time we're supervised. If we're given any presents they have to be given in.'

'When we go to the noviciate... if we are accepted... well, I don't know how often we can have visitors.'

'So many rules! Lots of prayers!'

'What do you expect, Agnes? It is a convent.'

'I don't know what I expected. Sometimes I just wish that we had some free time.'

'Oh! Uh! I can hear footsteps. Sr Laura must be on her way...'

Frankie was re-assured that everyone was speaking out. She began to think of all the things that she wished she could do or have.

I'd like to listen to my kind of music... the Beatles. If only I could chat to Margaret. If we were allowed to choose our partners when we go for a walk, we could discuss our problems and how we are coping.

She combed her hand though her hair. *My hair feels awful. Sr Laura chopped it off. Just as well that we do not have mirrors. Just imagine doing men's jobs pounding coke down an opening in the cellar. I hope I'm not made to do that again.*

'Frankie, Sr Laura is calling you.' Margaret nudged Frankie.

'Sorry Sister... I was... thinking.'

'Maybe you tell us all, Frankie?' said Sr Laura as she chuckled.

'I asked if you were a flower, which one?'

'Daisy... no, forget-me-not... oh, I love roses too. It's a difficult decision to make, isn't it?'

When they left the study to go to break, Frankie chose to sit by an open window. She was surprised to overhear a conversation:

'I terminated my contract in May.'

'You haven't?'

'Indeed I have. For the sake of your sanity, if for nothing else, why won't you see fit to leave this institutional set-up, Agnes?'

'You know full well, why.'

'It's the last time I going to warn you that you've already wasted your life and have already become regimented. Come on. Come home with me to real life where you can use your talents, Agnes. Please. You must ken that this makes sense?'

Oh my God! What am I hearing? I'll move away from the window before Agnes and Catherine realise that I can hear them. Wait until I tell Margaret.

Frankie used the signal that she and Margaret had agreed: tapping her two middle fingers on her forehead three times. She was relieved when Margaret responded.

Just then one of the nuns from the community came into the room. She whispered something to Sr Laura. Sr Laura beckoned to Frankie. Frankie moved closer to Sister.

'Sisters no go alone. Sisters home... Sour Mary... she need two aspirants carry meal to sick person... so you and Margaret forse ... perhaps?'

'Certo, Suor Laura!' said Frankie. She called Margaret

over. Delighted, they set off together.

Once the meal was delivered, Sr Mary returned to the community. Frankie and Margaret instead of returning immediately went to the statue of Our Lady in the kitchen garden. Once there, Margaret said, 'Frankie, I'm ready to explode. Three aspirants have left. They've disappeared. That is unforgivable. They should have been allowed to say goodbye.'

'I feel the same. I didn't think Mavis would go. You won't believe this. I overheard Catherine encouraging Agnes to leave...

'What? Another two?

'After Christmas I suspected that Catherine would hand in her resignation. But little Jeanette... well, she is too young. I'm glad she has gone home.'

'It's not just that, Frankie. Peter has been slipping notes to me via Angela Walker in sixth form. I have tried to forget him but I still have feelings for him. That bothers me.'

'Thank God for that, Margaret!'

'What do you mean, Frankie?'

'I told Fr Derek that I love Fr John and...'

'You did? What did he say? Oh, was it in confession? Maybe you... '

'No. He was very understanding. In fact, he clapped his hands and assured me that wanting to love and be loved at my age, is natural. You look as though you don't believe me. Honestly he did, Margaret.'

'Well. That's a change. I must be normal too.'

'What? You? After that lecture you gave us all when you came back from Lourdes, I nearly canonised you!'

'You needn't, Frankie! In fact, when I tried to do... what was it Sr Superior said we must do? Yes, *sublimate my feelings and think of my future spouse, Jesus, and ask for help to be pure from Mary Immaculate.*'

'These feelings, Margaret? What feelings? Do you daydream? Wish you were... ... well in the arms of ... and even more than that... is that what?'

'All of them! When Peter sends me these notes... '

'What does he write?'

'Do you want me to tune you? Music is the food of love. You are always in my thoughts...'

'Oh! Lovely. You're lucky.'

'Frankie, what are we to do? I've tried kneeling in front of the statue of Our Lady and mouthing the words of 'Where are you bound Mary, Mary, Mother of God'...but my emotions are too strong.'

'When things get bad, I want to go home. Then I wonder if I still have a home. Since my mother went to Kerry with some man, I don't know where I could go if I left. Mam hasn't told me if she has left the flat. When I can't find a solution, I lie in bed singing *All you need is love* and imagine I'm in the arms of John Lennon!'

'We're a right pair, aren't we, Frankie! I think I still want to stay and become a novice in September. I'm trying to convince myself. Others have done it. I still want to stick it out and be a nun. What about you?'

'Yes, I do too. Besides what have I to go home to? Let's say our prayer and begin again. Sr Laura has started me going to confession to Fr Derek. He is very understanding. Sr Rose is so natural too. Let's say our prayer and get back to the study before anyone notices that we're missing, shall we?'

20

MARRYING JESUS: NOVICIATE

'It's spooky in this attic, isn't it, Margaret?'
    'Typical convent attic, though. Someone's knocked the cobwebs down.'

'There's still a musty smell here. Whoever came up here to get our white dresses must have sprinkled this creaky wooden floor with water to keep the dust down.'

'Look at the state of those dilapidated wardrobes. Long time since they've had a lick of paint. What must they be like inside? Is it any wonder the dust has penetrated into the clothes bags and onto the white dresses.'

'White dresses? Are you referring to our wedding dresses? Our grey wedding dresses?'

'They're not up to much, are they? I bet Jesus was disappointed when He noticed the state of them! There's a brown stain around the hem of that one you're putting back into the plastic clothes bag. Countless novices must have worn them.'

'I think that a long time ago some nun was handed a bale of white cotton material and told to run up a batch of dresses on her sewing machine. The only difference between them is their lengths.'

'From far away, they do give an angelic appearance, though.'

'But, up close, they smell of moth balls, perspiration and dust. They've no shape. They are designed to fit various sized novices by drawing in a once-shiny, waist-band. Pity the nuns don't seem to have heard of dry-cleaning.'

'Could you hand me the box of pink and white crowns, Frankie.'

'Do you think we should check them before we put them away? The white one I was wearing was falling apart. A rose fell off it. I had to undo the wire and manoeuvre it back into the band.'

'They look disheveled. The white crowns really need replacing. They are the ones worn by those making their vows for the first time.'

'I wonder if that's significant, Frankie? Maybe the pink crowns are less worn because there are fewer nuns that persevere for six years.'

'Oh Margaret, you're not thinking of divorcing Jesus already? You're barely married!'

'Jesus has lots of brides! Do you think He would miss me! It's good to keep questioning ourselves, isn't it? I'm sure we all have our doubts from time to time.'

'Only six of us were professed. That's half the number we started off with as aspirants. I wonder how many of us will survive six years to make our perpetual vows.'

'And wear a crown of pink roses?'

'Have you forgotten about our insurance policy, Margaret?'

'Better than any that can be purchased commercially. Surely you've not forgotten? You know what we were told about... if we persevered in our vocation we...'

'We'd be saved and our entire family to the third

generation would be guaranteed of a place in heaven!'

'Our families are relying on us to stick it out. Otherwise we could be the cause of them missing out on eternal bliss!'

'I didn't dare tell my mam about that promise, Margaret. She takes enough liberties as it is. Besides if she got to know this guarantee of certain heaven, she'll make sure I never leave the Order.'

'Do you remember someone saying Benvenuta Madre… blow your snooter, Madre, on the day Mother Provincial came to see if we were ready for the noviciate?'

'Will I ever forget it? Whoever she was, she was nearly sent home.'

'How have we endured these two years in the noviciate, Frankie? We didn't know anything about rule books, constitutions, manuals, vows…'

'We do now.'

'We didn't really know what we were letting ourselves in for. I remember trying to explain to my mother that a noviciate was a place where you learn the theory and practice of the life of a nun.'

'Do you think she understood that, Frankie?'

'No. I'm sure she didn't. She was probably baffled. I suspect that when the Novice mistress read my letter to my mam, she inserted some explanation. Something must have happened because my mam never asked me again.'

'How did we ever survive?'

'We had fun, too. Maybe that kept us sane. Do you remember the sketches we did?'

'What about the joke I told you and Hilary? She told it when Mother Provincial came.'

'The one about the man going up the escalator in Euston Station? She was trying to put on an Irish accent? Go on… tell it again.'

'It went like this..' Frankie began:

'Late one night, Seamus and Paddy came off the boat

from Dun Laoghaire to Holyhead. They travelled to Euston Station. As they went up the escalator, Seamus caught sight of the notice saying; *Dogs must be carried*. He turned to Paddy and said, 'Where in the name of God, are we going to get a dog at this hour of night?'

'You sound hilarious. You can put on the Irish brogue. Hilary couldn't.'

'Can you believe that, at this moment, the nuns are discussing where each of us is going to be sent?'

'You're right. I hope they'll send us to Africa ... somewhere abroad. We've been locked up for ages. Most of all, I hope we'll be together.'

'Can't wait to find out!'

'The rest of our lives depend on the decisions that the nuns are making.'

'It's exciting and worrying at the same time.'

'Margaret. Can I ask you something? '

'What? Why the praying hands? We don't keep things from each other. Go ahead and ask.'

'Alright. Did you ever tell anyone about Peter, Margaret?'

'I got as near as I will ever get. I tried to tell you the other night, Frankie.'

'What happened? You've gone pale. Tell me. Let's sit on those stools.' Frankie pointed.

'I nearly didn't get professed, Frankie.'

'What? Are you serious?'

'This time two nights ago.'

'The night before our profession day... 7th December. I won't forget it... vigil of the feast of the Immaculate Conception.'

'What happened?'

'It was to do with Peter. Remember we'd been told that our vows wouldn't be valid if we weren't utterly sincere. If we omitted to say something... '

'Your love for Peter?'

'I panicked, Frankie. I burst into the Provincial's room sobbing and shaking. Mother Provincial stood up from her desk, looked over her glasses and nodded towards a chair. It was as though she was waiting for me? Perhaps she had witnessed similar scenes.

'Here,' she said, 'Have a tissue, Margaret, make yourself comfortable,' is what she said.'

'Gosh!'

'She waited until I dried my tears. 'You are making a big decision. I am not surprised that you are frightened,' she said.

'I blurted out, Mother Provincial, I can't make my vows.'

'Really? What did she say to that?'

'Something like...'All three of them or one in particular?'

'I said, 'All of them... especially chastity. I've had thoughts... yes, lustful thoughts and...'

'Coo... That was brave...'

'Do you know what she said, Frankie?'

'Tell me.'

'You have been tempted. Tempted, like Jesus was before he began his great ministry. We are all tempted. You know that the devil is always busy suggesting many things to us.'

'That's true.'

'Frankie, I didn't want to name Peter. I just couldn't. Instead I confessed that I am jealous of all the attention that my sister, Rosie, gets.'

'How did she respond to that?'

'She rested her chin on her open hand, moved nearer on her chair and looked straight at me, 'None of us are angels,' she said. 'I have my faults too. Sometimes I think that's why we are in the convent. To do penance for our sins. Life's a journey. You can only take one step at a time.'

'I'm surprised that she didn't ask you about your

228

problem with the vow of chastity. No telling off?'

'The opposite. She told me not to worry. God would reward my sincerity. But I hadn't told her about Peter. So I wasn't really sincere, was I? When Mother Provincial said, 'Today you are marrying Jesus. He is your spouse, I was still thinking of Peter.'

'I don't blame you, Margaret. It's hard to love someone you can't see or touch, no matter how hard you try. I admit that when I long to be hugged and loved, my mind wanders back to John or Fr John. Then I feel guilty. It's a real struggle. *Whenever I want you all I have to do is...*

Dream, dream, dream, dream... the Everley Brothers... lovely... my mam used to hum it..'

'When I saw you, Frankie, dressed in white, walking down the stairs from the dormitory to the chapel, I thought you looked so content and confident.'

'I was shaking inside, Margaret. I was wishing that I was wearing a proper, beautiful bridal dress ready to be given away by a father that I can barely remember.'

'I can tell you, Frankie, that when I caught sight of my father attired in his bespoke Savile Row tailored, grey suit, I had visions of him walking me down the aisle to tall, blonde, athletic Peter! I wonder what my father was thinking.'

'I could hear your mother sobbing. Rosie waved to you, didn't she?'

'My twin. Bless her. I wonder if she will ever marry.'

'My lot were all dolled up! Mammy, looking trim in a powder-blue costume, cream blouse and a pill box hat with a veil! I wonder where she got that outfit. Her friend, Joe, sporting tweeds. My sister, Mary, looked smart in a navy trouser suit and a floral blouse.'

'Can you really believe that we are now full members... professed members, of the religious Order of Maria Educatrice, Frankie?'

'We have professed... declared to all that we have

joined this Order of nuns. I'm really going to try to keep my vows: Chastity, poverty and obedience.'

'Me, too. I promised Jesus that I would try. I like these new grey habits.'

'Oh, I hope these stools are clean,' said Frankie standing, flicking her habit and looking round to examine the stool where she had been sitting.

'Just as well we're wearing our overalls. Was that the bell? Come on. We'd better be in time for tea, Frankie.'

'Where have you two been? We missed you.'

'Thank you for missing us, Stella. We were sent to put the white wedding dresses away in a wardrobe in the attic.'

'White? Grey and moth-balled, you mean. Need replacing.'

'I think I can hear someone marching this way… that'll be Sr Rita.'

Sr Rita announced from the door, 'In ten minutes time, Mother Provincial wants you all up in the study.'

'Oh! I'm scared!'

'I'm excited! Africa, here we come!' said Frankie as she waved her hands above her head.

'This Order has a house in Kenya. Love to teach there, but I'm not qualified yet,' said Margaret.

'I'm sure you could qualify on the job out there, Margaret. Wouldn't it be great if we were all sent there?' added Anne.

Frankie squeezed Margaret's arm. She said, 'That would be perfect. Let's go and find out.'

Frankie noticed Mother Provincial smile as she sat at the desk in the study. She seemed to have aged since she took over the task of looking after the six convents belonging to the Sisters in English-Scottish province. Steel grey whips of hair matched her pale complexion. The way she held onto the desk as she levered herself up onto the rostrum made Frankie suspect that arthritis had set in.

Frankie whispered to Margaret, 'I hope that our prayers are answered.'

Mother Provincial wriggled her tongue round the inside of her thin-lipped mouth and smiled down at the group.

'There is no need to look so apprehensive. You knew the day would come when your mission in this world will begin. You will be doing the Will of God.'

'Hope my will is the same as His,' whispered Margaret

'Before I tell you where you are going, there is an admin job to be done.'

Oh no... don't prolong the wait, thought Frankie.

Mother Provincial began to explain: In keeping with their vow of Poverty in the Order of Maria Educatrice. The Holy Rule states with regard to our possessions:

When a person makes the vow of poverty she may no longer administer nor dispose of anything belonging to her without the consent of the superior. In the congregation everyone is considered as though she literally possesses nothing having made herself poor so that she may become rich in Christ Jesus Our Lord.

'Not a problem for me,' Frankie whispered.

'Each of you will be called to sign the relevant document later. I will announce your future destinations now.'

She continued, 'Sr Margaret Blackburn: I hear that your passport is in order. Be ready to fly out to Kenya at the end of January. You are assigned to our Kenya mission to work in either Eldoret or Kitaled dioceses.'

Frankie joined everybody as they clapped.

'Thank you, Mother Provincial. I am grateful that you have chosen me to go to Kenya.'

Frankie knew that alphabetically it would be her next. She clutched her miraculous medal and prayed, 'Please God, keep us together.'

'Sr Frances, when the school reopens in January, I want you to join the three Sisters teaching in St Joseph's Infant school. We will assess your teaching ability. Initially you will observe and help Sr Sheila in reception class. You will gradually be prepared to teach a class. If you prove yourself competent, you will study for your teaching certificate at Digby Stuart College, Roehampton.'

'Teaching? Thank you, Mother.' Frankie tried not to show her disappointment.

Didn't they know I wanted to go with Margaret? Surely they've noticed that we are friends. I want to travel. The nuns must think I have sufficient qualifications to become a teacher. Perhaps later I'll be sent to join Margaret in Kenya.

'Oh Frankie it's terrible to be separated. We'll have to write to each other. When you're qualified, you could be sent to join me.' Margaret squeezed Frankie's hand tightly, tears forming in her eyes.

After the list of destinations to which the newly professed Sisters were going to be sent had been read the sisters were instructed to continue with the work that they had been engaged in.

'Margaret, before we go back to the attic, let's go down to our secret place ... to our shrine of Our Lady. I can't imagine life without you. Here, let me give you a hug.'

'Shall we say our prayer? We'll have to alter it now that we are professed nuns. Have you got your copy?'

'Should we perch on the stone wall over there? Have you a pen with you?'

'Of course I've got our prayer. It was you who suggested that we keep them in our petticoat pockets. And I have a biro.'

'Let's sit on my black shawl and wrap yours around both of us. The wool will keep us snug.'

'Look Frankie. See how the light from the moon is shining on Our Lady's eyes and on her rosary beads. It makes her look as though she's watching and praying for us. Maybe she is. '

A December silver moon and a slight breeze was pushing the clouds across the sky.

Margaret recited a verse of a poem: '*Slowly, silently, now the moon walks the night in her silver shoon; this way and that, she peers and sees...Walter de la Mare.*'

'Lovely, Margaret. We'll never forget this night. The statue of Our Lady of Lourdes dressed in white. Just as we were on our profession day.'

'Frankie, remember when we were learning how to crochet? I made you a little memento. It's very small. Here it is. Of course the 'F' is for Frankie.'

'Oh Margaret. I made one for you too! It's nearly the same. The initial I added in was 'M' for Margaret.'

'Oh. No matter what happens to us, Margaret; we must keep these lovely mementos together with our prayer.'

'Let's alter the prayer we composed way back when we made our promises and signals. Then we'll be ready to pray together. Shall we, Frankie?'

When they were ready, F. and M. stood side by side:

'Dear Mary Immaculate, we wish to renew the promises that we made on our Profession day.

I, Margaret Blackburn, ask that you will accompany me to the mission in Kenya and plead with your Son Jesus, to help me to be faithful to my vows of poverty, chastity and obedience. I also pray for my family, my father, mother, brother Peter and particularly for my twin, Rosie. Guard and protect them.

Margaret stepped back and nodded to Frankie. Frankie began in a quivering voice:

I, Frances Danivet, ask you to help me become a teacher.

My family needs the help of your Divine Son, Jesus. Grant eternal rest to my father, Frank. May my mother, sister Mary, brother John, be protected.

Together we pledge to do our best, to continue wearing our scapulars. We will carry a copy of this promise and our mementos with us wherever we go. Each day we will pray the first decade of the rosary for each other and all our intentions. Should we feel tempted, we promise to ask for help and support. We will write to each other as often as possible. Guide, support and plead for us, Mary Immaculate. Amen

22

SHOCK DECISION TO LEAVE

*F*rankie was meditating in the convent chapel. She became conscious of the pungent sweet smell from Arum lilies on the altar. They reminded her of the day when she received her first Holy Communion and when she made her vows in 1969, aged 19. That was sixteen years ago. She had often been told that the stem of the lily symbolises Mary's religiously faithful mind, the petals represent her purity and virginity. The scent of the flower represents Mary's divinity and the leaves signify her humility. Although she liked the peppery smell from these lilies, they seemed to be overpowering. She began to sneeze.

As Frankie pulled her hankie from her pocket, the crochet square that Margaret had given her 16 years ago came out, too. How she longed to see her. *Still in Africa,* she thought. She placed it on the bench in front of her. She prayed, *Thank you God for the good times.*

The privilege of teaching so many children. The enjoyment of strumming my guitar at liturgical services. For the Sisters in the community who share their lives with me... especially the good-natured and good-humoured ones.

Why am I sometimes so lonely? I miss Margaret. Why do I long to have a child that I could cuddle? I dream of being loved...

Frankie felt a tap on her shoulder. She turned round.

'Peter! What are you doing... ?'

The last time Frankie had seen him, he was playing the clarinet with Margaret.

'I hoped I'd find you. I didn't want the nuns to see me. I remembered that we used to cross the playground and that the convent chapel is always open... I... '

'What's happened, Peter? Why have you come? It's years...'

'May I sit next to you, Frankie? I have to tell you something that I suspect that you won't want to hear.'

'Of course. I'll move over. What? What, Peter?'

'Thanks'.

It is to do with Margaret. Strange that I have been wondering about her.

'Margaret isn't well? She's got cancer?'

'No.'

'What's wrong with her, Peter? Tell me? She never answers my letters.'

'I'm not going to beat about the bush, Frankie. It's very bad news. You'll want the truth.'

'Please Peter, tell me.'

'Margaret committed suicide.'

'Oh Noo! Not that, Peter. Why? Why? When?'

Frankie stared through Peter. She clasped her hands. She buried her head in her hands and burst into tears.

A long silence elapsed. Peter put his arm around her. He whispered, 'She went quietly in her sleep. The Sister, who found her, said there was an empty packet of aspirins. She left a note on the locker next to her bed. There was a little crochet square with the letter 'F' on it, too. Do you want me to read the note to you, Frankie?'

When Frankie didn't answer he read:

Thomas à Kempis.

Imitation of Christ.

All flesh is grass, and all its glory shall fade like the flower in the field.

I have tried and have been found wanting.

Please forgive me.

Margaret

'*Found wanting!* We've all been *found wanting*? She was always hard on herself. If only we had talked. Oh Peter, I should have persisted. That crochet square. I gave that to her. This is the one she gave me. I've just taken it out of my pocket. I've carried it about all these years. I could have asked the superiors. Oh... '

'She never answered my letters either, Frankie. I wrote and wrote and sent her presents... but... She was the one for me, Frankie. I waited for ten years, Frankie. I saved up to travel to Kenya to persuade her... but then she... I should have... The possibility of having children was ticking by ... Lulu... my wife... she... I blame myself ...'

'It's unbearably sad, Peter. I know she loved you. Even on the day we became nuns she confessed to me that she wished that she was walking down the aisle to you, instead of towards the bishop.'

'Deep down I knew that too. Oh God! I can feel my heart thumping... if only... she could be still alive...'

'Peter, I'm wondering if she ever was given our letters. You know that all our letters are opened before they are given to us?'

'Frankie, I learnt that early on. She must have told you that I found ways of smuggling them in to her. Now I found a...'

Frankie heard the chapel door open. Peter took his arm away from Frankie.

'There's something…'

'Oh no!' Frankie sighed.

'So here you are, Sr Frances.'

'Have you met Peter, Sister Superior? He was…'

'No. We've never met. I told Frankie…'

'Yes. Shall I show you out?'

'Well … I suppose…'

Peter bent near to Frankie. He whispered, 'I told you the truth.' He stood and turned. When Sr Superior looked away, Peter mouthed the word 'Truth' to Frankie.

The bell rang for supper. Frankie walked into the refectory. After Grace she stared up at the top table. She watched Sr Superior. She observed her stern face as she listened to the gospel being read. Soup was served.

Surely Sr Superior will tell the community about Margaret. I'd have announced it immediately.

Sr Superior rang the bell to gain attention. She stood, 'I have a sad announcement to make. I am sorry to inform you of Sr Margaret Blackburn's death. Her parents are flying to Kenya. Her funeral will take place tomorrow in the parish church in Kitaled Diocese, Kenya. She will be buried there. May she rest in peace.'

She said nothing about the cause of death. Suicide is a sin, reflected Frankie.

One of the nuns sitting at the same table as Frankie enquired, 'Weren't you the same year of profession as Sr Margaret?'

'Yes,' she answered as she caught sight of Sr Superior staring at her.

'She must be the same age as you? Was she another malaria victim?'

Frankie stared back at Sr Superior through misty eyes. Sr Superior beckoned her. She followed her out of

238

the refectory to a small parlour. Closing the door behind Frankie, she questioned her, 'Sr Frances, what did Peter tell you about Sr Margaret's death?'

'He said that she committed suicide. An empty packet of aspirins was found next to her bed. She left a note.'

'We do not know how Sr Margaret died. The cause of her death is being investigated. While proper procedures are being followed, I forbid you to spread rumours. Peter was not in Kenya. There is to be no mention of suicide. Do I make that clear?'

Frankie nodded. Sr Superior turned and left.

Frankie felt distraught.

This is radically wrong. Suicide is a sin. The nuns don't want outsiders finding out. Why won't they acknowledge that with me? This makes me suspicious. Was Margaret ever given the letters I wrote to her? Maybe she did write to me. I want to know the truth. Sister Catherine has recently returned from Kenya. I will contact her.

Frankie met Sr Catherine the following day in a local café.

'I knew you'd be in touch, Frankie. Margaret was always talking about you.'

'Talking? Why didn't she write?'

'Why didn't you reply to her letters, Frankie?'

'But I didn't receive any?'

'You didn't?'

'No. Never!'

'Gosh! When we first arrived in Santa Maria Mission, Kitaled, she used to get excited every time Superior handed out the post from England. As the years went by Margaret often used to whisper to me, 'I wonder what I did to hurt Frankie.''

'I can't believe this. What happened to my letters? I wrote monthly for seven years. Then for her birthday and at Christmas and Easter, on our Profession day for... we've been apart for 16 years. I know I had the correct address. I checked it in our book of addresses… the Elenco.'

'Maybe Sr Superior didn't approve of what you wrote.'

'I was aware that this could happen, Catherine. I was very careful. I wrote facts. They were formal letters… too formal. I even signed off 'Yours in Jesus and Mary'.

'I knew that to mention certain facts would inevitably bring to mind shared promises, pledges and experiences. I carefully slotted these between facts. Maybe this was the reason my letters were not given to Margaret.'

'You must be stunned by this news, Frankie.'

'*Was* it suicide, Catherine?'

'I'm convinced… all the community are. From the evidence, it looks as though Margaret did end her own life.'

'How?'

'She went to bed early. Because she suffered from migraine, we didn't disturb her. She didn't turn up for Mass. She wasn't at breakfast. We all went off to our various jobs. At midday one of the sisters went to check if she needed anything. She ran out of her room calling for Sr Superior.'

'Then?'

'Sr Superior went straight into Margaret's room. When she returned, she looked very serious and went immediately to the phone.'

'To phone the doctor?'

'And Mother Provincial, I suppose.'

'In the meantime the Sister who discovered Margaret told us about the empty packet of aspirins. When Sr Superior returned to us, we were warned not to say anything to anyone outside the convent.'

'The note? How did you find out about the note?'

'It was one of the native nurses who came to lay Margaret's body out. She told me.'

'How did Peter find out?'

'Peter… I'm … '

'Cathy, I … Margaret and I promised that we would always keep in touch. We composed a special prayer. During our years of formation we discussed things a good deal. We met before we became Aspirants. We supported each other. Because we were constantly warned about 'particular friendships' we knew we had to be careful so we agreed on a sign … Oh, maybe we were at fault… perhaps I'd better not divulge these things… it might let the Superiors justify their cover-up of Margaret's suicide.'

'Frankie, out there in the Missions, we were thrown much closer together. There were fewer of us. We were far away from home. We were like blood sisters. Even the Sister Superior confided in us. We never called her 'Sister Superior'. We regarded her so much at one of us. Margaret spoke often about you.'

'Did Margaret mention Peter?'

'She managed to get letters from Peter.'

'How? She didn't get my letters?'

'You addressed your letters to the convent, didn't you, Frankie?'

'Yes, of course.'

'Okay, Frankie. I'll tell you what happened. You can judge for yourself. After Margaret's death, Sr Superior told the community that she was going to our mother house in Ancona.'

'Why?'

'When I drove Sr Superior to the airport, I questioned her about Margaret's death. She remained silent on the matter. She looked weak. Her breath smelt.'

Frankie said nothing. Catherine continued, 'Frankie, I've written to the Pope. I can't take much more.'

Frankie lifted her face. She looked straight into Catherine's eyes.

'Frankie, I have decided to leave the convent. Others have left. I don't feel I can stay any longer.'

'Why? What will you do? Will your family help you?'

'My mother needs me. She lives on her own.'

'Is that your reason for leaving?'

'Some sisters have asked for exclaustration but I don't need to buy time.'

'This wasn't a sudden decision, Catherine?'

'No, Frankie. This cover-up over Margaret's suicide, caps it all. I was professed aged 19, two years after you in 1971. This year, 1987, aged 35, I've been a nun for 16 years.'

Frankie began to calculate how long ago it was since Margaret and she had entered the convent. 29th August 1966 aged 16.

'Margaret and I entered the convent in August 1966. … I am… she was 37. We were professed 16 years. Oh Cathy, I can't believe Margaret is dead.'

'She loved teaching. She laughed a lot. When her parents brought her sister, Rosie, out to Kenya, she was very proud to show them around.'

Frankie was conscious that they had been sitting in a café in Lavender Hill, Battersea, in silence for some time. The waiter asked if he could get them anything else. Catherine ordered two scones with jam and cream. Frankie pulled off her big, woolly, black cardigan and rested her head between her elbows.

'Catherine, just how much did Margaret confide in you?'

'She talked about you often, Frankie.'

'Did she tell you about our prayer? I need to be sure. I'm frightened that Mother Provincial will blame us for being so supportive of each other.'

'Frankie, you can talk to me. I told you that I am leaving… here… read this. This is a copy of the letter I wrote to the Pope.' She pulled it out of her bag. 'Maybe this will convince you. Look. Read it.'

'Sorry Catherine. When I entered the convent I was

a strong person. But over the years … all the rules to be obeyed…'

'You've got used to being told what to do. It must be stricter here than out on the missions.'

'Yes. Maybe that's it. A lot has happened in our English Province recently. Some nuns have disappeared without any announcement. I've been wondering what's causing this.'

'Perhaps we are more aware of what's going on in the world around us now. Remember we weren't permitted to watch TV until a few years ago.'

'You're right. Maybe that has something to do with it. One minute a nun seems to be fervent and convinced, the next minute, she's gone.'

'Perhaps we are more open with each other. We tend to discuss things more openly.'

'One sister, Sr Marie, did tell me that she was leaving. It was obvious that she was struggling. She became thin and pale. From being a cheerful healthy member of the community who enjoyed strumming her guitar at the parish folk Masses, she eventually looked like a miserable skeleton.'

'I suppose it's inevitable.'

'Yes, it's true, life in the convent is modernising. Instead of leaving, one of the Sisters got permission to live outside the community.'

'Completely outside the community?'

'For most of the week she had a room in Digby Stuart College. She lectures in education there.'

'The nuns are adapting.'

'Good. You're smiling, Frankie.'

'Did you hear about Sr Aileen Collins? A Sister saw her taking legs of lamb and other cuts of meat from the fridge and giving it to her family when they visited.'

'She was caught stealing?'

'Yes. Soon after, she left the convent.'

'Our nuns, out in Africa think nothing of wearing ordinary clothes... even shorts.'

'Sisters here in England, have begun to take off their habits and wearing ordinary clothes when they visit their family. Three Sisters have been granted permission to live apart in a flat.'

'Catherine, I've been asking myself this question for a long time. Do we have to stay in a convent in order to do good?'

'I've noticed that there is a lot of unfairness. Some of those who came from better-off families are allowed to keep gifts like radios, books and wear clothes that have been given to them.'

'Frankie, what is happening here is mild to what goes on out in the missions.'

'I bet!'

'I've witnessed romances between nuns and priests. Priests forced to admit that a child is theirs. One of the Sisters regularly went places with a priest. He used to drive up to the convent for her on her day off. No one was surprised when she announced that she had obtained dispensation from her vows in order to marry him. He admitted that they were planning to marry. She left to join him back in England. Sadly he reneged on his promise to marry her and to father the child. Instead of leaving, he became parish priest in another area.'

'That's awful.'

'If only Margaret had married Peter.'

Frankie did not expect an answer but Catherine responded, 'Her long time friend, Peter did marry.'

'Margaret told me that he always held a torch for her.'

'Before he married he wrote twice a month pleading with her to leave and come back to him. By that time she despaired of ever hearing from you again.'

'Margaret loved Peter.'

'She desperately needed to be loved and to love. For her, love was a drug that she needed to quell her feeling of guilt. She always held herself responsible for her twin's accident and consequent disability.'

'How did she get Peter's letters?'

'One of the priests in St Anselm's Church, in Tooting Bec has a brother who works as a missionary in a nearby community. Peter addressed them to her to be collected there.'

'She mustn't have wanted Peter to marry someone else.'

'My understanding is that 'love at distance' proved to be safe for Margaret. Besides she probably confided in Peter about the guilt she felt about her sister.'

'Maybe she unconsciously used this as an excuse to keep in touch with him?'

'I think you may be right, because, soon after Peter married, Margaret seemed to form a close friendship with Fr Gerard.'

'Were they tempted to leave?'

'Who knows? Margaret became happier than I had seen her for some time. We were all happy when Fr Gerard formed a folk group. We began going over to his community to rehearse hymns to sing at liturgies and Masses.'

'This was a house full of males... priests and brothers?'

'Yes. Sometimes we returned the invitation. The priests and brothers came to our community house. We sang other sort of songs too. Mixed groups singing accompanied by strumming guitars and African drums gave us a whole new release.'

'Did Margaret play her clarinet? She was brilliant!'

'That was it. When Margaret played *Steal Away'* to accompany Fr Gerard singing, we all realised that this song had special meaning for them.'

'So she was going to leave, Catherine?'

'Within a week Fr Gerard was moved to another

mission. He never even said goodbye. The singing was abruptly stopped. No reason given.'

'Margaret needed to be loved. Let me read your letter to the Pope, Catherine.'

For the attention of His Holiness, Pope John Paul 2nd,

I, Catherine Gilhooley, want to be released from the vows of poverty, chastity and obedience that I made in December 8th 1966 as a member of the religious Order of Maria Educatrice.

I have struggled with my commitment for a number of years. After consultation, counselling and for health reasons, I have concluded that I can no longer continue as a member of this congregation. For the good of the Order and my own sanity, I request that I be granted permission to end my commitment.

I await your reply.

Yours respectfully

Catherine Gilhooley

22

IN OR OUT?

'*C*atherine! How did you find me?'
'I was sent to this Retreat Centre, too. When I heard that you were on retreat in Wales, I guessed it was the same place.'

'Mother Provincial told me that other religious Orders send their members here.'

'Yes. It's a good place to reflect and evaluate our priorities. I'm not surprised that Margaret's death has taken its toll.'

'I wasn't eating or sleeping, Catherine.'

'Were you seen by a doctor?'

'The doctor said that I needed a complete break. Mother Provincial sent me to this Retreat Centre.'

'Did you travel here by train?'

'Yes. Bus, train and a pick-up car.'

'Are you able to relax?'

'To some extent. I'm struggling, Catherine.'

'Are you okay to chat? I don't want to intrude.'

'Come. There's plenty of room on this bench. I'm

grateful that you have come.'

'Good.'

'I like being out outdoors. Someone I met here described this to be a formal garden. I think that's heather in those oblong-shaped beds. I love the fresh air. The wind blowing over the Welsh mountains.'

'What did our nuns tell you about me?'

'Only that you were here.'

'Did you get my letter, Frankie?'

'Yes. I was encouraged yet frightened by your letter to Mother General. In or out? Burning my bridges? Leaving a life that I have become so accustomed to. I'm angry when I reflect on what the nuns are stating about Margaret's death. Perhaps that's hampering my ability to make a balanced decision?'

'When I was here, I availed myself of counselling sessions. I found that talking about my concerns helped me to arrive at my decision to leave the Order.'

'I've been re-reading the letter you sent me. The bit where you said, 'I imagine that you are riddled with guilt and petrified with fear …''

'Was I right?'

'Yes, I am angry. Mother Provincial's announcement, 'Sr Margaret Blackburn 1950-1986 RIP died of a heart attack.' That is not true.'

'Heart trouble? She loved. Is that a crime? I wonder if the nuns told her parents the truth.'

'I don't know what they said to them.'

'The Catholic Church is reluctant to bury those who commit suicide in Catholic graveyards.'

'I'm sure her father must have been told that she took her own life. I heard that he insisted on taking over the organisation of her funeral. He chose the readings. He spoke about his lovely daughter at the Mass. Apparently it was a heart-rending eulogy.'

'The family must have been devastated. They have always been good Catholics. Suicide would be very difficult for them to accept.'

'Did Peter travel out to Kenya for the funeral?'

'I don't imagine he would have arrived in time. You know what it is like in hot countries. Three days is the most time that lapses between the death and the burial. But I really don't know the details, Frankie.'

'I wish I had been there. I still can't believe that my best friend, Margaret, is dead.'

'No. I'm sure you can't. What did you think of my letter to the Pope, Frankie?'

'Thank you for letting me read it. Seeing your application to leave, is forcing me to decide what to do. Have you received a reply?'

'Yes! I should have told you that straight away! My dispensation came last week!'

'How d'you feel?'

'How do I look?'

'Clapping your hands... you look excited... how do you really feel?'

'Excited and bewildered... the unknown, you know. I'm leaving the convent within the month.'

'Are you peaceful?'

'Yes. Once I made the decision, I felt better. It was the right thing to do. I hope that, like me, once you have made your decision, you will experience peace. I feel so much better now.'

'I don't know. I keep changing my mind. Years of obeying orders. My life has been so structured. I sometimes feel that I am at the edge of a pool but I have forgotten how to swim. I can't jump in... the water is too cold. It's got hidden depths. I can think of many excuses.'

'Once a swimmer... it's like riding a bike... Margaret told me how resourceful you are, Frankie.'

'Was. I've become institutionalised. Besides, I have no home to go to. My mother…'

'Wouldn't she benefit? You're a qualified teacher with a salary.'

'I don't know what she thinks. She will likely realise that I have a regular wage. No doubt she has been showing a photo of her 'daughter who is a nun' to everyone.'

'Use this retreat, Frankie. Pray. Talk to yourself. Maybe you should make a list of the pros and cons.'

'Good advice.'

'Good luck, Frankie. I'd love to promise to help you whatever your decision. I don't have any definite plans. Once I have sorted myself, I will try to make contact again.'

Frankie admired Catherine's stylish green jacket as she watched her step confidently into an awaiting taxi. She was impressed by how assured she appeared to be.

Frankie sat for a long time puzzling her future. It's different for me, she thought. Catherine's family will help her adjust. My mother seems to be going back and forward to Kerry. She has lived at five different addresses over the past sixteen years. I wonder if she stays with my uncle when she is in Ireland. She always settles in a council flat when she is in England. She seems to be busy looking after herself. Whenever she writes, she tells me to ask the nuns to pray for her. I think they have given her money, too.

At the evening meal, Frankie sat next to a woman wearing a mid-length dark blue skirt and knitted jumper. She held out her hand to Frankie.

'How are you, Sister? I'm Gloria. I'm a nun too. I no longer wear a habit. I'm here to discern whether I should renew my vows.'

'Is everyone else here for the same purpose?'

'*Discernment* is the buzz word. Everything is changing so rapidly in convents and monasteries too. I expect your Sisters are also adapting to modern ways.'

'Our convent routine has changed over the years. Some Sisters have permission to live at home with their sick, elderly parents. Others have left the community to experiment with living in a flat. It has become accepted that the Sisters studying at university can *live-in,* only returning to the convent for retreat days.'

'It's not the life we signed up to, is it?'

Next morning another nun enquired: 'Are you alright, Frankie? You've pushed that toast round and round your plate.'

Frankie put her hand to her forehead. She wasn't aware that people were watching her. 'I've an awful headache. I'll drink my coffee and take a walk outside. Thank you.'

After breakfast Frankie circled the garden. Then she went to her room and started writing her letter to the Pope. She copied part of Catherine's.

The opening hymn at Mass in the convent chapel that morning began with: *I am calling you to step out on deep waters.* The refrain was *I shall be your light…*

Frankie looked over to admire a monk plucking his guitar accompanying one of Damian Lundy's inspirational new collections of hymns.

That monk has curly hair and strong limbs. *He reminds me of the sepia photo of my father that my mother gave me. If only I could be friends with such a talented fellow. What shall I do? My heart is beating faster… but my head is reminding me of Mother Foundress's words*:

'*Sublimate your emotions to a higher level and remember that Jesus is your spouse and the love of your heart'.' Live the present moment. Live it with love!' But that is what I am doing! Didn't God make us to love one another?*

'Here. Rub some lavender on your forehead when you go to bed tonight, Frankie. It helps me sleep. Try it.' It was Gloria.

'Thank you.'

'What have you been up-to today?'

'Walking round these lovely grounds, thinking, praying. I go home tomorrow.'

'Have you decided to leave the convent?'

'Gloria, I think that I will stay in the convent. I'll go back to London and try again.'

Back in the convent, Frankie was called to the phone.

'Hello. It's Sr Frances.'

'It's Sr Rosina, I used to be the Sister Superior in the Kenyan community, Frankie.'

'Kenyan community? Are you in England?'

'Yes. Sr Frances... Frankie, is it possible for you to meet me in St Mary's Church in Clapham tomorrow morning? I feel that I need to explain something to you.'

I hope she is going to tell me the truth about Margaret's death, thought Frankie. *The Sr Superior of the English Province told me a lie.*

Frankie dreamt of Margaret. After Mass she caught the bus to St Mary's Church. When she walked through the gates, she recognised the nun wearing the habit worn by members of her religious Order.

'You must be Sr Frances.'

'Sr Rosina?'

'Delighted you've come. May I treat you to a coffee?'

'That would be lovely, Sister.'

Sr Rosina led the way to the church café. Frankie followed. 'I came here yesterday. The background music you hear is from an album released by Benedictine monks, based in Norcia, Italy. Their chanting is meditative. Do you like it?'

'Love soothing music. Sonorous male voices.'

'Tea or coffee, Frances?'

'Coffee please.'

252

'Once they were served, Sr Rosina pulled out a letter from her bag.

'Sr Frances, I felt I ought to show you this letter. It's the last letter that your friend, Margaret, RIP handed in to be posted to you.'

'Margaret's letter to me?'

Frankie felt faint. She grabbed hold of edge of the coffee table. The church café was windowless.

'Oh, Sr Frances, you are shocked. How stupid of me. Don't faint on me, will you? Drink some of your coffee.'

Frankie felt a shiver shoot through her body. Sr Superior sipped her coffee. Frankie sipped hers. After a while Sister said, 'Frankie, I asked you to meet me because I suspect you want to hear the truth.'

'This letter.' Frankie pointed. 'When was it written? Why wasn't it posted?'

'You want the truth? Your letters to each other were routinely burnt.'

'Burnt?'

Frankie took a gulp of her coffee and screwed her eyes tight as she scrutinised Sr Rosina's face.

'Burnt? Why?'

'I know, Frankie. I was given strict instructions not to send on any letters that Margaret addressed to you. I didn't agree then and I don't agree now but you know the fears that the Order has about 'particular friendships'.'

'We were miles apart… a continent.'

'But as Superior of the convent I had to obey. *Blind obedience*. That's what the Holy Rule calls it.'

Frankie reached for Margaret's letter. 'Why didn't you burn this letter?'

'I don't know why.'

'It's opened! Who read it?'

'I'm sorry. I knew I had it. When they said it was suicide, I knew I had this letter. No one else knew and I…

that's why I needed to speak to you, Frankie. I want to know what you make of this awful, unnecessary death.'

Frankie pulled at her miraculous medal from inside her blouse. Clutching it, she was transported back to the convent kitchen garden where on Easter Monday, March 1967, she and Margaret pledged to always be there for each other.

She placed Margaret's last letter, still in its envelope, down on the coffee table. She felt a trickle of tears beginning to flow down her cheeks.

Frankie began to signal to Margaret as she had done so often. She crossed her second and middle finger, placed them on her forehead and tapped three times.

'Margaret and I pledged to be there for each other. I don't care what you think about that.'

Then Frankie carefully lifted Margaret's letter from its envelope and read:

Dear Frankie

I imagine you busy teaching those little one in your class. Sr Rita told me that you are an excellent teacher. I too, although not a qualified teacher, love teaching our lovely children here in Kenya. Thank you very much for the books and other equipment that your school sent to us.

I always pray for you and want to send you good news but lately I have begun to feel a little tired. It can't be old age! I pray a good deal to Mary Immaculate, remembering our visits to her statue in Putney Convent kitchen garden. As I tap my forehead, it is all coming back to me. When we pray the sorrowful mysteries of the rosary, maybe we can remember each other? Our vows, our pledges need to be renewed and recalled especially if we want to relive them. I always make sure that I have the crochet piety bag with the 'F' on it, in my pocket. I expect that you receive our Kenyan Bulletin so you will be up to date with our mission here. Of course, when we receive the Provincial accounts from England, I often see pictures of the community ventures there. When you have time, I would be grateful if you could to write to me. I value and really look forward to a response this time. I heard that Sr Mary Kelly is coming out to join us, so to save a stamp perhaps, you might be able to ask her to bring me your reply.

Mary Immaculate keep us united at least in prayer. You never know the minute or the hour when God will call us to Himself.

Margaret Blackburn FMI

Frankie held the letter in her left hand. With the other, she rubbed her cheek trying to blot her tears.

'A totally unnecessary death! How could you? That was her last plea for help. You prevented her getting the support she cried out for. How could you?'

'Frankie, I'm sorry. I didn't realise. I was obeying orders from on high. Remember, I didn't read this letter until...'

'Until it was too late! Why don't you trust your sisters? All this rigmarole about loving God and your neighbour. How do you square this with a sister's call for help? Would Jesus have acted as you did?'

'No..I..'

'It's like being in prison. It's worse than being in prison. Even after 16 years of profession and miles apart, we were prevented from writing to each other. You have her life on your conscience, Sister. How does that feel?'

Frankie thumped the table as she stumped out of the restaurant, banging the door behind her. She continued her angry walk until she reached Clapham Common where she slumped herself on a bench near the pond. After walking and crying she took the tube back to the convent and wrote her letter to the Pope. She longed to get away from nuns who had killed her friend, Margaret. She longed for the day when she would be free of them and their subtle cruelty. She intended posting her letter to Vatican City before the four o'clock collection. As she returned she became aware of the carefree warbling of a robin and felt that Margaret was with her.

23

COLLAPSE

'Are you alright, Sister?' Frankie felt herself losing consciousness.

'Maybe it's the heat… just a little dizzy…'

'Why don't you take a seat. I'll get a glass of water.'

Dizziness, feeling weak this morning at Mass. What's happening to me?

'Thank you. What an entrance I've made to this exhibition! Yes, I'll sit here for a moment, if that's alright.'

'You are still feeling shaky, Sister? You look pale. I've brought you a strong cup of tea instead of the water. Two lumps of sugar. Sweetened tea will be better for you. Have you come alone?'

'Thank you. Yes, I'm alone.'

Yes. Very alone, she thought. *My mind is addled. I can't switch off my brain. Worry is eating into my very fibre. Should I remain in the convent or is it better to leave? I was a determined person. I seem to have become so indecisive. I've written my letter to the Pope asking for dispensation.*

Frankie took two sips of tea. She felt nauseated. She

pushed the cup aside. Weakness snaked at top speed through her body. She put her head on the table and slowly curled in on herself.

She lowered herself onto the floor. Her hands felt the hard, industrial type carpet.

People are peering down at me. A lady is leaning over me … and another woman. Asking for my identification card. It's in my bag. Why don't they search my bag? I can't talk. My head is reeling. They're calling for a First Aider. Mumbling. An Irish accent. Oh it's Mrs Kelly.

'Sister probably taught her son. Call her over. She'll know Sister's name.'

'That's Sr Frances from the convent on Dante Road.'

Frankie felt a man's hand on her arm.

'Sr Frances, I'm George. I'm going to help you onto this stretcher. Slowly, slowly… not to worry. We'll be at the hospital in no time.'

Frankie could hear voices. She tried to talk. Her eyes wouldn't open. She wondered if she was dying.

'You're doing well, Sister. We're going to lift you into the ambulance. Off we go. May I ask you some questions on the way? Just nod. Try to keep awake… '

Frankie felt the ambulance speeding along. Then it stopped. Someone said, 'At the hospital now. The trolley is waiting. We'll ease you on. In we go.'

Frankie heard someone else say, 'The left side of her face has dropped. Check there's no blockage in her lungs.'

Frankie prayed, *Dear God, I am dying. Why are you punishing me for berating the nuns for the death of my friend, Margaret?*

'Sister, we're going to take you to have a MRI scan. Just going to check your responses.'

Frankie thought*: I don't care anymore. I can't even open my eyes.*

'I'm Doctor Donovan. Smile if you can hear me. Good.

Can you wiggle your toes? Excellent. Lift your arm… either one. A miracle! That's better… you've a lovely smile.'

Frankie felt herself being wheeled along on a trolley. She tried to open her eyes. She heard another man's voice. 'We're putting you in the Intensive care units (ICU). They'll take good care of you in that ward.'

The next voice she heard was a woman's, 'Hello Frances. I'm Nurse Amanda. I'm going to push a cannula into the vein on the back of your hand so that I can attach a drip. You will feel a little prick.'

Frankie felt the nurse push the cannula into her hand. It felt cold. The nurse's arm was warm. She wanted to sleep. All her energy seemed to have gone.

Frankie could hear the wheels of another trolley. Someone said, 'Nil by mouth. Nothing for her. I'll leave her a jug of water.'

Frankie assumed that they must be the catering staff. *I can't swallow. When I try to drink water, I want to vomit.* She ached, felt weak, sleepy and nauseous.

Frankie was woken. A gentle voice said, 'Hello, Frances. You need to drink. I'm going to feed an anti-sickness solution through the cannula into your blood stream. It's to prevent your stomach bleeding. We'll monitor you every hour until you're stable. Alright?'

Frankie tried speaking but couldn't. Her eyes opened. She nodded. She heard the trolley again. She thought: *Every time the food trolley goes past, I feel sick. I heave when I smell it approaching.*

Frankie felt sleep over-powering her again.

She heard a shrill voice. She felt a cold hand touch her arm.

'Hello Sr Frances? 'How are you feeling?'

Frankie recognised Sr Superior's high pitched voice. She was trying to distinguish the gentle voice of whoever was with her. Was it Sr Mary?

'How do you feel? You gave us a shock, you know.'

Frankie thought: *I can't answer. I can't move... I can't see them properly.*

'She squinting, I don't think she can see us... she's probably too weak to speak.'

'Better ask one of the nurses. There's one over there.'

Frankie was wondering why she couldn't move and had begun to shiver.

'There's no point in staying. She's not speaking. Phone us when you have a diagnosis.'

Another voice said, 'I filled in Frankie's details. Fr Dan is the chaplain. He'll keep an eye on her.'

'Who did you put down as next of kin?'

'I put my name down. Sister Superior. I told the staff that I have the responsibility for the nuns in our community. Frankie tells us that her mother is often in Kerry.'

Frankie could hear the sounds of their shoes on the tiled floor as they moved further away from her. She thought: *They are talking about me as though I am about to die. Mammy will want to know that I'm in hospital. Mary could visit me. Who will tell her? No one, probably. Dom is too far away but he could be told. Next they'll be planning my funeral. Am I going to die?*

'Goodbye, Sr Frances. We'll be praying for you. You're in God's hands. He'll take care of you.'

'Wave. She's trying to blink her eyes open. Goodbye.'

Frankie thought, *I'm in God's hands. Hopefully He works through the nurses. Maybe God is punishing me because I am planning to leave the convent.*

Frankie felt a little stronger. She began to move about in her bed. *She thought: I must have been in here for days. I've managed to drink a little water. I need the commode. I can speak now.*

'You can walk into the toilet, Frances. You must try. I'll help you up.'

'Oh… I don't think I can, Nurse.'

'Move your legs over to this side of the bed.'

'Oh Oho I …'

'That's it. See, you can. Put you feet on the floor. Hold on to me. I'll take you the first time.'

'I'm going to fall. I can't balance.'

'You can. See. One foot after another. Keep going. Try again. You're here. Cling on to the rail. Take your time. I'll close the door. In you go. Press the button if you need help.'

Frankie reflected: *By clinging onto everything, I've managed to get back into bed… such a struggle. Will I ever be strong again?*

Lying back on her bed, Frankie tried to assess what was going on around her. She had become conscious of noisy days merging into disturbed nights. The woman opposite asking for her pillow to be adjusted even when the nurse dispensing medication from a trolley couldn't leave it unguarded.

When the doctor did the rounds he stood at the foot of Frankie's bed. He pulled up her medical record card from the rack, 'Good news. You can go home to-day, Frances. I am aware that your sense of balance has not returned yet. You'll be supplied with walking sticks. The physiotherapist will come this morning to assess your needs.'

When the doctor had moved away, Frankie questioned the nurse, 'I didn't really understand what the doctor said that caused me to collapse. Can you explain again, nurse?'

'That kind of condition is referred to as vasovagal syncope resulting in the malfunction in the autonomic nervous system causing a drop in your blood pressure and a reduction in your heartbeat. This leads to a temporary interruption to your brain's blood supply.'

'I don't think I'll remember that, nurse.'

'Not to worry. I'll provide you with a leaflet on vasovagal syncope.'

'I'm Pam. A physiotherapist. I need to get you fit to go home. First I would like to see you walk up and down this ward. Then I'll take you along the corridor to stairs. I'll show you how to manoeuvre up and down... '

'But I can barely walk to the toilet. I have to cling on… I… ' , stammered Frankie.

'I know. It's scary, but I'll provide you with a stick. See, I have brought this one. I'll measure you. Before you go home, you will be provided with one that is the correct size for you.'

Later, she returned. 'Your stick is here, Frankie. Your medication has come from the pharmacy. Good. I see you have dressed and packed.'

'Thank you, Nurse. I am very grateful for all that I have received. You do a grand job. God Bless each of you.'

'Sister Frances, the nuns from your convent rang to say that they will come to take you home after they have finished their prayers. They also said that community meals finished earlier. They requested that you eat here before they come.'

'Oh… I…'

'Not a problem, Sister. We need your bed for a new patient. If you don't mind, we'll move you to the little table down at the end of the ward. I'll see that you'll be provided with a meal. You can wait there until the nuns come.'

Frankie felt her cheeks becoming pink with embarrassment. The nurses seemed to be more caring than the nuns.

Back in her own bed in the convent, Frankie wondered why none of her family had come to visit her while she was in hospital. *They would have come if they had been informed that I had collapsed.* She was glad that she had not posted her letter to the Pope. If she left the convent, she would be alone in the outside world.

She heard a knock on her bedroom door.

'Come in! Catherine! Drag that chair nearer.'

'You're surprised to see me?'

'Yes. I thought you had left. When you came to see me in the Retreat Centre in Wales, you said you were very busy preparing to leave the convent. I wanted to talk to you but I thought it was too late.'

Catherine began, 'That I am a *persona non grata* is obvious from the reception I received from Sr Eileen, just now. What is wrong with our nuns? We spend half our lives saving the world but once we decide to leave the Order we are treated like... well it's better I don't say, Frankie.'

'Oh no! Well, I'm delighted to see you.'

'You wrote your letter?'

'I wrote to Mother General and the Pope for dispensation... but Catherine, since I collapsed I wished that I hadn't. I didn't post it. I'm so scared.'

'What Frankie? I can't believe you still have doubts. After all the deception piling up over your best friend's death. I thought you would have lost all faith in this outfit.'

'I feel very muddled, Catherine. Your circumstances are different to mine. You have a family behind you. They will help you. Not one member of my family even contacted or visited me while I was in hospital. Sr Superior told me that she hasn't even got a contact address for my mother.'

'Frankie, don't rely on your family. Be your own woman. You're an experienced teacher. You've been educated. Guided others. You're resourceful. You can earn your way in a secular society.'

'Resourceful? I suppose I was. Years of obeying rules and regulations seems to have hampered my...'

'Frankie, let's get things straight. When you entered the convent as a teenager, your family presumed that you had chosen a new family with a different lifestyle. They may even have envied you for all the privileges and respect that you accrued. If they are believers, they may also wish that they too could be certain of a heavenly reward at the close of their lives. What they don't know is that nuns live solitary lives, denying their feelings and inclinations in the belief that they will merit heavenly bliss when they die.'

'Life does have its difficulties for people outside the convent too, Catherine. My mother asked me to pray for my sister's marriage.'

'Agreed. I'm not doubting that.'

'In spite of the possible problems that could be involved I still long to be loved... just to be normal and to have a child... oh... I don't know... Yes I do... maybe...'

'You're making my point, Frankie. We all have made choices and we have to take the consequences.'

'Maybe that's true... but aged 16?'

'Well, we opted out of enjoying certain pleasures believing that we'll be rewarded *after* we die. Does that mean that those who are not nuns, have a doubtful existence after death?'

'That's true, too. Who is to know? We live alone in a community... denied real friendships.'

'Can you honestly tell me that in the 16 years that you have laboured in religious life that you have ever been special to another human being?'

'Initially, Margaret and I confided in each other as much as we could...'

'But you were not supposed to be friends with her. In fact, that was the reason why your letters to each other were not delivered. Might that be the cause of Margaret committing suicide?'

'Don't remind me, Catherine. I feel guilty. I blame myself for not doing more to make sure that these letters were delivered to Margaret. When she didn't reply I should have realised that she had not received them. I don't know what I could have done. She needed me. I don't want to collapse again.'

'Okay, Frankie. I won't stress you. Just take time to

reflect on the alternatives from living with nuns who are prepared to wait for their reward in heaven and to what life outside the convent will be like.'

'You're right, Catherine.'

'Margaret was always singing your praises when we were out in Kenya. From the accounts she gave of you, I learnt that you are a quick-witted, talented and a determined person. Understandably, you're dithering now because you have been under the influence of a regime. It's much the same as having been in the army. You can break out. Let the real Frankie show her determination.'

'Thank you, Catherine. I suppose that, were I to leave, the nuns would help me. They are well aware of my dysfunctional family background. There must be some provision for folk like me. If the Order doesn't help, surely there must be some organisation within the Catholic Church that will.

'Why are you laughing? That's a raucous laugh, Catherine. The nuns will come in... Watch that chair... You're going to fall backwards... Throwing your hands up in the air like that... what is so funny?'

'Frankie, you're so naïve... surely you've contacted others who have left the convent?'

'No, I haven't. Why?'

'If Sr Superior was here today, I would not have been permitted to visit you. Once a nun leaves, or is on her way out, the other nuns shun her and she is made to feel that she is betraying those who remain.'

'No! I can't believe that. I've lived beside these nuns for half my life.'

'Wait until the news gets out that you have applied to leave. You'll see.'

'I suspect some must know already. Sr Superior must have been told. I didn't notice any change in her attitude to me.'

'But you were in hospital. You collapsed, Frankie.'

'I could do very little this time last week. I couldn't talk, eat, walk. I thought I was going to die, Catherine.'

'Precisely. Hopefully, you are nearly back to enjoying good health again. Let me tell you about Angela Collins.'

'She was in the Bermondsey Community. Tall and well spoken.'

'She told me that she was not allowed to say goodbye to the other Sisters. She said that she had to leave when the other nuns were away on retreat. On the morning that she was leaving, she was called into the Superior's room and instructed to hand back her habit, the crucifix she had worn together with her Divine Office book, Prayer book and her copy of the Holy Rule.'

'She would no longer want to keep her habit... but not to be allowed to say goodbye... that's not right.'

'All she was given were a pair of worn bed sheets and two towels. Money-wise, she was handed a cheque for five thousand pounds. The nuns had agreed to pay the rent in a one bed-roomed flat over a butcher's shop for six months. After that she was on her own.'

'Oh... What should I do, Catherine?'

'I cannot tell you. No one can, Frankie. Besides, you are still recovering.'

'Each day I feel a little better.'

'I shouldn't be telling you all this. Sorry, Frankie. Rest as calmly as you can. Weigh up what is best for you.'

'Maybe, I should stay... but on the other hand...'

'Fortunately, we are both teachers. As long as we are employed, we have a better chance of managing.'

'That's a plus. We've got to thank the convent for that.'

'I looked up the ads and found myself a new teaching post and a flat within walking distance.'

'Good for you, Catherine.'

'When Sr Teresa McShane left, she married within a year. She has a lovely little boy now. She married an ex-priest. Apparently they were in love before they left. He lectures at London University while she is a stay-at-home-mum.'

'You're right Catherine. There is a different life to lead outside the convent. I must get my act together.'

When Catherine left her room, Frankie surmised that because of the awful reception that Catherine received from the nuns, she wouldn't hear from her again. She tried to sleep. She was restless. Stretching over to her locker she took her letter to the Pope from her copy of the Bible. When Sr Norma came in with her tea, she asked her to post the letter.

Ten days later Frankie heard a knock on her study door. It was Sr Superior.

'Two letters for you, Sr Frances. They look official so I thought I'd better bring them in myself.'

'Thank you, Sr Superior.'

Sr Superior stood waiting in attention.

Frankie thought, *she knows that these letters are from the Pope and Mother General. Their insignia is on the envelopes. I suppose she want to see my reaction.*

'If you wouldn't mind, Sr Superior, I prefer to read these letters on my own.'

Sr Superior turned. She left the room.

I want to tear the envelopes open and I don't want to. I can feel my heart beating faster.

Which letter would it be better to open first? Maybe the one from the Pope.

I'll never forget this moment. I'll open the envelope carefully. Lovely paper. It's headed with the Papal insignia. Two Crossed Keys, one gold and one silver, bound with a red cord. It all looks so official. Oh it's written in Latin! But there's translation provided:

Congregatio Pro Institutis Vitae Consecratae

Translation of the Pope's letter:

Most Holy Father,

Sister Frances Danivet, a perpetually professed member of the Congregation of Maria Educatrice, begs your Holiness for the indult allowing her to leave the Institute so that she may freely and lawfully return to the secular state in view of the motives set forth...
The Congregation for Institutes of Consecrated Life and Societies of Apostolic Life, having given careful attention to the considerations set forth, has given a favourable response to the request so that the suppliant, having laid aside the external form of the religious habit, remains separated from her Institute.
In addition, let the regulation contained in Canon 702-1 and 2 regarding fair and evangelical charity be observed.

This present rescript, unless refused by the suppliant in the act of its notification, by the law itself, carries with it dispensation from the vows and from all obligations arising from the Profession.

Not withstanding anything to the contrary.
Given at Rome August 1987

So that it. It's final. I have to leave now. I might as well open the letter from Mother General.

The door to Frankie's bedroom was opened.

'Mother Provincial has come to speak to you, Sr Frances.'

'No need for you to move, Sr Frances. I see you have read the letters. They are official letters.'

'I haven't read the one from Mother General...'

'She accepts the dispensation from your vows granted by His Holiness. I have just been speaking to Sr Superior.

We will now begin procedures for your leaving process. Consideration will be given to the fact that you have not been well and you are recovering.'

'The letter from the Pope is so official… cold … factual… '

'What did you expect, Frances? You made your decision. The Holy See has granted your request. I have to go now but I will speak to you again. We can arrange matters when you are a little better.'

'Mother Provincial, I would like to ask you… '

'Sorry Frances, I will send you an appointment. We will speak in my office.'

Frankie watched the door close behind Mother Provincial.

What will happen now?

24

FRANKIE'S DISMISSAL

*F*rankie was delighted to find two of her favourite nuns relaxing around the convent kitchen table. She remembered that only a few years earlier there used to be a tiny room sectioned off in the far corner of the kitchen. Sr Superior or Mother Provincial often slipped in there to sip a cup of coffee in private.

'An bhfuil aon sceal agat? What's the story?' enquired Sr Anne. She was sitting beside Sr Brigid at the kitchen table. Frankie winked. She raised her hands, pretending to play the bodhrán while twirling round.

'Sure, there's not much that I can tell you two.'

'Delighted to see you performing, Frankie, but you're still pale. Is there something troubling you?'

'Three days in hospital. Ten days in bed recovering from my collapse. Is it any wonder?'

'Not at all, a chara. It was most likely stress that caused you to end up in hospital.'

'Sheer determination got me going, today.'

'Well done!'

'Hearing your voices cheered me up. I don't think I'll ever thank you two enough. It's true when they say that the kitchen is the heart of the family.'

'Ah... will you stop all that plámásing! You'll prevent my progress towards reaching the thirty-three degrees of humility! Pull that stool nearer,' joked Sr Brigid.

'You're safe to gossip here. You'll have a cup of coffee, won't you?' encouraged Sr Anne.

She stood, opened the oven, pulled out a shelf and tossed a loaf of soda bread onto a cooling stand. She placed the stand on the counter that ran along the side of the kitchen where there were windows.

'Smells good, Sr Anne. I see you've put currants in that one.'

'You prefer the fruity one. It needs to cool down. I've opened the window. With a whiff of the bread, no doubt the nuns will be looking forward to a slice or two at teatime,' answered Sr Anne.

Frankie noticed that Sr Brigid's arthritic hands were crippling her. She used both hands to lift the coffee pot. The handle of the cup that she gave to Frankie seemed to have been glued back on. Frankie wondered if it was a reject from a set of ware used in the parlour.

'Thank you! Go raibh maith agat! I've nearly forgotten all my Irish. You two have always been so good to me. How's the leg, Brigid? The fleabites must be painful.'

'Ah well, you can't reach my age without some affliction. Come on now. It's you, we're concentrating on. Tell us all.'

Sitting opposite them both, Frankie marvelled at how Sr Brigid always seemed good humoured. No doubt standing on hot tiles in front of the oven for many years had caused her legs to swell.

Frankie sat. She reached for the coffee. She laughed as she remembered the first time she met Sr Brigid.

'What's tickling you?'

'I was thinking back to when we met, Sr Bridie. I hope you won't mind me telling you this. I never knew when you were codding me. You're always so straight-faced. You've got a wicked sense of humour. As we Irish say... *the craic is mighty!*'

'Maybe it's my glasses? I used to be told that there's a twinkle in my eye.'

'But we can't see it through those tinted glasses. It's hard to gauge what you're thinking when you peer through...'

'Ah go on... Bridie wouldn't harm a fly... ' interjected Sr Anne.

'Sure, I know that, now... but way back...'

'You were never afraid of me... why's that?'

Frankie wanted to explain to Sr Anne that she seemed to smile more easily. She was also short, plump and cuddlier.

'I don't know. I suppose it was because you don't wear specs it was easier to guess what you were thinking,' Frankie replied.

'Never mind about us, Frankie. Stop rolling those lips... isn't that a sure sign that you've something to tell us?' said Sr Brigid.

No doubt over the years, especially after the changes brought in by the Second Vatican Council, Sr Anne and Sr Bridget must have watched many nuns leaving the convent, thought Frankie.

'I want to thank you both for all the times you both took good care of me. Whenever I took to my bed, you two made sure that I was fed.'

'Ah, come on now, Frankie. Weren't we only doing what is expected of us?'

'No! Many Sisters interpreting the Holy Rule thought that anyone staying in bed during the day could only remain there if they were genuinely sick. Furthermore, it was assumed that if you were that unwell you didn't need to be fed. But you...'

'The difference was that you *were* sick. Worry can wear you down, Frankie. You needed building up.'

'I'll always remember your kindness.'

'You'll remember? You're leaving us too, Frankie, aren't you?'

Frankie stopped sipping her coffee. She looked at both of them.

'My guess is that you already know what is happening to me?'

'We have our suspicions but we want to hear it from you, Frankie.'

'I've been warned by Mother Provincial, not to breathe a word. I can't keep my secret any longer. I'm leaving on Saturday. There now, I've said it!'

'So soon! We knew you're leaving but we didn't know when. We've put two and two together, Frankie. When you collapsed, we surmised that whatever caused you to be rushed into hospital, affected you seriously. Then we heard about Sr Margaret's suicide. It was all hushed up but one of the priests let it slip when I took him his breakfast in the parlour,' confessed Sr Brigid.

'We know the signs when Sisters are leaving. You were searching for accommodation last week, weren't you? '

'You knew that too?'

'Sure, wasn't I instructed to put bed linen and towels aside for you, Frankie.'

'You two really don't miss a thing! Yes, I've a room in the house of Evelyn Renaldo in Wimbledon. Perfect location: Just round the corner from the St John The Baptist Church and a short walk to Wimbledon Tube Station. She's a good Irish Catholic married to an Italian.'

'Sr Noreen told us all about the shenanigans that went on there... '

'Oh did she now?'

'You were circling adverts for suitable accommodation

in the newspaper each day. Then phoning up and making enquiries after 6 pm each evening. By which time they had gone!'

'I was trying to save money. Calls made after 6pm are at a cheaper rate...'

'It was only when you phoned Evelyn, during the morning that you got an appointment to view the flat last Tuesday evening.'

'Did Noreen tell you that we didn't wear our habits? We went in clothes taken from the wardrobe where the clothes that are handed in are stored ready to be given to the needy?'

'Yes, and that when the landlady was showing you round, she mentioned that there was a man living in the flat next to the one she was showing you ...'

'Noreen saw me pulling a face. She said that I looked scared. I told Evelyn that I had never lived close to men. When I said that, I felt I had to inform her that we were both nuns.'

'Fortunately, all ended well. Noreen wasn't annoyed. The landlady understood. She suggested that you take a room in her own home,' congratulated Sr Anne as she clapped her hands.

'In the end, it turned out for the best. The Provincial bursar, Sr Mary, put down the deposit for my room. My rent will be paid for the first two months.'

'Will you have enough money for everything else, Frankie? Will you be able to carry on with your teaching job in Battersea?'

'I hope I will. It will all be new to me.'

'Thank goodness, you are a qualified teacher.'

'And thank God I am employed. I'm to be given six thousand pounds to start. Then I'll have to manage on my own.'

'Your mother, Frankie. She knows you're leaving the convent?'

'I was instructed to inform her. I sent a letter to her Irish address.'

'Haven't you a brother and a sister? Surely, they'll help you? Did you ever discover yon man your mother travels with backwards and forwards to Ireland. Is he your uncle or… ?'

'I don't expect much help from my family. Dom and Mary are struggling to cope. As for my mother… I really don't know what she's up to now.'

'Isn't it a sad state of affairs, Frankie? You've spent half your life with us. Now you are about to venture out on a life of your own.'

'Tis sad, but I can't live a lie. After the cover-up of Margaret's death, I can't continue to live here. It's taken its toll. When I collapsed, I realised that my body was reacting. I have to leave. I am nervous. There's no doubt about that. However, I am determined to cope.'

'It will be our loss, in so many ways, Frankie. You've gained spiritually. You've been educated and trained. You've grown-up with us. We'll have one less salary coming in now. Sr Ella remarked that our nuns are ageing and fewer are earning. Some will resent your leaving us after all that you have received. But what you have gained you will take with you and will no doubt help you to continue to try and make this world a better place.'

'Thank you, Sr Anne. After all that has happened I realise that I cannot stay in the convent.'

'You're right if you feel like that, Frankie. Look what happened to Sr Regina…'

'… she really must have struggled with all the criticism from the Sisters and our Superiors when her sixth formers put on that performance at the end of term.'

'Who would have thought that she'd end up in Springfield Mental Hospital in Tooting Bec? God love her. After all she did for the congregation, to end up there.'

'Poor soul. Remember all the dance drama that she directed with the sixth formers when she was in charge of religious education?'

'Yes, wasn't their final performance called 'The Creation'? Some of the nuns criticised her because the students wore tight fitting Lycra costumes?'

'Frankie, I just want to be sure. I hope you don't mind me asking. Was it your decision to leave? You haven't been asked to leave, have you?'

'Yes, it is my decision. I have chosen to leave. I wrote to the Pope.'

'I'm happy to follow my vocation. Nonetheless, I respect your decision,' declared Sr Brigid as she joined her hands in prayer.

'I'm happy too, Frankie,' echoed Sr Anne. She tapped the table and continued, 'Some Sisters adhere too strictly to the rules. That is probably what the Superiors did with regard to Margaret.'

'It takes courage to leave. You'll have to start again.'

'I am going to put every effort into finding my way outside the convent.'

'Frankie, you're wise enough, to realise that most of the community try hard to serve God. Many succeed in doing great work. But there'll always be bad apples.'

'Look at you two! Aren't you a credit to the Order?'

'More plámásing!'

'No I really mean it. The congregation owes you two a debt of gratitude. How many of us have received sound advice here in this very kitchen!'

'It's like the new fangled face-to-face confessional! No, joking aside, I pray that God's Will be done,' declared Sr Brigid.

'I know you pray. You both do. Let me confess: I've been disillusioned for years. It's been building up. I sometimes feel alone in community. Does that make sense?

Being loved, being in love, sublimating longings for love, with love of God. It's difficult to puzzle out what nuns are expected to do about love.'

'Explain yourself, Frankie. Talking about things like this can clarify notions that you may be harbouring. What do you mean when you ask 'what nuns are expected to do about love?''

'Okay. Remember the other night when a few of us watched 'The Thornbirds' on the television?'

'Only five of the community chose to watch. It showed a priest falling in love with a woman. Priests have taken a vow of chastity. They should keep their promises...'

'Sr Anne, there were a lot of things happening to me during that film. I closed my eyes when the kissing was going on. I was embarrassed.'

'Why? Was it because it was a priest kissing a woman?'

'I don't know. I got all hot and bothered. My emotions... my imagination was running wild. I wanted to be hugged and loved.'

'Hugging and kissing is natural. That's what people do when they are in love. But this was a priest...'

'Precisely. Why did the priest seem to need this type of loving? Did he commit a sin? Is the love that I feel welling up inside of me sinful? Margaret fell in love. Should she have left the convent for that reason? Would she still be alive had she left?'

'So many questions!'

'Now we're getting to the nub of things, Frankie,' commented Sr Anne. 'When I watch love scenes in films like the *Thornbirds,* my emotions are aroused, too. When I see people kissing, I remember how lovely it was when I was kissed. It is then that I tell God that I have chosen to love Him alone.'

'Do you feel guilty?'

'No, Frankie,' said Sr Anne.' Remember what it says

in the new Rule Book of our Order, *'Chastity for the sake of the Kingdom of heaven is a precious gift of the Father, which we accept in faith. ... '*

In return, we offer our 'powers of loving' as our grateful and joyous response,' joined in Sr Brigid.

'Maybe, I did not receive this 'precious gift' of chastity? Perhaps Margaret didn't either?' said Frankie, as she scratched her head.

'We've both celebrated the silver jubilee of our profession last year. When we made our vows, convent life was very different. At the Second Vatican Council the church made new rules,' said Sr Brigid.

'It is even rumoured that one day some priests might marry. Who knows what will happen in the future?' added Sr Anne.

'You're both very broadminded.'

'We've been around a long time!'

'Will you miss me?'

'Of course we'll miss you, Frankie. Come here 'til I give you a hug. We'll pray for you, won't we, Anne? You have to be true to yourself.'

Reaching to hug her too, Sr Brigid said, 'We'll miss you. The community will miss you. Keep praying. As we say, 'Keep the Faith!' Remember that we're all on a journey through life.'

The final day. Frankie was leaving. She looked around her narrow bedroom. She left her bed undone, as instructed. She picked up her briefcase and walked down the worn-carpeted stairs and along the corridor. She knew that Sr Mary Louise, the bursar, was the only other Sister in the convent that morning. There was a smell of Brasso coming from the sacristy. As Frankie passed the door in the corridor leading to the Mother Provincial's room, Sr Mary Louise put down the chalice that she was polishing and called out, 'Oh Frankie! You're ready. Let me come along with you.'

'Thank you, Sr Mary Louise.'

They sat and waited in silence outside the office. They heard Mother Provincial ring a bell and call out, 'Come in'.

Sr Mary Louise stood and waved to Frankie as she went in. She hoped Sr Mary Louise would be there when she had been dismissed.

Frankie felt strange, dressed in a brown suit and lemon blouse. There were no mirrors. She didn't know how she looked. When she searched in the box handed into the convent for the next jumble sale, they were the only clothes that she could find that fitted, what her mother had called, her thin and lanky frame. She wished that she could have gone to a hairdresser. Sr Mary Louise had lopped off some of her mousy brown hair. Up until then it had been washed in a thick green shampoo for many years and covered by the veil. It was brittle with split ends. She was disappointed that the rest of the community had gone to the Streatham Convent for their monthly retreat. Only Mother Provincial and Sr Mary would witness her departure.

'Good, Frances. Please place your habit, crucifix, copy of the Constitutions, Manual and Prayer books here. Have you still got any other book or item belonging to the Order?'

'No, Mother Provincial.'

Frankie noticed that Mother Provincial looked serious. *She did not call me 'Frankie'. She is not looking at me. She's just issuing instructions.*

'In observance with what is prescribed in the Constitutions of our Order, article 105 as dictated by the norms of Canon Law, 'evangelical charity is to be observed', I am giving you the sum of six thousand pounds. I understand that you have already been given some essential items to start you off in the room that the congregation is providing for you. Sheets, towels etc.'

'Thank you, Mother Provincial.'

Frankie put the cheque carefully into her briefcase. She realised that she would have to open a bank account. She had heard one of the staff talking about taking money out from the 'hole in the wall.' She would have to find out about that. This was the first time she had been given money. She had always handed the envelope containing her teacher's salary unopened to Sr Superior. Six thousand pounds seemed a lot to her. She wondered what it was like inside a bank. She planned to go there soon in order that she would not lose the cheque that she had been given.

'You are now free to leave, Frances. I hope that you will manage to cope.'

Frankie felt bewildered.

This farewell is so cold. Mother Provincial shows no warmth. She hasn't even thanked me for all the years of my life that I have worked hard in this Order. Why is she behaving so legalistically?

Frankie looked at Mother Provincial. They both stood. The silence felt awkward. Frankie decided that she was going to say goodbye in the way she felt was right. *I'm going to hug Mother Provincial.*

Frankie stretched out and embraced Mother Provincial. 'Goodbye, Mother Provincial. Thank you.'

Mother Provincial smiled and returned the hug. She held Frankie at arms length. *Were there tears in her eyes? Maybe she does care?*

'Be careful, Frankie. God bless you.'

Frankie struggled to hold back tears. She turned and opened the door. She smiled back at Mother Provincial. She held onto the handle of the other side of the door until she had steadied herself.

Sr Mary was waiting for her. She opened her arms. They gave each other a warm, meaningful hug.

'Goodbye and God Bless you, Frankie.'

Frankie glanced back at Sr Mary as she gently closed the convent door behind her.

25

NEW WORLD

*T*he bright September sunlight made Frankie blink. She felt sad to leave the family that she had belonged to for 19 years. *I am 35 years old. I'll miss the nuns. But if I am to make up for lost time, get married and have a child, I'll have to start my new life today.*

An-end-of summer breeze blew. Frankie reached to hold her veil down. She smiled as she realised that she no longer wore one. As she crossed the road, she nearly toppled off the pavement. She was not used to wearing wedged-heeled shoes. She felt her straight skirt restricted the length of her step. She wished that she was carrying a handbag instead of her tattered, brown, school briefcase. The last time that she had worn a jacket was when she was a pupil at school.

Dismissing the suspicion that walking under a ladder would bring her bad luck, Frankie came very close to a man climbing down the scaffolding with his underpants showing. She didn't know where to look. He must have noticed her blushing. He whistled. She walked swiftly round the corner.

Frankie kept walking with her head down, hoping that she would not bump into any of the children that she had taught or their parents. Frankie found herself walking in the direction of Putney Tube Station. She kept squeezing her eyes into focus. Why had she not been thanked for all that she had contributed to the Order during the 19 years in the convent? *Why didn't the nuns drive me to my new home? I am leaving almost by stealth on a Saturday morning when the rest of the community are supposedly unaware. This is the cold goodbye that Catherine warned me would happen. The kind of cold goodbye that must have been experienced by Mavis and Jeanette, Brenda and Pauline.*

Frankie stepped into the entrance of a clothes store. She looked at the selection of brown and orange skirts and jackets displayed in the window. She leaned nearer the window to admire the autumn coloured leaves scattered around the display. She wondered how much the orange blouse would cost. It looked silky. The buttons were shiny. She thought that it might have been good to wear with the suit that she was wearing. She caught a glimpse of herself in a side mirror. She smiled at her slim trim figure. She wondered if she might be considered attractive. She felt like skipping.

She walked further down the street and decided to go into a chemist shop. She stopped at the cosmetic counter. She tried to see if there was orange lipstick on the rack. She wondered if the pale lipsticks that were fashionable long ago when she went to her first disco were no longer suitable now. She thought that bright orange might help her make a bold statement and go well with her green eyes. She was trying to remember how she used to cover her freckles when a young woman with a 'Clarins' badge moved to the front of the desk.

'Can I help you, Madam?' she enquired. Frankie replied, 'Not today. Thank you.' She turned and left the shop. She realised that she was almost at Putney Bridge Tube Station.

'Dear God,' she prayed, 'I'm all alone in this world. I know that I have chosen to leave the convent. Please don't punish me. Help me, please.'

As she passed a café, Frankie smelt coffee and fresh bread. She felt hungry. She had only eaten a bowl of cornflakes that morning for breakfast. She peered into the café. A young man with chestnut curly hair caught her eye. She looked away. He looked handsome. She didn't want to go in alone. She realised that from now on she would have to cook her own meals in the microwave oven in the room she rented. She had not cooked for herself since she entered the convent. She remembered that there was a branch of Sainsbury's on the road leading from Wimbledon Tube Station to her new home. She planned to buy some food there.

As she turned into the tube station, Frankie felt the wind swirl round her legs. She put her hand up to hold her veil down. Again she remembered that she no longer wore a veil. She combed her hand through her hair. She rubbed her eyes. She blinked into the comparative darkness of the station. She was glad that she had her zone 2 and 3 rail ticket and that Putney was on the same district line that connected to Wimbledon.

When she showed her ticket at the barrier the man on duty seemed to look her up and down and smiled as he said, 'Thank you, Madam.' This was the second time that anyone had addressed with that title. She wondered if he liked her. She nodded and tried to walk away confidently in her wedged-shoes.

As the train swished into the station, the wind blew Frankie's hair around her face. This time she shook it back into place.

She found that she was sitting opposite a young couple on the train. They hugged and kissed each other. She tried to avert her eyes. She felt embarrassed at their open demonstration of love. She wished that she had not sat near them. She longed to be hugged. Why am I embarrassed? These two love birds are not afraid to show their love for each other? *Will I ever fall in love?*

When Frankie stepped into Sainsbury's she did not know what to buy. As she walked round the store carrying her basket and brief case, people brushed past her. She remembered that there was no fridge in her room. After examining everything carefully she decided to buy half a litre of milk, two long brown rolls, two bananas and a tube of liver pâté. Then she noticed that there was an offer on chocolate flaky bars. As it was a long time since she had been able to indulge herself, she reached out and added two of them to her basket.

Are these a bargain? Am I being overcharged?

When she joined the queue she put her basket down on the floor in order to unzip the pocket of her briefcase and take out the plastic bank bag containing the twenty pound note that Sister had also given her together with the cheque. Someone from behind pushed their basket into her back. Frankie realised that she needed more time to open the plastic bag containing her money. Using her foot, she nudged her basket to one side and stepped out of the queue. When she was ready she tried to get the attention of a man in the queue. He looked straight ahead. He did not make eye contact. Frankie stepped in behind him.

A woman shouted, 'You can't just barge in. There's a queue!' Then she seemed to count the number of items that Frankie had in her basket. 'Oh for goodness sake, you might as well carry on.'

Frankie felt hot and embarrassed. She thought that everyone was watching her as she walked out of Sainsbury's. *If I had been wearing my habit, maybe people would not have been impatient with me. If only they knew that this was the first time for many years that I was shopping for food for myself.*

Frankie twitched, blinked and rubbed her eyes. She found it hard to focus on her surroundings. She began to walk towards her new home. She noticed a bench. Feeling tired she sat and pondered why her eyes were troubling her. She reasoned that it was most likely because she had been embarrassed. The artificial light in the store could also have triggered off a reaction when she emerged into the sunlight. Shopping was such a new experience.

As she sat on the bench, no one said 'Hello Sister'. Nobody smiled at her. She felt that without her nun's habit, she had become anonymous.

The white façade of 31 Acacia Road gleamed in the noon sunlight as Frankie approached her new home. It was one of twelve houses facing each other in a quiet cul-de-sac. She lifted the latch on the waist-high wooden gate and inhaled the smell of lavender mingling with roses as she stepped through the garden. As Frankie turned the key of her room she thought: *I will turn my life round. My new life has begun.*

Her new home was silent. Her landlady had helped her carry her belongings to her room the previous day. She presumed that the landlady's husband and son must not be at home. She walked resolutely up the stairs and opened the bedroom door.

Sunlight streamed through the window. It bounced off the gleaming white paintwork of the shelf above her bed and her dressing table. Frankie glanced at the photo of Margaret that she had cut out of the convent magazine and framed. She picked it up and kissed it.

If only you were with me Margaret! I will never forget you. Look down on me from heaven. Guide me in my new life. You are close to God now. Intercede with Him for me.

Frankie placed this photo next to the crochet piety bag

that had been found on Margaret's locker on a a little table near her bed. She looked at the letter *F* embroidered on it. She whispered, *I love you, Margaret.*

Frankie put the photo of her mother taken with her on her First Communion Day on the shelf above her bed. She wished her mother could help her. But she guessed that if she told her that the convent had given her six thousand pounds, she would probably plead with her to give her some of it to her. Besides, she didn't know whether she was living in England or in Kerry.

Feeling hungry, Frankie put a towel over the desk next to the window so that crumbs from her rolls would not fall onto the lovely maroon-coloured carpet. She plugged in her kettle and made herself a cup of tea. After peeling one of the bananas, she made a sandwich and sat overlooking the family's beautiful long back garden. It looked well cared for. There seemed to be a vegetable patch at the far end. Many lovely coloured blooms thrived around the border. The lawn had been mown recently. A couple of blue tits were feeding from the bird table.

When Frankie looked back into her room to admire her floral duvet, she noticed the card on which she had listed her belongings. She picked it up and read:

2 mugs, a big and small plate, a tray, an electric kettle, fork, knife and 2 spoons, duvet, two pillows, a pair of used sheets, a bath and hand towel and hair dryer. Radio, alarm clock, Bible, dictionary, A to Z Street-finder, Photograph albums Stationery, pencils, pens, rubbers, sellotape. Two skirts and tops. A pair of shoes. A jacket and two changes of underwear.

She hid the money that she had been given under her pillow. Then she decided to put the milk and pâté in a box under the bath to keep them cool.

Frankie placed the prayer that she and Margaret composed many years ago in the convent garden, on the shelf above her bed. As she knelt down and leant on the bed her knees sunk into the lovely pile on the carpet. She undid her blouse and clutched her miraculous medal. She bent down and kissed it. Remembering Margaret, she prayed, *'Mary, Mother of God, my mother and guide, please intercede for me with your Son, Jesus. Thank Him for giving me the courage to start a new life. Remind him that I will need His support and guidance. Amen.*

ABOUT THE AUTHOR MARION DANTE B.ED.

Marion Dante hails from Limerick and has lived in England since 1955. When her family arrived in Shepherds Bush, London, there were signs on some door saying 'No Blacks. No Dogs. No Irish.'

Aged fourteen she began training to be a nun in the Salesian convent in Chertsey Surrey. After her aspirantade and noviciate, Marion made her vows of poverty, chastity and obedience in Friar Park Henley-on Thames in 1965. (These premises were later purchased by George Harrison.) She finished her three year teacher training course at Digby Stuart College in 1970. Having taught in Chertsey, Henley on Thames, Battersea, Rotherhithe, Glasgow and Farnborough she gained her degree in education (Bachelor of Education) London University in 1979 and continued to teach when she left the Salesian Order.

Many changes brought about in the Catholic Church as a result of the second Vatican Council resulted in Marion pondering on her future role in the convent and the realisation that she did not have to be a nun in order to live a fulfilling life. Mother Provincial of the Salesian Sisters strove to help her to prepare for life outside the convent. Initially, Marion was sent to Ireland to study theology and related religious studies. She graduated from Maynooth University, Kildare 1987. The following year she completed a Secretarial and Business, Pitmans word-processing and typing Course at Language, Secretarial and Business Centre, Balfe Street, off Grafton Street, Dublin 1988.

On returning to England at some financial cost to the Salesian Sisters, Marion benefitted from further support, counselling and various therapies in a Heronbrook House in the Midlands. While there she became convinced that she could no longer remain in the convent and eventually wrote to the Pope to be dispensed from her vows in 1991.

Anxious to equip herself for her future life, while still teaching, Marion gained further qualification from several courses: Two years at Tavistock Clinic to meriting Counselling Aspects in Education certificates. City and Guilds Further Adult Education run by University of Surrey in Family, Language and Literacy. TESOL qualification enabling her to teach English to speakers of other languages. Information Technology at Brooklands College Surrey.

While teaching in St Patrick's School, Farnborough, Hampshire, Marion was diagnosed with breast cancer in 1995. She eventually retired but continued to teach privately. Soon after becoming a member of Camberley Writers' she began to pen her autobiography. Encouraged and supported by Charlotte McDowell, who had been her radiographer and became co-founder of The Fountain Centre in St Luke's Cancer Centre in the Royal Surrey County Hospital, Guildford, she enlisted and continues to be a volunteer helping to raise funds for this therapeutic centre. To this end she was sponsored when she climbed Machu Picchu and on three occasions endeavoured to trek the last hundred kilometres of the Camino Compostela in northern Spain.

Marion Dante's autobiography 'Dropping The Habit' was well received in Ireland, England, USA and was translated into Polish. She is invited to give talks to many different groups:

Women's Institute, The Townswomen's Guild, Probus, Rotary, Inner Wheel, Tangent and various retirement groups.

Marion was on RTE television and radio as part of the publicity at the launch of her autobiography.

She has featured in BBC Programmes such as Heart and Soul BBC World Service, Radio Four Saturday Live and this February 2017 to speak on BBC Radio Surrey taking part in the BBC Listening Project. (Stored in the British Library).

She is a member of The Three Counties Cancer Support Group, The Kindred Spirits Choir, Camberley and Farnborough U3A in which she takes part in Italian, yoga, walking and ukulele groups. Marion also attends aqua aerobics and is a Member of National Women's Register discussion, dining and reading group.

ACKNOWLEDGEMENTS

The late Barbara Large, MBE, was my tutor for over four years. I owe a great deal to her. Barbara Large was the Founder-Director of the Winchester Writers' Conference for 33 years. She was director of CreativeWordsMatter and a member of The Society of Authors and The National Association of Writers in Education.

Bead Roberts, writer, tutor, broadcaster and lecturer encouraged me to write in my own voice and conversational style. I am indebted to her for giving me the title of my autobiography 'Dropping The Habit'.

My parents Frank and Patricia Dante (nee Colivet) and my brothers Tim and Des RIP.

My sisters Pat Stay and Ber Collins.

Jenny Hattersley tutor, preacher, lecturer, friend and much more.

Barney Cantillon for the checking my use of the Italian language. I take full responsibility for my mistakes.

St John Bosco founder of the Salesian Order St Mary Mazzarello Co-Founder of which I was a member for thirty-three years.

My nephew Mark Stay for formatting the first editions of both books and imparting his vast knowledge of publishing matters.

Ray Lane who has always been on hand for technical support.

In producing my second edition I am grateful to the following:

Joanna Barnard editor and critique.

Christine Hammacott of The Art of Communication graphic design consultancy.

Andy Bowden for the cover design.

Milton Keynes UK
Ingram Content Group UK Ltd.
UKHW010635141123
432548UK00004B/249

9 781999 647100